Philippa.

CHILD IN MY LIFE

CHILD IN MY LIFE

Valerie Church

Copyright © 2024 Valerie Church
The moral right of the author has been asserted.

Apart from any fair dealing for the purposes of research or private study, or criticism or review, as permitted under the Copyright, Designs and Patents Act 1988, this publication may only be reproduced, stored or transmitted, in any form or by any means, with the prior permission in writing of the publishers, or in the case of reprographic reproduction in accordance with the terms of licences issued by the Copyright Licensing Agency. Enquiries concerning reproduction outside those terms should be sent to the publishers.

This is a work of fiction. Names, characters, businesses, places, events and incidents are either the products of the author's imagination or used in a fictitious manner. Any resemblance to actual persons, living or dead, or actual events is purely coincidental.

Troubador Publishing Ltd
Unit E2 Airfield Business Park,
Harrison Road, Market Harborough,
Leicestershire. LE16 7UL
Tel: 0116 2792299
Email: books@troubador.co.uk
Web: www.troubador.co.uk

ISBN 978 1805143 130

British Library Cataloguing in Publication Data.
A catalogue record for this book is available from the British Library.

Printed and bound by CPI Group (UK) Ltd, Croydon, CR0 4YY
Typeset in 10.5pt Garamond Pro by Troubador Publishing Ltd, Leicester, UK

ONE

London 1939

Last night I dreamed my mother loved me. That she did not, I am now certain, though exactly when I realised this is hard to say. Why she did not, took me nearly forty years to discover.

We didn't speak much of love in the days of my childhood, not sibling or parental love. Mid-20th century children took it for granted, I suppose. Mothers were there to feed us, keep us clean and tell us off for misdemeanours, which mine did much of the time. Love us? Never thought about it.

But the love we did know about was romantic love, it was featured every week in the cinema, the 'pictures' we called it in those days. Films were about 'falling in love', which was what grown-ups did. Which was what my parents did, one night in August 1939, after meeting each other at a dance at the People's Palace, in the East End of London. Soldier on leave meets pretty girl having a night out with friends, they have a dance, two, three perhaps, surely the last one, ending the evening most probably with a kiss. Who knows? I didn't, simply imagined it all.

Kathleen Quentin and Jeff Francis, young, naive, puzzled, that the seemingly unchanging world they had been born into was now a country on the brink of war. Jeff had joined the British Expeditionary Force shortly before the beginning of conscription, one of the 160,000 men sent to France when Britain declared war on Germany in September 1939. He and Kath knew his time left in England would be short, and that if they were to be married, it should be as soon as possible. With the German troops overrunning Europe, who knew what the future might hold? Grab what happiness you can, while you can.

The wedding took place in St John's church in Poplar early that month. Almost immediately afterwards, Jeff disappeared with the first British troops to engage with the Germans in France, coming back on leave in December to find his new wife pregnant. A few happy days together, and he was off again to join the rapidly expanding army in Europe to fight on the disastrous Maginot Line, where he was captured and sent to one of the German prisoner-of-war camps on the Belgian border. He was not to return to England for the rest of the war, husband to a woman he had known only for a few months and already father to a child he had never seen. My mother had told me how she had said goodbye to him on the platform at Paddington Station, and he'd tentatively suggested a name for the baby she was carrying.

'If it's a boy,' he'd said, 'I'd like to call it Winston. If it's a girl, call her 'Kay' – it would remind me of you.'

'Did you agree?' I'd asked Mum.

'Suppose so,' she said, 'I was crying too much to care about names. Or anything else... except that the train was carrying him away from me. Our hands were pulled apart.'

Did she really tell me that? Or was I imagining the drama being played out in that noisy, smoke-filled station?

His war, Dad told us later, was a long weary wait for peace, filled with boredom, discomfort, apprehension. They feared, the prisoners, not only for their personal safety, but for that of their families back in England, and the outcome of the war. The news that filtered through to them was of massive air raids. For Jeff, days passed performing the routine maintenance jobs allocated to him, exercising in the prison yard, sleeping, thinking, talking to his fellow prisoners, writing letters to his young wife, and pondering on the exigencies of being an absent father to a little girl growing up without him. Would I have been a different person if he had been there from my birth? At least I would have been loved.

Meanwhile, I was emerging into a conscious being, learning the language I needed to understand and make my way in the world, a world at war, most of which I was too young to remember. For me, Kay Francis, four years old, awareness of living in a country at war emerged amid the noise and nightmares of 1944.

In a final desperate effort – not to win the war, it was too late for that – but to stop the massive Allied bombing of Germany that was paralysing its economy and the morale of its citizens, Adolf Hitler was relaunching his air raids on London.

Nights were spent listening. First, for the fluctuating wail of the air raid sirens warning us of the arrival of the German bombers. Then came the anti-aircraft fire, sharp fierce cracks aimed at any plane caught in the focus of the searchlights sweeping the night sky. Next the half-heard, half-felt vibrations, the thump of bombs exploding over the city, the crackle of incendiaries, the scream of fire engines. Finally, as the sounds grew fainter, the single prolonged note that told us that tonight's theatre of fear had closed its nightly performance.

We could have a few hours' peace from the attacks that killed, among so many, my maternal grandparents.

We survived, that summer, my mother and me, rarely leaving the basement flat we rented. Not for us the nightly safety of the underground tube station round the corner, the close proximity of sleeping strangers unacceptable to a woman to whom familiarity did not come easily. Found people 'nosey', she said, didn't mind their own business, always asking questions. The camaraderie of East End Londoners was not her style. 'Keeping yourself to yourself' was one way of demonstrating the social status she aspired to. That the absence of contact with other children might affect the development of her own didn't occur to her, the psychology of childhood was unknown territory.

Days were lived through somehow or other, wartime routines established which must have seemed strange to those remembering the peace between the wars, but to a child as normal as cleaning your teeth. You didn't just draw the curtains when it got dark, you went outside to check that not a glimmer of brightness was escaping through a careless gap. You didn't want those Germans in the city skies to see where your house was. Nor did you want to attract the attention of the local air raid warden, appointed to spot any escaping beams of light, bang on the door, and scold the culprits. A ghostly figure who patrolled the streets after dark, tin-hatted, with a torch to find his way down area steps and up to front doors. A real and constant threat, which scared me far more than the German planes overhead.

'Mum, what would he *do* if he found some light?'

'He'd tell us to pull the curtains properly.'

'The curtains don't cover *all* of the windows, Mum, we have to keep finding things to cover the gaps. Should we get some new ones?'

'We haven't got enough money for new curtains.'

'How much would they cost?'

She rubbed her forehead, in exasperation, as she always did when I persisted in a conversation she didn't like.

'Oh I don't know, do stop asking questions Kay. I've got a lot to do.'

She always had a lot to do. What it was I was never quite sure, but it stopped her from spending much time with me. I became a self-sufficient child, living in a world peopled with a multitude of characters and animals, some of them toys, some household objects, others existing only in my imagination. I remember them all quite clearly. 'Good morning, Henry, good morning, Charlie' I greeted the taps in the kitchen sink where I washed each morning. Well, the taps were clearly identified by their initials, H and C, thin black letters on shiny round ivory-coloured caps.

What is there about our early years, the rooms, the houses, streets, all the locations of childhood, that are the background and context of so many of our dreams, persisting into adulthood and old age? Even today I dream of my first home, appearing in all its strange perspective, seen from the eye-level of a three-to-four-year-old. A child's world unknown to grown-ups, for how could they be as familiar as I was with the *underside* of things, places where only a very small person could go? I knew every scratch and blemish on the crossbars that braced the legs of the wooden living-room table, adding my own marks, partly, I think, to make a small home for myself with its own familiar features, and partly as tentative experiments on the nature of substances. Attacked with a knife, carpet produced twine and fabric debris, wood splintered, and concrete simply damaged the knife.

I played with the fluff that accumulated under my bed, forming it into a soft grey image of myself, and using wool pulled from my jumper to simulate my own mop of red hair. Frequent power cuts required candles to be brought out and lit by Mum with the instruction that they were not to be touched. But they were discreetly played with when she was out of the room, and I loved the smell and malleability of the candlewax. I threw surreptitious pinches of rationed sugar on to the open fire in the living room, exulting in the small explosions of flame. Lying in bed, I would pull out thick threads from the white bedspread, knotting and weaving them into new patterns. Small secret exploratory delights, most of which went unnoticed by my mother, but which, if she discovered them, led to scolding and punishment. The acts themselves were trivial, but taken together they added up to Disobedience, a major sin.

I watched my mother. Wondered about the two vertical lines that often appeared in the space between her eyes. Noticed the magical dimple that appeared when she smiled at visitors, showing the small white teeth she was so proud of. Her clear unblemished skin was maintained, she said, by copious splashes of ice-cold water before bedtime. To avoid her displeasure, I splashed dutifully and noisily at the kitchen sink before bedtime, judiciously avoiding any facial contact with the icy water. Her unfashionably straight black hair was crimped by the application of metal 'tongs', heated over the gas ring. The result of all these procedures was, I thought, quite beautiful.

Many of my activities annoyed and angered her. I told stories. Most were the consequence of loneliness and an overactive imagination, but they were real to me, as I acted them out in my domestic theatre. I met King George and Queen Elizabeth, I told her, on one of their visits to the bomb-ravaged parts of London. I'd asked them in for a cup of tea, but they had politely declined as their little girls, Elizabeth and Margaret, were waiting for them at home in Buckingham Palace, and they would be worried if their Mummy and Daddy were away for too long.

I related such stories to my mother as if they had actually happened, and she angrily dismissed them as lies. I talked of companions in my adventures, I talked of Nellie, who was often with me, joining in my exploration of the world, sometimes following me, sometimes cross, with small acts of bullying, jealous of my mother's attention. My imaginary playmate, real enough to feature in my adult dreams, even today. She came, and went, for no apparent reason, depending on how my imagined world was engaging me. Not always welcome, for there were threats to 'tell' on me if I transgressed some rule or other, anthropomorphism of my conscience, I thought, when I was older.

On the mantelpiece in our living room was a photograph of a man in army uniform. This was Daddy, my mother told me, and one day he would come back from the war and live with us. All sorts of things would happen 'one day', but how far away one day was I had no idea. Things would be different then, you wouldn't have to draw your curtains every night, or run home when the air raid sirens sounded. There would be bananas in the shops – I had never seen one but there were pictures of them in my books. They were yellow, like fat fingers. There would be lights in the streets, and you would be able to buy as much margarine as you could afford. Butter was out of our reach anyway, so its measly ration wasn't an issue.

Aeroplanes above us would fly straight and level, not ducking and weaving in dogfights, dropping out of the sky, nose down, trails of smoke issuing from their tails. I remember one day in the park, looking anxiously at the small silver plane crossing the London sky. A kindly passer-by smiled reassuringly, and commented

'It's all right, it's one of ours!'

What a strange life one day would bring.

Daddy? I dismissed him into the unreal world of streetlights and bananas.

The pattern of air attacks changed. Suddenly we were listening for the danger of silence. You were O.K. if you could hear the monotonous clatter of those plane-shaped missiles we called doodlebugs – as long as they kept moving across the sky you were safe. It was when their engines cut out that you dived under the table. No warning at all with the next and last German effort to avoid defeat, you never heard the V2 bombs coming. The deployment of this desperate and hopeless missile lasted only a few weeks, and then, gradually, – the skies fell silent and empty, nights strangely dark. Searchlights ceased to sweep the sky, gone were the barrage balloons, those fat grey elephants that had helped to keep London safe, it was said, though I couldn't see how. They hadn't stopped a bomb falling on a house at the end of our street, shattering our small living room window. Mum made a temporary repair with some cellophane, and I was given the job of picking up shards of glass that covered the floor. Most of them Mum managed to brush into the dustpan, but the rest had to be located and retrieved by hand. A slow process, as I was obliged to put on my winter woollen gloves in case I cut myself. The odd sparkle would occasionally appear long after the window had been replaced, stuck between floorboards or some overlooked corner. The glittering eye of a malicious sprite, reminding us of a death we had narrowly missed.

V.E. Day came, Victory in Europe, that formal marking of the end of the war with Germany. We walked to Victoria Park, where we heard relayed the familiar gruff voice of Winston Churchill, addressing the nation. We joined the waving and cheering, along with the rest of London. I asked my mother what would happen now.

'Back to normal, I s'pose.'

Normal? Whatever was that?

The nights were so quiet, it was hard to sleep for the silence. Lights were turned on again. In the street where we lived, other people's Daddies were arriving home from the war. Ours would be one of the last, Mum said, because he had lots of special jobs to do first. During his time as a prisoner of war he had been learning to speak German, and made himself too useful, so England decided that he should stay until all the prisoners had arrived home and the Germans could do without him to organise things. I was nearly five before I met him.

Just before he came home, Mum and I made a long, memorable journey out of London. We were going to visit a friend, she said, a former neighbour, and the place wasn't in England, it was in Wales. A different country, and some of the people spoke a different language there, Mum said.

It was the first time I'd been in a proper big railway station. Enormous, glass-ceilinged, noisy, with such a strange distinctive smell, part smoke, part something that made my nose sting. So many people walking in different directions, on different levels, how did Mum know where to go? And the train, with all those linked-up sections, and the smaller spaces inside where you could sit down. Peering into each bit, Mum managed to find an empty carriage, where we took places beside the windows, opposite each other. Other people drifted in, filling the empty spaces.

We sat down and waited for the train to start. I felt an initial jerk, and we were off, feeling the metal-on-metal grind of the wheels beneath us. So many houses at first, with views into back gardens, sheds, lines of washing, all appearing and disappearing between gaps in the narrow band of trees and bushes that separated these glimpses of backyard life from our curious passing eyes. After a while, the dense mass of houses thinned out into separate clusters, with patches of grass between them, and then I had my wonderful first sight of cows.

'Look, Mum!' I shouted in amazement, 'there's cows!'

An embarrassed 'SSh!' was all I got in reply, but the other occupants of our carriage smiled.

The train whistle shrieked, and suddenly we were engulfed in blackness. I shrank from the window I'd been glued to, there was a smell of smoke. In fright I grabbed my mother's hand.

'Don't be silly, Kay, it's only a tunnel.'

Equally suddenly the outside world was restored, with our eruption into the sunlit pattern of fields, woods, sheep, real farms, my picture books magically brought to life.

I exclaimed at every new delight. Whizzing past tiny railway stations, brief blurred snapshots of sheltered waiting rooms, a few enamelled adverts for long-forgotten food and drinks, time barely registered. We ate a sandwich from the package Mum had brought, only half, the rest had to be kept for the return journey. At some point we changed trains, but the only seats we could find in the new train were between other travellers, spoiling the immediacy of the views, eclipsing them with the folding and refolding of newspapers, and distancing them in a blue haze of cigarette smoke.

Eventually, the gradual appearance of back yards and kitchen windows told me that we were approaching another town. Mum started to gather our belongings.

'We get out here.'

'Where are we Mum?'

'Shrewsbury.'

A walk up the hill to a bus stop brought us to the next stage of our journey. Once again beside a window, I looked at the passing black-and white timbers of the town's ancient houses, and wondered at the upper storeys so dangerously tilted above the pavements. Was it safe to walk beneath? Winding our way out of the town we were back in the countryside I had seen from the train. How untamed the grass, hedges and trees seemed, compared with the managed greenery of Victoria Park, up till now my only acquaintance with unpaved earth.

We left the bus about an hour later, and, stopping occasionally to ask for directions, found the house where Mum said our old neighbour was now living. A very small cottage of stone, away from the village and only a short walk from a river. By this time, I was replete with new experiences and bursting with questions. None of these were answered satisfactorily and some not at all. The journey had taken so long that there wasn't time to go home that day. We spent the night in the tiny cottage, both of us squashed into a narrow bed. Next morning Mum gave me my sweets ration book and two pence to spend at the shop in the village, didn't want me hanging around, she said. But when I arrived at the shop my eye was taken by local picture post-cards. Sweets would be gone by the time I got back, but a card would remind me of these amazing two days.

I would have liked to *choose* one, but was obliged to take the only card I could reach, the lowest from the tall rack where the shop's collection was displayed. I was pleased that it showed a picture of a river and distant hills. I could fill in more interesting detail from memory – and very probably, imagination.

I gave the shopkeeper my two pence, and he told me that the place where we were staying was called Newfield, and the river was called Severn, which puzzled me as I wondered where the other six were, but I was too shy to ask. The card showed a picture of the river I'd seen from a bridge on the walk from the bus stop to our destination. I'd not been allowed to linger.

The colours didn't look right but I wanted the post-card to look at when we were back home. I put it in my pocket, I wouldn't show it to my mother, guessing she'd be cross for one reason or another, so back in the little house I showed it to a spider who was climbing up the wall, to the hearth-brush in the fireplace, and to Nellie, my imaginary playmate who had turned up to keep me company.

'Look, Nell, I bought this post-card. Isn't it nice?'

'Dunno what you want that for.'

'To remind me of here!'

'Dunno why you want to be reminded of here. It's nothing special. Bit boring if you ask me.'

She never understood the things I was keen on, bit like Mum.

My mother barely spoke a word on the journey back to London, and I had enough to think about to keep me quiet. Back home I wondered about the children who were sent away to the country, away from the bombs.

'Sent away without their Mummies? Don't the children mind going?'

'Sometimes they do, sometimes they don't.'

Time passed. There was a smile on many faces, a darkness on others, our train was coming out of a very long tunnel. Letters from Daddy were becoming more frequent. He was coming home. The 'one day' I'd been told about became 'soon', then 'next week', and finally, '*tomorrow*'!

We got up early on the Day. Mum put on her best frock, and did a few necessary jobs and some unnecessary ones, switched on the wireless, switched it off again. Moved things. Moved them back. Sat down, something she rarely did during the morning. Looked flushed, nervous.

I wandered aimlessly around the kitchen, the bedroom, and went, reluctantly, to the outside toilet. I didn't want to miss the anticipated knock at the door. I positioned myself at our basement window, from where I could see the feet and ankles of passers-by. Sooner or later one pair of boots would not pass by, but descend the area steps, a soldier home from the war. I tired of the vigil and was back in my own world of imagined happenings when a sharp, loud knock at the door broke the uneasy silence. It made me jump. Daddy was home!

A wise man, my father. I had retreated in alarm to a corner, and gazed in awe at the large intruder. He kissed Mum for a long time, longer than necessary, I thought. Arm still round Mum, he looked at me and smiled. 'Hello Kay' he said. A few seconds passed, the man in the picture on the mantelpiece had materialised in front of me. Looked a lot older than the image I was used to. My mother looked at me.

'Say something to your Daddy, Kay.'

I considered the situation. He was very big. Would there be room for him in our tiny basement? Where would he sleep? What ought I to say? What did my mother usually say to visitors? Much consideration needed here, for I was frequently reprimanded for saying the wrong thing to people who called.

'Would you like a cup of tea?' I ventured, hoping that this would be a polite and acceptable greeting.

My father smiled at me again. 'What a good idea' he said. 'Would you like to show me where the tea things are?'

During the following days I watched him closely, questions forming in my mind. I dared not ask him yet all the things I wanted to know. He told me that he had thought about me every day during his time in the prisoner-of-war camp. He had a photograph of me, he said, taken on my second birthday. But there was one thing the photo didn't show because the picture was in black and white.

'I didn't know you had such beautiful red hair!'

'Auburn,' corrected my mother. 'And freckles to go with it.'

'Hello freckles' said my new Daddy, and kissed me.

Then I was on his knee, and in deep conversation, for here was a grown-up who was interested in me, and listened to what I had to say. One who was never too busy to answer my constant questions.

'Daddy, why were the Germans so wicked?'

'Not many of them were really wicked. They had been told wrong things, so they believed things that weren't true. They made a lot of mistakes, but maybe we did too.'

'Did the Germans think the English people were bad? Is it alright to kill people if they are bad?'

I don't remember all his answers, but I realise they were all considered, and never dismissed. He was introduced to my toys, real and imaginary. I told him about Pluto who was sometimes an elephant and sometimes a dog. I explained that when he was an elephant, he was too big to fit in our living room, so had to become a dog. I'd dispatched him to London Zoo, where he would have more space.

'What happened to Nellie?'

'Dunno. Jus' gone.'

'Where did she live?'

'Here of course. Slept in the same bed as me. We had to whisper, 'cause Mum got cross if she heard us talking.'

'Will she come back?'

'Might do.'

My imaginary playmate never came back. Why should she, when I had a real playmate who occupied all my days with the happy anticipation of his return every evening from his new office job. Watched for the feet that didn't pass the house, but came down the area steps, waited for the arms that picked me up and kissed me, and the gentle voice that asked me what I had been doing all day.

I hadn't known that a Daddy in the house meant joy.

TWO

London 1945 – 1948

Were *they* happy, Jeff and Kathleen Francis? What did they know of each other from those brief few weeks together after the wedding, and one or two home leaves before my father was whisked away to the front line?

There had been letters. Batches of them, via the Red Cross.

'What does Daddy say?' I used to ask her.

'Oh, the usual things,' she'd answer vaguely. Which wasn't much help as I didn't know what the usual things were.

Back home, Dad didn't talk much about the prisoner of war camps, but told us about how life had revolved around the arrival of Red Cross parcels of necessities, particularly, cigarettes. 'It was our form of money,' he explained, 'you bought what you wanted with cigarettes. Food, paper, pencils, whatever was available, the guards brought stuff in for us, and you paid for them in cigarettes. You could buy special privileges, like lights out an hour later, extra exercise time, or a new football. Money would've been no use at all. Didn't buy much for ordinary Germans either.'

The rich people were the non-smokers, he told us, they got their ration of ciggies from the parcels, but didn't use them, so they accumulated like money in the bank.

Dad reached for his current pack, lit up while I watched the curling spirals of blue smoke on their journey towards the ceiling. I thought they were rather beautiful. Do people use cigarettes because they like to see the smoke, I wondered. Mum was looking cross again.

'Wish you'd stop it,' she said, 'waste of money.'

'Yes,' he said, looking despondent, 'but it's not that easy.'

I wondered why.

Dad went on, telling me of his occasional happy days in the prisoner-of-war camp.

'A packet of fags and a letter from your Mum, that's what made my day. I kept all the letters in my pocket and read them over and over again, till they got so tattered and dirty that I had to throw them away and wait for the next batch to arrive.'

I can see now that things weren't easy for either of my parents after Dad's return. Harder perhaps for Mum, whose rôle had changed and now had to include that of wife as well as mother. She did her best, her housewifely abilities stretched, now that she had another person in the house to cook for, and to accommodate in our tiny basement flat. She watched nervously over our new relationship. Thousands of other young children were coming to terms with an intruder into the only life they had known. There were stories of toddlers afraid of the big new men who were occupying so much of their mothers' time, of anger, jealousy, and tantrums. Was she afraid of something of the kind? For she seemed to worry if my father and I spent time alone together, wanting to know what we had been doing, what we had talked about. Back from the shops, she hung up her coat and asked him

'Kay been telling stories again?'

'Of course. She's grown out of her little story books, so she makes them up for herself. She's got quite an imagination.'

'Bit too much sometimes. You don't want to believe everything she says.'

'I'm not supposed to. I think we understand each other.'

I guess that my mother had expected the end of the war and the return of her husband to mark the beginning of a new life, an ordinary, pleasant life that mirrored her own before the war. Nice things, nice neighbours, nice ways. All lost to her with the death of her parents in an early air raid, having to supplement her meagre income as an army wife with what she could earn through her own sporadic efforts. I sometimes wonder if she had seen marriage as the only way out of the miserable basement flat she was renting when she met Jeff. Things would change, she believed, once her husband was home again. Things did change, differently and more profoundly than she could have imagined.

Dad's first task was to find a job.

'The Army didn't teach me much,' he observed regretfully, 'It wasn't their fault. All I got from the war was fairly fluent German. Spent some of my ciggie ration on lessons from one of the guards. Nice bloke, he was, used to be a teacher.'

We didn't know if his determination to learn the language contributed to the offer Dad finally took up. It was an office job, approved of by Mum, and offering security for the future. He passed a written examination and was taken on as a clerical officer in the Civil Service, near Edgware station. He arrived home each day, late and tired, usually after I'd gone to bed. He'd always come to my bedside to say goodnight, and if I was awake, tell me a story.

'We'll need to move,' said my mother, 'you can't be making that journey twice every day.'

The search began, the hunt for a small house on the other

side of the city, one that would pass her domestic criteria. Dad added another.

'Schools,' he said, we must look at the schools in the area.' The move is just as important for Kay. As well as any future addition to the family.' He smiled, looking hopeful. There was no response from Mum.

During weekends, the three of us would take a train and alight somewhere not too far from where Dad worked. Footsore and weary, we looked at houses to rent. One or two seemed good candidates, some were too far from a school, others in a neighbourhood that was considered unsuitable. The search dragged on. Dad seemed restless, Mum wrapped up in her own problems, finding it difficult to relax. Still basking in the sunshine of my newly arrived Daddy, I pottered around happily at home in our tiny basement flat, talking to my toys and imagined friends, much as I had always done.

Dad hadn't taken to his new job. Felt stifled, he said, stuck behind a table in a big room with dozens of other people all doing the same thing, dealing with forms, copying down numbers which were sent to another roomful of people, all girls. 'What do they do with the numbers? I asked him. 'They punch holes in cards!' he told me, laughing at my incomprehension. How strange it all seemed. Making holes in things usually resulted in a telling off. 'Why do they do that?' I asked.

He frowned with the effort of trying to explain the elements of digitisation to a seven-year-old.

'The holes all mean something' he said, 'so the cards with holes in the same places all have the same information on them. Machines sort out these cards and can count how many there are with holes in the same places.

'There are lots of things you don't understand yet because you don't know enough for them all to make sense. When you know lots more, some of the ideas you find difficult now will get much easier. It's exciting that scientists are making machines now that do all kinds of jobs much more quickly than people can.'

I thought of the jobs I wasn't very good at, and which would bring about a scolding by my mother for being slow, like washing the dishes and drying them afterwards.

'Will there be a machine for washing up?' I asked him hopefully.

He laughed.

'Sure to be,' he said, 'and drying the dishes too. Shall we go for a walk in the Park?'

It had been a beautiful place, once. But Victoria Park, the green lung of Stepney, had been taken over by war-time defences, and public access reduced to a few tree-lined paths, limited by the various temporary structures that had housed air raid shelters, anti-aircraft guns, the detritus of war. There had been a prison-of-war camp along one side, where, if you were lucky, you could spot a real live German or Italian. Evil monsters? They looked to me like perfectly ordinary people. The wide grassy areas and flower beds now grew vegetables for hungry Londoners, huge posters exhorting them to 'DIG FOR VICTORY'. You could still find a few untouched areas, though, a rogue daffodil or two, a small clump of snowdrops. We walked, the three of us, along the Regents Park Canal, throwing bread crusts to the imperturbable ducks. Before bread rationing kicked in.

Walking back, through half-demolished streets, places still too dangerous for local kids to explore, the big problem that was the background to all we did and said, emerged once more. Dad kicked aside a stray brick, plaster and flowered wallpaper still attached.

'No place to bring up children' Dad said to Mum.

'You're right' she replied.

'We should move.'

Her face lit up. 'We will, won't we? When you've got the right job?'

'I can only keep trying.'

Which he did, week after week, till our basement flat seemed knee-deep in pages of job adverts. Trawling through them, my reading abilities had plenty of practice, as I painstakingly read out work that I thought my Dad would like.

Dispiritedly, he said to Mum -

'But I've got a job, don't like it much, but at least it's something. Same goes for the flat. Got to be careful that we don't rush things and make mistakes. I'll keep on looking at vacancies, and if there's anything that sounds possible, I'll apply. Not sure what I want to do, but it's certainly not what I'm doing now. I'm bloody bored here.'

I could see why. All those cards with holes in them. Not much fun, I thought.

Time passed and I'd almost forgotten the idea of a move, but it surfaced again, unexpectedly, over one Sunday breakfast. Dad had lit his morning cigarette, finished his cup of tea, and was reading his Sunday newspaper. Mum was trying to clear the breakfast things. Dad spoke.

'Australia' he said.

'What?'

'Australia' he repeated, looking at Mum. 'Would you like to live there?'

'Dunno' she said. 'Not much point in thinking about it since we never shall.' She poured him another cup of tea, crossly removing the cigarette ash from the saucer. 'Wish you'd use the ashtray.'

'It's not out of the question. They want people. Look at this.'

He showed her the headlines in the paper. She peered at the words, reading them wonderingly.

'POPULATE OR PERISH'

I heard and looked at the words, but was no wiser. Dad explained.

'They're short of workers in Australia, they want people to come and live there, particularly people from this country.'

'Are you saying that *we* could go?'

'Don't see why not. Read it, Kath. It says there's plenty of jobs. Australia has lovely weather, there'd be outdoor life for Kay. Bit of an adventure for all of us.'

Mum's face changed. Suddenly, she seemed younger, jumped from her stool, eyes alight with hope. Leaned over Dad's chair to look again at the words that had grabbed Dad's attention.

'Oh Jeff! D'you mean it? We could really leave here? How on earth could we afford to go?'

'I'll send for the information tomorrow. We'll have a look at what it says.'

It was as if the sun had broken through into our dull basement room. Mum smiled her lovely smile, eyes shining. During the next few days, the atmosphere changed. She seemed easier to get on with, less impatient with my questions. She talked to me a bit. Met the postman every morning before he had a chance to drop anything through the letter box. Grabbed delightedly at the fat envelope that eventually arrived and met Dad at the door on his return from work.

'Jeff! It's come!'

Dad opened the envelope, studied the contents, and smiled.

'I can't see any problem,' he said, 'Our passage would be paid for.'

She wept, which puzzled me. But then, grown-ups

sometimes did – how on earth could you know what they were feeling?

Dad hugged her. 'New start,' he said, with a huge smile. 'New life. We'll forget the war. And all this...' He gestured towards the sunless window.

'Kay will buy new hats to protect her beautiful freckles, and all the fine Aussie boys will fall in love with her.'

'Will it really happen?' she whispered, 'could something go wrong?'

'I don't think so, love. We shan't be the only ones to go, Australia wants lots of people. I'll send for the application form tomorrow.'

Life entered a new dimension. Mum started to sort her few possessions. Looked at her thick woollen coat and laughed. Threw out the fake fur gloves Dad had given her for Christmas.

'I won't need all these in Australia!'

Hats, boots, warm sweaters, all joined the pile of discarded clothing, all products of such careful consideration at the time, all acquired through precious clothing coupons in our ration books. Discarding them seemed to me a risky procedure, a bit premature, but there was no stopping her.

I looked over my few clothes and asked her if I should take them.

'Might as well. You'll have grown out of them soon enough.'

'Mum, why do you want to go to Australia?'

Her expression changed, as it often did, as though her mind and spirit were suddenly absent, in another place.

'It's as far away as possible from England. And the sun shines every day.'

'Daddy says that they have Christmas in the middle of summer. Why don't they change it to the middle of winter, same as us?'

'Oh for goodness' sake Kay, I don't know. Ask your father. Now do go away and let me get on.'

That night I had gone to bed in my cupboard-sized bedroom, but I could hear every word they said. In reply to his wife's main concern Dad told her

'We'd only have to fork out ten pounds. And there's help with expenses to get people settled.'

'It'll be the best thing that happened since we got married.'

'Another good thing could happen. We could have another child.'

There were no more words, and I fell asleep. In retrospect, I guess they made love.

I think he was fond of her, though there were things that sometimes puzzled or annoyed him. She didn't manage money well, though it's likely that he didn't fully understand the difficulties of the immediate post-war period. Food was still rationed, and the shortages were even more severe than during hostilities. Bread rationing was imposed.

'But where has all the money gone?' he asked her once, during an argument. She cried, and said she did her best.

'You don't have to do the shopping! You don't know how difficult it is to get things! Supper's always on the table when you come home, it all seems so easy to you.'

However, all such irritants and frustrations disappeared on the day that another envelope was pushed through our letterbox, telling us that our application to emigrate to Australia had been approved.

I got out my school atlas, and located this new place. It was many pages away from the map of my own country, the paper clean and pristine, with no fingermarks. Strangely empty of place-names.

I lived in a whirl of sorting, washing, packing and shopping. No goodbyes were said, there was no-one to say them to.

Feeling temporary, Dad hadn't bothered to make friends, for different reasons Mum hadn't got round to it either. 'Not our kind of people', she'd commented once.

However, on the morning of our departure, and realising that I would not see my old home ever again, I said goodbye to the only friends I had left in the house.

'Goodbye, Henry, Goodbye Charlie,' I said to the taps in the kitchen, wondering at the strange empty feeling in my stomach as we climbed the area steps for the last time.

Tilbury docks were awash with families. Feelings all on the surface today, – hope, apprehension, tears, laughter. Children, like me, puzzled at their parents' unusual reaction to a trip out. Knowing we wouldn't be going home again, but we'd be somewhere or other, not too different, we supposed. Australia? A long way away, we were told, but so was France, the destination of a day trip for Mum's thirtieth birthday. At least they spoke English in Australia. It couldn't be that far away.

We were all herded up the gangplank over a sinister gap to the safety of a ship that was so big that it didn't look like a boat at all, just a huge house whose windows were all circular. Most of the people were congregating along the side of the boat, leaning against a barrier I could only just see over. Many were laughing, some were in tears, waving, calling to those left behind. A hooter blasted just above our heads, we heard the rumble of engines starting up, there were vibrations beneath our feet. The gangplank, our only visible connection with the dockside, was pulled back into the ship. The dark gap widened. Dad picked me up so I could see the edge of the shores that seemed to be moving away from us. 'Say goodbye to England,' he whispered. I waved, with everyone else.

The abandoned crowd became smaller, their cries fainter as we moved away from our old life. At the time we didn't know that we were among the lucky ones. Some families were shipped out in converted troopships, with only the most basic amenities. We were in a former P&O liner, with all the luxuries of a hotel. I could hardly believe my eyes. There were books and magazines lying all over the place. You could *choose* what to have for dinner! There was a swimming pool, which terrified me. A cinema. So much to see and read and do. Surely heaven on earth. Or rather sea, as I looked out every day for six weeks at the unchanging horizon.

Mum seemed to flourish. She became less suspicious of strangers, talked more easily to our fellow passengers than she had to our London neighbours and the occupants of the air raid shelters we'd sometimes been forced to use during the war. She made the most of the luxuries that were free. Sunbathed on deck, when possible, though carefully, she had fair skin to go with her dark hair. I suspect that one or two male passengers might have wished for further acquaintance, but she behaved impeccably.

Dad was clearly frustrated by inaction. He tried some ball games, had a chat with some of the crew, asked questions, was given a private tour of the mysterious processes that drove the ship. Thought about embarking on an engineering apprenticeship. Apparently there were a variety of options for immigrants who were prepared to work hard. There were rumours, too. Stories from previous English families of disappointment, bad experiences. Some authorities were unprepared for the impact on local areas of so many incomers. Dad said we must be ready for anything, but that with patience and goodwill we would survive the difficult initial period.

It was only my second trip out of London. I had made sure my Welsh post-card, still unknown to my mother, was safely stowed away in one of my luggage cases. The only picture of Britain I possessed. The only link with a past that I didn't understand.

THREE

Melbourne, Australia, 1948

Melbourne, my second home.

The first few months didn't match up to the temporary paradise we'd been enjoying on our two-month journey from London. Our accommodation in small Nissen huts on the outskirts of the city was cramped and we shivered, but the coldness was a manifestation of discomfort and disappointment, rather than temperature.

Mum was despondent. I went to a temporary school for immigrants, where I was taught about life in Australia, and how not to be a whingeing Pom. Our miseries would pass, Dad said, they were only to be expected by incomers to these new and unfamiliar surroundings. There had been conditions to our settlement; immigrants were supposed to work in whatever job the government had allocated to them for at least two years. Not to worry, Dad said, there are ways and means of getting round restrictions.

'Be patient,' he said, 'If you're not happy in a year's time we'll think about going back. There's loads of work around. I'll get the best-paid job I can find, don't care what it is. With the settlement grant, it won't be long before we can find somewhere nice to live.'

Melbourne was changing. A Victorian city, densely packed with terraced bluestone buildings, its centre was being systematically demolished to make way for modern steel and glass-fronted emporia.

This was where the money was, Dad decided, and got a job on the latest building project in Collins Street. This, with the obligatory overtime, left him exhausted but with more cash in his pocket than he had ever dreamed of; within twelve months we were house hunting. Frantic and exhilarated, we toured the growing suburbs surveying what seemed to us like a city of palaces!

We found it, our new home, indistinguishable from most new houses in the suburban sprawl, and unrecognisable as a place that we could ever have hoped to occupy. Space between the houses! A kitchen to die for. A room of my own, where I could keep all my possessions, my books, my pictures. A small kingdom, mine.

New beds, tables, chairs – Dad called a stop to our purchases, we were spending too much, some things would have to wait.

They did, but the money kept coming in, and it wasn't long before our lifestyle caught up with it. We adjusted to our change of fortune, and the good life started to feel like a normal one.

I went to another school; classmates laughed at my accent and asked me to tea. They laughed too because I couldn't swim, had never been to a beach, didn't know what a 'barbie' was. One or two called me 'Pommy'. But it wasn't long before things stopped seeming odd, and I started to take it for granted that outdoors was where people had most of their fun. My freckled skin reddened, I got used to using sunscreen and wearing a hat.

Dad was happy with his new job, quickly mastering new skills until he was moved to the company's headquarters. He flourished there, given new responsibilities. Developing latent talents, he moved into the field of property management, going from strength to strength. There was no shortage of money now. We bought a family car, and Mum learned to drive. I recalled the London days when our shopping was piled into the pushchair I had occupied on the outward journey. 'Remember, Mum?' I asked her, 'how awkward it was to get it all down the area steps?'

'Don't think I want to remember those days' she replied shortly.

'Lots of us had bad days during the war', Dad said. The prisoner of war camps weren't exactly a holiday. But even during the worst days there was usually something to laugh about. Misery isn't so bad when you've got someone to share it with. You two must have had a bit of fun between the air raids.'

We didn't, but I wasn't going to say.

Relations with my mother had seemed better after our move to Melbourne, she was as relaxed as I had ever seen her. She refused to talk of our London days, comparisons were unwelcome, even from a new and improved viewpoint. We picnicked on the beaches, I learned to swim. We took boat trips on the muddy river Yarra and strolled along its tree-lined banks. Made a few friends, mostly ex-pats like ourselves. Mum didn't talk easily to the neighbouring Aussies who made the occasional friendly overture. I suspect she couldn't place them in a social hierarchy that she didn't understand, even if it existed at all.

We bought the occasional English newspaper to see how the old country was getting along without us. Well, they've wheeled Churchill out again, Dad said, but reckoned the old boy was getting on a bit for the job.

A decade passed. Meantime school was endured or enjoyed, depending on what I was doing at the time. English Literature was undiluted pleasure, maths a bore I could put up with, science a mystery I was willing to worship but not study. Sport was a misery. Less to do with the nature of the activity I was expected to take part in, than the world in which it existed, where classroom alliances disappeared, normal civilities abandoned, new rules, obvious to others, unrecognisable to me, took precedence over normal daily school relationships. An attitude I have never quite lost; for me organised physical activities have always seemed oddly threatening.

I lost my London accent. I was no longer an object of curiosity; I was left alone by the more vibrant members of my class, retiring into a quiet life of observation and reading, which suited me fine. I still told stories, as I had been doing ever since I can remember. Now, at school, they were being written down, and to my amazement and pleasure, meeting with approval from my teachers. Putting ideas on paper, so that they were always there in my exercise books, came soon after I had learned to use a pen. Next came the discovery that the choosing of words, the ordering of them, was a new source of fun and excitement. Teachers had liked my stories, end of term reports had contained favourable comments, which pleased and puzzled me, as I didn't know what it was that I was doing right.

Dad had been delighted, my mother remaining unimpressed. 'Scribbling's not going to earn her a decent living,' she sniffed. He had responded, irritated,

'Can't the child do *anything* right?'

I read hungrily, all the stories I could find. I wept with Griselda, suffered with Dorothea Brooke, was condescended to by Lady Catherine de Bourgh. I laughed with Waugh, lost myself in the future worlds of Wells and Verne, and went through a stream of consciousness phase. By my seventeenth birthday I was editor of the school magazine, and even had one short story accepted by a women's magazine, spoiled by the fact that they had cut out what I considered to be the best bits. Dad was delighted at each small success, my mother observing that sooner or later I would have to think about getting a job. She was right, of course, but her route for me was not mine.

Her comments presaged the return of her old, half-forgotten periods of anxiety and depression that had marked our days in London. She became restless, wanted to move again. Dad was happy to indulge her fancy for a more secluded location, somewhere bigger, posher, nearer the coast.

Again her mood lightened, we looked at possible homes for her approval, smidgeons of fun beginning to reappear. We found a suitable house, moved in, I started a new school.

Dad was now managing the properties he had once helped to build. He started to look at investments for the accumulating cash in his bank account. In material terms the future looked bright.

I had a friend, Cherry Donovan. Why we became close I never really understood. We were at the same school but seemed to have little in common.

She was beautiful, I thought, envious of the blonde locks that suffered a great deal of tossing in the presence of the opposite sex. Together we shopped for clothes, hers bought for the fun of it, since nothing in the sphere of fashion mattered, her face and figure being enough to turn heads. I bought more carefully. As far as my appearance was concerned, I considered that there was distinct room for improvement. Cherry was consoling.

'You under-estimate yourself, Kay,' she said, 'You're small, but with a nice figure and a face that's pretty and *interesting*.'

I was not sure I wanted to be known as that girl with red hair. But then I wasn't sure how I wanted to be known. I suspected that making a name as a writer was the undisclosed goal I was aiming for.

We both fancied Uni, for different reasons. Cherry hankered after a whirlwind social life, I wanted to write better. Writing had taken hold of me, and this was the activity where I was truly at home, my other world. You knew where you were with stories, you were in charge, you invented the mysteries, solved the puzzles you had devised, and when the stories were finished, unlike life, they did not return to haunt you, but went back between their covers and stayed there.

Cherry spent much of her free time at our house, her parents leading an unpredictable lifestyle, frequently absent from their grand house in Footscray, leaving Cherry well provided for, but a touch lonely, I thought. She was a sociable soul. She knew that in our house she'd have nice meals round the family table, a welcome from Mum, gentle teasing from Dad and confidential fun with me.

My mother adored her. This puzzled me, but I welcomed the lightening of the atmosphere when she was around. Mum deplored my lifestyle, shaking her head over my inadequacies.

'I wish you could get Kay to have a bit more fun,' she remarked to Cherry one day. 'She's always got her head stuck in books.'

'Kay's clever, Mrs Francis. She'll walk into Uni. If I'm to get there, I shall have to do a lot more work than I'm doing at present.'

I had long ago concluded that I was not the sort of daughter my mother wanted. I saw the puzzlement in my father's face when school successes were met on her part with indifference.

I'd showed her my latest school report. Barely glancing at it, she'd put it down without comment, and changed the subject. I felt hurt, it had been a *good* report.

'It's not personal, Kay,' Dad said, later. 'I believe it's depression.'

'Couldn't a doctor help her? Prescribe medication of some kind?'

'I did suggest that once. But she went berserk at the idea. Haven't dared mention it again. All we can do is be patient and hope it'll get better. It usually does, after a while.'

She didn't go out of her way to be unkind, but the ups and downs of my life were not something she appeared to give much thought to. After all, what more could I want of life? A comfortable home, a good education, and licence to do more or less whatever I wanted. She used to comment, with a smile, to acquaintances,

'She's a real Daddy's girl'.

I certainly wasn't Mummy's.

Exams were sat and passed, Cherry and I moved into higher education. English literature for me, Drama for her. She had always been keen on acting, and thought that a course in that field and the career that she hoped might follow would produce the fun and excitement she loved. Bigger and better parties for her, another equally exciting but different world for me.

Once at University, I lived in the library, my time there not so much consciously pleasurable as passing so quickly that I surfaced from my reading as though waking from a dream. Cherry flourished on her drama course, though our daytime paths rarely crossed. Her weekend visits offered me a view of her university life, very different from mine. I think she saw it as her mission to introduce me to a more normal round of student activities. I listened to her stories of each party she went to, and what I supposed were standard experimental sexual activities, but I was not much inclined to join in. Later, I thought, when I'm surer about who I am. Being grown up seemed so *complicated*, so many things to think about at the same time.

'You lead an exhausting life' I told Cherry one evening. Don't know how you stand the pace!'

She looked appreciatively at her reflection in the mirror, carefully applying her new lipstick.

'And I don't know how you stand the lack of it! You could pass your exams in half the time you're spending on them.'

'Cherry! You know perfectly well it's not the exams I care about…it's just that I *like* what I do.'

'And is this how you're going to spend the rest of your life?'

An expression of horror at the thought appeared on her pretty, newly made-up face.

'Don't know. But it'll do for now. One way or another I want to write.'

Cherry heaved a deep sigh.

'If you're going to write books you've got to *live* a bit. There'll be so much you can't write about because you've never *done* it.'

'You may have a point there. But that doesn't worry most writers. You don't have to murder people to write crime fiction. I have to say that there are times when it seems I don't know what I *think* until I've written it down.'

'Well, sometimes I don't know what *I* think until I've *done* it!'

'Sounds bloody risky!'

A rare, fleeting discussion of abstractions.

I helped her replace the lids and stoppers on the assembly of her beauty products.

'You really don't need all this stuff!'

'Wait and see what it does for me!'

We laughed at each other, as we headed off for a morning's shopping, hand in hand. Celebrating our solidarity with the purchase of identical green t-shirts, sloganed with some newly popular revolutionary message.

Our incompatible relationship continued, Cherry's boy friends came and went. My apparent lack of them intrigued her, but I wasn't happy discussing the few overtures made by the more enterprising of my male colleagues, even less about the ones I fancied. She took my reticence as lack of opportunity, – not the case, but I preferred to leave my private life undiscussed. I was making too many mistakes in that direction. Why, I asked myself, did Cherry, extrovert and charismatic, choose a quiet, bookish, insecure girl as a close friend? Was I a foil for her performances? I examined the idea, and concluded that it was completely wrong, that somehow or other there was a spark of understanding between us, invisible to others, even to ourselves, that kept us together as a unit. 'Girls need friends,' she once said, if we don't look out for each other, who will?'

Why had I not been more careful?

Cherry had a new boyfriend.

'Another?' I asked.

'This one's special.'

'How special? What's he like?'

'He's... he's just lovely.'

'That doesn't tell me much.'

Previous boyfriends had been enthusiastically described in detail, and I decided that either Cherry had been rendered speechless by the new candidate's perfection, or that there was nothing outstanding about him that could move her into descriptive mode. Time passed, it became apparent that Chris was indeed special, and that Cherry was in love.

She brought him to our house one weekend. I was introduced as 'Kay, my best friend', a description I felt I barely deserved, but was grateful for. Well, I thought, I can see what *you* see in him. Older than most of her contemporaries, he was already on the academic ladder – a lecturer in the Politics department at Uni. With black curly hair, a bit longer than convention required in the early sixties, his film star good looks were marred only by the slightly crooked teeth revealed in his ready smile. What a stunner, I thought!

He was carrying flowers for Mum, which he presented her with as he came into the house, exuding charm.

He coaxed her into more contributions to the conversation than was usually the case in the company of visitors. He talked politics with Dad. Charmed me, too, I was seriously envious.

The visit was judged a success, and my mother was delighted.

'Wish you could find someone like Chris,' she commented next morning at breakfast.

'Give her time,' my father replied. 'Kay's not in a hurry, are you, love?'

The pair became regular visitors. Chris was interested in the research I was doing in the field of children's literature. I was intrigued by animal characterisation, and how it reflected or implied criticism of the society of the day. He offered to help with this where he could. I valued his comments on my work, and was pleased that Cherry had found someone whose company was not only enjoyable but useful too.

'You've had to slow down a bit,' I teased Cherry. 'Don't you miss your old life?'

Cherry laughed.

I'd miss Chris a great deal more!'

'Do you think you have a future together?'

'I hope so. Things are going so well at the moment. Finals this year, maybe we'll make some decisions afterwards.'

Chris and I frequently met at the University café at lunchtime, Cherry's drama course being held in distant university premises, she rarely joined us.

Intrigued and flattered, I was aware that we puzzled our fellow diners with our arguments over the experiences of Mole and Ratty, and why the occupants of the fields and the Wild Wood were all male, and permanently on the move.

'Hunting and gathering of course,' said Chris, 'no time to stand and stare. You might be grabbed by a predatory female.'

We laughed, recalling the Wind in the Willows of our respective childhoods. With a sudden change of mood, he spoke, thoughtfully.

'We have a lot in common, you and me.'

It should have been a warning, but we started talking about one of his teaching colleagues who, Chris commented, was Mr. Toad in person. His description of the unfortunate man escalated into mutual helpless laughter, which turned a few heads in our direction.

We walked back to our house one evening, where Cherry would be waiting, together with friends, to celebrate two events. One was Dad's birthday, the other the publication of my first book, a collection of stories for children. I had dedicated it to him. Mum had made a birthday cake.

It was a good party, friends arrived, spilled into the kitchen, the entrance hall, the garden. Dad had a bit too much to drink, made a speech, hugged Mum and me, spoke of our journey over the years since we arrived from London.

Among his presents was a recently written collection of stories about England since the war, looking at how it had changed. I saw that in holding it, his eyes were suspiciously bright.

I sauntered through the next few weeks in a fog of self-satisfaction. I fancied Chris, of course I did. I was flattered that he liked my company, made me feel grown-up, worth listening to. Finals came and went. I scarcely noticed how quiet Cherry had become.

The news came from my mother. She was pale with fury, as I returned from a day in the library. Cherry had called, weeping. She and Chris had split up, and she was heartbroken.

'It's all your fault!', my mother shouted at me.

'What are you talking about? What's it got to do with me?'

We faced each other across the hall, in an eruption of buried dislike, guilt and anger.

From my mother's disjointed accusations, I gathered that Chris had told Cherry that he was becoming unsure that they could make a go of it, that he needed time to mull things over, he must be absolutely certain, he had said, that they were right for each other. I responded to my mother's tirade with contempt.

'The usual crap! He's just bored with her.'

'It's more than that! Cherry said he's in love with you. *Infatuated*, she said. How could you do this to your best friend? I'm ashamed of you.'

I hit back.

'You always have been! God knows why.'

She turned away, feeling for her bedroom doorhandle.

'Rubbish! I shouted after her. 'There's never been anything between us. Don't blame *me* if he's gone off her.'

She disappeared into her bedroom, weeping.

I woke up. There was a tiny pinprick of guilt at the back of my mind. And some confusion. There had been moments, once or twice, a silence when there should have been words, a hand over mine, a glance that I recognised as a question. I think the truth is that if I had recognised these signals for what they were, and had backed off, I would have lost this very pleasant and undoubtedly flattering acquaintanceship. I wasn't even absolutely certain they had really happened. Was my imagination playing tricks again, as had often happened in the past? How many times I had asked myself the same question, how many times had I been unsure of my recollection of experiences? Whatever had been going on, I had not behaved well.

Cherry refused to speak to me, I felt guilty and confused. I sent her a note. I said I would be by the Old Bandstand in Fitzroy Gardens at lunchtime, and that I hoped she would come because I was sure that everything could be put right, back to the way they had been before.

The sun was uncomfortably hot. With a layer of sunscreen and a wide-brimmed hat I set off for the Gardens, located the old bandstand, sat down on a bench inside, sheltered from the blazing sun, rehearsing what I had decided to say. There had been nothing between Chris and me, people seeing us together in the café at Uni were simply imagining an affair. It was nothing more than literary banter. True, after a fashion…

I spotted her in the distance, walking fast. I rapidly rehearsed what I'd planned to say. Give Chris a bit of time and space, and whatever you do, don't make a big fuss. Stay calm, he'll come round. Sure to. This patronising waffle was never said. Cherry's face was pale, unrecognisable in its misery.

'You didn't really want him. Why did you take him away from me? Just for fun? Just to show me that you could?'

'Oh Cherry. You won't believe me, but I didn't recognise what was happening. To say sorry sounds so feeble. I thought … no that's a lie. I just didn't think. I was stupid, careless, enjoying my life, basking in the reflected glory, in the company of a star.'

My voice thickened as I felt the tears coming.

'So I heard. Other people noticed. I'd heard rumours before Chris spoke to me. I didn't believe them. You were my friend.'

I looked at the dishevelled figure in front of me; the beauty shadowed, the light extinguished.

'I hope you suffer for this. One day you'll pay for it. I hate you.'

She turned and walked away. My best friend, who'd wanted me to like the man she loved, and to share her happiness. What was wrong with me, that I hadn't seen clearly what had been going on? Or had I seen it and chosen to do nothing? Cherry couldn't hate me any more than I hated myself. I believed, with utter certainty, that we would never meet again. There were notes from Chris, but I neither read nor replied to them. Mum didn't speak to me.

She still cooked our family evening meal, refusing any help from me. Dad and I were sitting in our garden while waiting for the call to dinner – three-way conversation was now difficult, recent events still disturbing my mother's attitude to both of us. I guessed she would have wanted Dad to join in her punishment of me.

We watched the breeze playing in the eucalyptus trees, heard the chatter of the ubiquitous budgies. Thin cirrus marbled the sky, would it rain tomorrow?

I was wondering how long the current stand-off between my mother and me would last.

'Sorry to put you through all this, Dad.'

'It's not *all* your fault, Kay. Relationships are infinitely complex. It's even possible that one day, looking back, you'll see things a bit differently.'

'It's always been clear Mum doesn't like me. Some of it has been my fault, some of it hers. A kind of genetic misfit. A bit of bad luck too, I suppose. It goes back a long way.'

'I know, Kay. I've thought about it so much and wondered. I noticed it only a few weeks after coming back from the war. I thought at first that my homecoming had somehow disrupted the relationship between the two of you, and that it would all settle down when we got used to each other. But it didn't, did it?' He was silent for a moment or two, then smiled, sadly.

'I'd have liked a brother or sister for you, but Kath said she'd got enough to deal with, moving to a new country, making a new home. One day, perhaps, she said, but the day never came. I wish I could help you, Kay, but I feel out of my depth.' He took a packet of cigarettes from his pocket, Craven A, his favourite brand.

'And my latest stupid behaviour with Chris Martin hasn't helped.'

'We all make mistakes. Some can be repaired, others we must live with. *All* of us.' He was silent for a few moments. 'If things can't be put right, we must just get on with life. We owe it to ourselves, and to those around us. Pick yourself up, and carry on living each day that passes. That goes for you, for Cherry and me, too, each of us in our different ways.'

'Can't see that advice taken on board by Mum. She seems rooted in past misunderstandings, things she can't break free from. I'm sure some medical advice would help, I wish you could persuade her to see a doctor.'

'So do I.' He sighed, looking towards the house where the clatter of pots and pans indicated the readiness of another silent meal.

'I do realise that you'll leave home one day, and I shall miss you. But congratulate myself that you've grown an independent woman, which once was the only goal I had for you, until I realised you had goals of your own and were well on the way to achieving them. I am proud of you, Kay.'

I smiled gratefully at him, thinking that my mother wasn't. Ashamed of me, she'd said. But this was the first time I'd done anything to warrant it. Her dislike had deeper roots. We made our way back to the house. Dad put out his cigarette.

FOUR

Melbourne 1960 – 1971

Our family unit became fragile. I spent longer at Uni, still researching the field of children's literature, but beginning to feel the pull of adult writing. I must make the transition, I thought, I have spent too long in the generation of a world which is not mine. I had written a few short stories and put them together in a collection. A small publisher in Birmingham, England, had taken them and sold them successfully. Run-of-the-mill for him; a huge achievement for me – the first tentative steps towards my life's goal. A novel must follow, I told myself, mustn't put it off any longer. How on earth do I get going?

The answer, I decided, was to start researching life, rather than literature. I recalled, with sadness, one of Cherry's comments – "If you're going to write books you've got to *live* a bit.'

She'd been right.

I'd dropped in at our local bookshop, and started reading, as usual. The proprietor, Bradley Crawford, emerged from the back of the store to tease me, I assumed, for reading and not buying.

'If all my customers were like you,' he assured me, 'I'd be bankrupt within a week!'

'Sorry, Brad. But look – I'm a published author now! You should feel honoured to have me here in your shop!'

'Your stories have been published? Congratulations, Kay! When shall we see them over here?'

'Soon, I hope!'

The shop door tinkled discreetly, a customer was coming in. Brad eyed him for a moment, turned back to me. The customer was examining crime thrillers, seemed absorbed. Shop policy, I knew, was not to descend on customers the minute they entered – better to give them a few moments to look around, settle down by the books that interested them.

'I have a problem, Kay.' He lowered his voice. 'It's been on my mind for some time.'

'I've a suggestion, an offer, a proposition to make. Spend as much time as you want here, read yourself silly. I need an assistant. I'm so stretched at the moment – I want to go to Frankfurt Book Fair, and can't find anyone suitable to cover for my absence. I need a permanent helpful presence in the shop, giving me time for other things. A bookshop's a commercial enterprise, not just a local amenity. I'm offering you a job.'

He leaned back against the Cookery shelves, displacing Elizabeth David's culinary – and other – adventures.

I considered his suggestion. It fitted well with my new determination to explore new avenues; practise being grown up. I didn't need to think about it.

'Offer accepted! I'll do my best, Brad.'

'Bless you, Kay. I can't think of a better person to look after my customers. I'll check out rates of pay locally. Can you start *now*?'

His glance flicked over to the customer in the front of the shop.

I tried not to giggle. Writers do not giggle, they smile perceptively, they laugh knowledgeably. I walked over to the customer.

'Were you looking for something special? Or just browsing? Let me know if you need any help.'

I made my first sale. I went back to Brad, triumphant. His eyes were bright with joy. We shook hands, he held mine for a moment or two.

'Brad, I'll start tomorrow if you like. I must go home now and announce to my parents that they no longer have to clothe and feed a jobless dependent.'

I stepped out into the sunshine.

A new way of life for me. I must get up promptly and on time. Not that I was ever a just-another-five-minutes person, but I could do with a bit more self-discipline. Breakfast no later than seven-thirty. Clean clothes more often than usual. A touch of lipstick? My thoughts turned irrevocably to Cherry; I couldn't dismiss my many memories of her.

I announced my news.

'Mum, I've got a job. You'll be pleased. Brad at the bookshop needs some help and he's offered me the post.'

'So you're going to be a shop assistant. Thought you'd have wanted something a bit better than that!'

I didn't bother to argue, it never resolved the disparity of our views.

She asked a few questions, particularly about how much I would earn.

Dad was delighted. 'A bit of routine'll be good for your writing. Brad's a good chap. The work's ideal for you.'

It was.

My proposed novel flourished under the pressure of having to fit it into a firm routine. The characters were uncooperative at first, but eventually became resigned to the discipline. The story was one of characters torn from their roots, a bit of biography of course, as most first novels are.

I finished it and submitted it to Jonathan Parfitt, my English publisher.

He accepted it without a great deal of enthusiasm.

Well, it's a first novel, he pointed out over the phone. 'It'll do.'

I was a published novelist! Well, almost. The months passed slowly while changes were made, details discussed, contract signed, and words finally printed on paper. The book arrived in Melbourne.

'We must arrange a book-signing event. Never had one before.' Brad announced with pleasure. 'It'll bring in loads of customers.'

Well, in the event It brought in a steady stream. I wondered how many of them would actually *read* the book I was signing. Brad was delighted.

'Can I take you out for a super meal afterwards? – we need to celebrate!'

It was certainly a good dinner, in a hotel with a table by a window overlooking the ocean. First course and pudding were consumed with appreciation. The book-signing we were celebrating was barely mentioned. I had a hunch that it wasn't the true purpose of the event.

'I've a question for you, Kay.'

'Yes?'

'Will you marry me?'

This was not a bombshell. I had suspected that the proposal would come sooner or later. And, of course, I had wondered what my answer would be. In many ways it would be an ideal alliance, we had mutual interests, got on well together, had separate but compatible ambitions, his to open a chain of bookshops, mine to be a *bette*r writer. But there were other implications within marriage.

I had often thought about having a child. It would happen sooner or later, I'd thought. At this moment I couldn't think of a nicer father for it. But, *marriage*?

Brad was looking at me hopefully. He'd taken his glasses off, they were for reading books, not faces. The waiter was hovering, – I waved him away.

'I don't know, Brad.'

He was silent for a moment.

'Well, at least that's not a refusal!' he said. Would you like a coffee? While you think about it?'

'Do you love me?'

'You bloody well know I do!'

'Well, you might have mentioned it!'.

That somehow struck us both as funny, there was a muted burst of laughter from both of us. An unromantic proposal, an unconventional response. I tried to give Brad an answer that was honest and affectionate.

'Tell you what, Brad. I'll come home with you. See how we get on.'

He looked joyful.

'You're always full of surprises, Kay, but this one's the best ever!'

It was my first sexual experience, and, to my mind, worth the wait. He was kind, considerate and gentle, I'd told him I was a virgin.

'A wise one,' he'd said. 'Let's hope the wisdom stays now the virginity's gone!'

I returned home next morning, quite early, Mum and Dad were finishing breakfast.

'Celebrations go well?' Dad asked cheerfully.

'Yes, Dad. And there's one more thing to celebrate. I'm moving in with Brad.'

'We were pretty sure this would happen, love,' said Dad.

'I'm so glad for you. It's not only a practical move, but an obvious and happy one.' He gave me a hug and a kiss.

'We shall miss you, but with much happiness.'

'Not much room over the shop,' Mum remarked.

'It'll do for now,' I told her.

'Aren't you going to get married?' she asked.

'Perhaps – but not immediately. That would be a big step.'

The sixties were well and truly swinging in London, I'd heard, wasn't very sure to what extent they had been swinging in Melbourne, but I was pretty sure that Mum wouldn't approve, whatever I did.

I transported clothes, books, and my typewriter to Brad's small living area above the shop. Gone was the sense of space I'd enjoyed in our new Melbourne house, the fine kitchen, the tree – filled garden. It didn't matter, there were other rewards. Brad organised me.

'You must have a couple of clear hours a day for your writing, Kay. I'd never forgive myself if that suffered in any way.'

As I remember, the only occasions when my writing time was compromised was during Brad's occasional absences. I was anxious to make sure the shop flourished during these periods, and was quite proud of myself for managing it without disaster. The new life filled my waking hours. I felt grown-up.

But what of the mythical child that popped into my mind from time to time? Could I cope with the enormous changes that getting pregnant must bring about? Nervously, I broached the subject to Brad.

'We should discuss a family, Brad.'

He was non-committal, observing 'I'd lose my shop manager!'

Hardly an enthusiastic response, I thought.

'We'll be fine,' he said, 'Just deal with things as they happen.'
Nothing happened.

We needed a holiday, I decided. We found a willing friend to run the shop for a couple of weeks while we took a break, visiting some of the amazing sights our country has to offer. Ayer's rock, Sydney's Opera House, the outback and its unique wildlife. Back home, I spent an evening with Mum and Dad, telling them about it all and showing them photographs. Mum was quiet, went to bed early, she was tired, she said. Dad took a packet of cigarettes from his pocket.

'Kay, I'm really worried about your Mum. I don't think she's well.'

Has she ever been, I thought.

'Let's go and sit in the garden.'

We sat in our usual chairs by the eucalyptus bush, now grown into a tree. Time made visible. I see it passing in the mirror every day.

'Haven't you noticed anything, Kay? She's gets confused, forgets things. Loses track of what she is trying to say.'

'She talks to me so little, Dad, save to remind me of how I had spoilt her pleasure in life by being the reason for the cessation of Cherry's visits. Remember when she packed a couple of sandwiches and drove to the beach where we used to swim and picnic, in the hope of bumping into her? What she was intending to say I can't imagine.'

'It's worse than that now. While you were away there was a phone call from the police. She'd parked the car in the town centre illegally and seemed unable to explain why. She told them that her husband would come and fetch her as she'd got lost and didn't know the way home.'

'That's worrying, Dad.'

He told me of other things, many trivial, but they added up to something more serious.

The message was clear, we had to accept the onset of mental deterioration.

As the weeks, the months passed, I tried hard to be patient with her, sorry for a life gone wrong for reasons that were beyond me.

One day I came home to find her sitting at the kitchen table, writing a shopping list. She looked at me blankly.

'What's up Mum? You O.K.?'

'Who are you? What d'you want?'

It had to happen sooner or later. A stark confirmation of all we feared. Moments of forgetfulness, we all have them, she had them too often, now they had exploded into a frightening memory loss, a massive displacement of the context of her daily life, of where she was, of who she was. She recovered, more or less, from this particular episode, but could not remember that it had happened.

These events pointed in one direction. This was dementia. I must negotiate a relationship with a changing person. I answered her question, smiling at her.

'What I really want is a cup of tea,' I said. 'I missed lunch today. Stay there and I'll make one for both of us.'

Dad received my news resignedly. 'We must accept this,' he said, and decide the best way to cope.'

Inevitably, her illness started to impinge on my daily life. I visited my parents more frequently, squeezing my precious two hours of writing into a session with her that was full of interruptions. Things she said she needed to do that she had already done. Trips to the toilet forgetting why she was there. Moments of distress.

Strangely, our relationship improved. She always knew who Dad was, but although she knew she had a daughter, sometimes it was Cherry, sometimes a person strange to me. It was manifestly not me. And, oddly, the animosity started to fade. She began to treat me as a visitor to whom she must be polite and friendly. 'Nice of you to call', she would say, 'Would you like a cup of tea?'

One day I found her crying, and I was able to put my arm round her, something I could never have done in earlier days. I could only imagine the fear and distress of a person who was becoming lost within the world they had always known, a stranger in their own history. 'Don't cry, Mum,' I said. 'You'll be feeling better soon.'

'You're very kind,' she replied, 'But it's too late. Do call again, it's so nice to have someone to talk to. I have lost my daughter. I don't know where she is.'

Thus began the fragmentation of a personality that had once known love and hope.

A couple of difficult years passed, during which I was able to do little but deal with her increasing physical and mental problems. I spent less and less time in the bookshop, soon none at all. Brad was understanding but obliged to hire a new assistant. I felt my time with him was coming to an end. Neither of us said that one day I might come back, take up my old life again. I kept writing, it was my only pleasure.

Dad seemed lost, spending little time at work.

'They can do without me,' he said, 'they know where I am if I'm needed. I can be more useful at home.'

She died, more peacefully than she had lived. Dementia had been diagnosed, expedited by depression and anxiety. We missed her, suddenly bereft of the duties of care.

My father was saddened, but not devastated. He had been patient with his wife's difficult moods, disappointed, I imagine, with her lack of enthusiasm for the challenges of their new life, and her restlessness. I have often wondered if he had considered separation or divorce, but, as far as I know, there had never been another woman in his life. I think he had loved her.

Suddenly I was free. Not only from the chores of nursing, from my responsibilities of a shop, from constant decision making, but from the cloud of disapproval that had followed me all my life. I could go out, have dinner with friends, come home – to someone who was pleased to see me. It felt strange. I felt a hundred years older than the feckless girl who used to go shopping with Cherry. What did I want to do with my life now? Strangely, I felt no desire to go back to Brad and the shop. It closed off too many possibilities. We had been fond of each other, but what I wanted now was a new world, challenging, unpredictable, demanding from me skills I hadn't yet learned. The child must wait.

I had a dream one night. It was a dream of fields.

I thought of starting again in that old, old world, the one I was born into. Should I go back to England? But I wouldn't go alone, Dad would be overjoyed to come with me. He had been homesick for so long. We both needed to kick-start a new life. Back in our chairs in the garden, I broached the subject.

He rose from his chair, gazed into the far distance, where we could just glimpse the blue line that was the ocean. He was silent for several minutes, then turned to me.

'Australia's been good to me, but for a long time I've wanted to go home.'

I thought of the day twenty-three years ago, when the reverse situation had been suggested. A grey, chilly day in dreary post-war London. Mum's unexpected joy at Dad's tentative proposition, that we should look for a better life on the other side of the world. I had often found it surprising that my mother, someone who usually saw any change as a threat rather than a challenge, should have taken to the project with so much enthusiasm. Never for a moment, I'm sure, did my father envisage his rise to a situation where he could do whatever he wanted without noticeably depleting his bank balance. Not that he had ever wanted much, a world tour had once been suggested to Mum, but she had shuddered. 'All those people', she had said.

Wherever we decided to live, it wouldn't make any difference to what I would be doing, and maybe both of us needed a new focus, a new life. What did I know of England, other than a slum basement in London's East End? I thought of other British immigrants who had returned from a nostalgic holiday in the old country. They'd had a good time, looked up old friends and relatives, but were glad to be back. We too were Australian now. Would we fit in, back in that old country we had left so hopefully?

'Shall we give it a try?' I said.

The shopping, the sorting, the packing started again, twenty-three years after our original nervous steps out of England. We took little with us, my books, my typewriter, a few objects I had grown fond of. We could buy necessities as and when they were required. We sold the house. If our new venture didn't work out, and we decided to return, we didn't want to come back to the place we had left. Too many memories there.

Eight weeks to travel to Australia twenty-three years ago. Less than a day to return. One person lost in the interim.

FIVE

London, Shrewsbury, 1971 – 1972

London, on our arrival, seemed unbelievably crowded, cold, and rather grand. We stayed in a hotel for a couple of weeks, doing the usual tourist round, and finally, from curiosity and a taste of nostalgia, visiting our old home in the East End.

Arriving in our hired car, we found a parking place a couple of doors away from the house. *Found* a parking spot? This was the first shock – the whole area would have been empty of parked cars in the old days. New buildings now sprouted from areas devastated by bombs, and even in those streets that had been spared, there seemed a sharpening of outlines, a redrawing of details – the odd green plant outside front entrances, new door trims, freshly painted lamp posts. The battered victim of the 1940s was coming back to life.

We left the car and walked to the railings that enclosed our old area steps. Looked down at the window that the sunshine never found. A large potted fern sat by the basement door.

At street level, a man came out of the front door, asking if we were looking for someone. I told him the reason we were standing outside his house and commented on the distinct improvement that we could see around us.

'Yes,' he answered, 'the place is certainly changing, we've noticed this in the short time we've been here. House prices going up a bit. We're new to London, and with the economy buoyant, I'm predicting that London is on the brink of prosperity. We like it here. Nice cosmopolitan atmosphere.'

I could see the evidence of his remarks. Black and brown faces on the trains, the buses, and in shops and offices. Faces that would have caused comments and stares in the old days, when we first encountered those black American soldiers who were part of the nation that was winning the war for us.

With the increased traffic, it would seem dangerous for children to play in the streets as they once did. Not me, of course, my mother would never have allowed it. This particular restriction hadn't bothered me; I was shy, and didn't talk their street language. On the few occasions I came across them by myself, walking to school, in local shops, they would tease me without mercy and with contempt, I was not one of them. I saw no children in the streets today. Where did the kids go to play now?

'So you lived here during the war?' our new acquaintance asked.

'I was in the army,' my father said, 'an early prisoner of war. My wife and daughter lived in the basement of this house, they managed to survive the air raids, thank goodness. I joined them when I got back from Belgium after the war was over.'

The man smiled at us. 'Would you like to see inside?'

I laughed. 'We've never been in the main part of the house,' I told him, 'the basement is the only part we ever saw!'

'Well, come in and have a coffee,' he said, 'in the basement.'

This was an offer I couldn't refuse. I glanced at Dad, who looked quite happy at the invitation. Our host indicated the steps that led to the main door, and the three of us stepped inside.

There had been stairs leading up from our basement rooms, but the door at the top had been permanently bolted from the other side. I saw it now, unbolted, and half-open. Our host introduced himself.

'My name is Patel. Adam Patel.'

'Our name is Francis. I'm Kay, and this is my father, Jeff.'

We followed him down the stairs to our old home. It was now – just the kitchen. Not as magnificent as the one we had left behind in Melbourne, but palatial in comparison with the place where I used to spend my days.

'We have made some changes,' said our host. In due course we hope to make more. I see this house as a good investment if my forecast proves correct. The area is ripe for development.'

There was a new window looking towards the backyard that had once housed our toilet. Today it showed us a tiny, paved garden, filled with pots of lettuce, tomatoes and bright flowers.

I remembered all the other uses of the space where we were now standing – a bedroom, a kitchen, a large cupboard which was called my bedroom, and a miniscule, enclosed area we called 'the scullery' – I don't even know if the word is in use today. It had contained little but a tap and a chipped white enamel sink. Its function was unclear, but it had its uses, particularly when the weather discouraged outdoor trips. I suspected that it now housed the abandoned facility from the back yard.

Dad and I spoke a few words of recollection to each other.

'Well, one thing is obvious,' said our host, 'You've spent the intervening years a long way from here!'

I smiled. 'We left for Australia in 1948. I suppose in those days my accent was Cockney. Translation to Australian would have been easy and quick!'

I think I'd expected to be moved at the sight of the place where I was born, however changed it might be. In truth, I felt no nostalgia in my renovated home. We sat at a large central table, drinking our coffee, talking of wartime days.

'Living in the basement must have been a tight fit for you,' he said.

'There was only my mother and me,' I told him, 'It was when my dad came home that we felt it was time for a move.'

Our host frowned for a moment. 'Just a minute,' he said, 'Francis, you said your name was. This rings a bell. My wife has spoken of some letters addressed to someone of that name, letters she found lying around, that had arrived, presumably, after you left. I think she kept them. Just in case, she said, you never know whether the former occupants might turn up. I got a telling off for suggesting that she should throw them away. I don't know where she keeps them. If you're interested, I'll find them and put them in the post, or you could pick them up if it's convenient. Laila will be delighted to be vindicated.'

'No good posting them at the moment,' Dad laughed. We have no fixed address.'

We told him of the purpose of our exodus from Australia, that we were looking at the possibilities of making a home here in Britain. Not in London, but perhaps another city, or a small town. Maybe the countryside – it all depended on how we felt after living and breathing English air for a few months. We were not in a hurry.

'If you would kindly keep them for a bit longer,' Dad said, 'we'll drop you a line when we are able to give you an address. Since we've lived for twenty-five years without them, I can't think they contain anything of world-shattering importance. Probably just advertising stuff. Hope there aren't any bills.'

We thanked Adam Patel, and left, pleased with our experience. A pleasant man, we thought, his wife seemingly possessed of an unusual respect for moral and social niceties. Were they the only ones to have lived in the old place? I couldn't imagine a series of occupiers keeping a few old letters.

We had decided to travel around the country for a bit, seeing if we could find somewhere that appealed to us as a new base. Together? Or should we look for separate but not too far apart homes? We decided that looking for two suitable houses would be complicated and time-consuming.

'We'll find the right area,' I suggested, 'buy a good-sized house for both of us, then if we like it there, one of us can set up on our own. Let's play it by ear!'

We had a look at some of the most popular country towns. A dazzling few months of holiday, I suppose, we fell in love with one place after another. We thought about Cambridge, but I took the view that to live in close proximity to an academic community without being part of it would be somehow unsatisfactory. Devon appealed, particularly on account of its mild climate, but Dad said he didn't fancy living in the picture on a chocolate box. Hereford was a winner, until I suggested that we have a look at Shrewsbury, the town where Mum and I had left the train on that memorable day out just before Dad's return from Belgium. My precious post-card still with me, I wanted to locate the place that was becoming more dreamlike as I grew older; before it merged into that strange territory of things, places, people, events that inhabited my imagination, though not the real world. I had clung to my post-card as a lifeline to reality.

Once more, we packed a car with maps and travelling gear, and set off on the motorway that would take us towards the Welsh borders.

Shrewsbury delighted us. Yet another ancient and beautiful English town, should we ever be able to make a choice? Over dinner at our hotel, we looked again at our plans, our vision for the future, and asked ourselves what we were really searching for. We had, perhaps, been seduced by the cities we had seen, comparing one with another, this cathedral with that abbey, this city wall with that castle, this view of the mountains with that glorious stretch of river. The history of each town and city was researched and discussed over our evening meals, leading to fierce partisanship in the matter of the Civil War and the Battle of Hastings. We didn't know a lot about the Battle of Shrewsbury, and Dad's information, as he readily admitted, was based on the plays of Shakespeare. Unreliable, I told him. The Shrewsbury clock? Could have been any one of a dozen.

'Are we so besotted with English history,' I suggested, 'that we want to live in one of the towns where so much of it happened? Be part of its reflected glory?'

'Maybe you're right. We're not thinking enough about how we want to live, day to day. What we want to see when we look out of the windows.'

I thought of the basement flat of my childhood. I remembered our last house in Melbourne. In both places the world had felt very close. I had grown out of my childhood and adolescent shyness, as most people do, and I wasn't an unsociable being. However, the thought of living without close neighbours had its appeal, the idea of keeping a nominal distance from the clamour of the world. Slowly, as this picture of a putative new life developed, I described it to Dad.

'I think I want space. I want to see the earth, not concrete beneath my feet. What I want is to step out of my home into seasonal rhythms, into winter, spring, summer, not into the demanding restlessness of a city, however timesaving it may be.'

Dad nodded. 'I know what you mean. 'We'll look at some villages, at the countryside. See how we feel about rural life.'

'Well, now we're here, I must find Newfield, the village I told you about, Dad, the place Mum and I visited just before you came home. I've got my old post-card with me. No idea where the place is, except that it's by the River Severn. Can't be too far away.'

'We'll make it our priority tomorrow.'

We found Newfield on our map, a village a few miles on the Welsh side of the border. We left the town via Welsh Bridge, taking the road that led to mid-Wales, past a notice that welcomed us in two languages, one seemingly unpronounceable. The village was not far from the English-Welsh border, and to my pleasure and relief, I saw the river, and there on the skyline was the outline of my remembered hills. We found the village pub and decided to spend the night there.

Waking early, I set off on my own exploratory walk. I was hoping, I suppose, for a revelation, for a small patch of landscape that exactly matched my vision of the place I remembered. I had long ago discovered the anomalies of a child's view of the world, and was prepared for disappointment. I turned a corner, and I was that child again.

It was lovely in the early morning sunshine, there were pale yellow flowers along the grass verges, which I knew to be primroses. In the hedges were small white flowers stuck haphazardly along sharply angled black twigs. These were blackthorn, the precursor of sloes – a bitter wild fruit, I discovered later, to be immersed in gin, and drunk at Christmas time. And there, only a field away, the Severn, bright and shining, Britain's longest river on its circuitous journey to the sea.

I was back on that far away day, the moment when I realised that a stream, a field, a wild tree with blossom along its branches were not just pretty pictures in books, but a reality that changed with the weather and the seasons. A place where real lives were lived, just as real as mine had been in the then unchanging grey streets of London.

'It's so nice here, Mum, can we come back again soon?' I had asked my mother.

'No', she had said, 'There'd be no point.'

There was a point now, Dad and I needed somewhere to live. And what we wanted, we finally decided, was not one of those fabulous cities, but somewhere quiet and rural, a house with space enough for two people to live without treading on each other's toes.

We promised ourselves a visit to an estate agent when we got back to Shrewsbury. Driving the car carefully along the narrow lanes we passed the gated entry to a house. I slowed down and stopped.

We spoke simultaneously.

'That house we just passed! it had a 'For Sale' notice!'

I reversed the car for the short distance, and we looked over the gate. We saw an unpretentious old building, not one of those eye-catching half-timbered houses that we had noticed and marvelled at on the outward journey. It was a modest but confident dwelling, part brick, part stone, with no apparent contemporary modifications. We had observed, with some dismay the addition of fine conservatories, swimming pools, picture windows, to some of the old traditional buildings, and Jeff had turned to me with a smile.

'Bits of Australia stuck on to Wales!'

We liked the look of the place sufficiently to follow it up with a call to the house agent. Apparently, it had been empty for six months. A viewing confirmed my suspicion that it had the outlook I coveted. From the living room, you could see the distant hills, through the kitchen windows the river was just visible, probably a mile away as the crow flies. The house had been built on a slope which bounded the wide river valley, catching the afternoon and evening sun, but open to the full force of the westerly winds which brought the rain for which Wales was notorious.

The property included a small paddock, adjacent to the garden, and accessed through a wooden gate. Whatever we had had in mind as a new home, it certainly wasn't this quiet, remote old building. However, we came back for another look. And another. We continued touring the narrow lanes of the area which had taken our fancy, investigating various properties. The older ones had names, in Welsh or English, that indicated their function in days gone by, when people expected to find whatever they needed locally, before transport to the towns became quick and easy. The shop, the smithy, the old pub. The house we had our eye on was called, unimaginatively, I thought, The Cottage. It had an older, Welsh name, but the agent said he didn't know how to say it. On our fourth visit, Dad turned to me.

'I like this place. It has a homely feel. I like the area too. Forget all those fine cities we looked at. I like it here.'

I stood in the hallway, slate-floored, doors leading to kitchen, reception room and to the small recently added room that I fancied for my study. A fourth door led to the garden at the back of the house. Dad disappeared up the fine Victorian staircase that led to the upper rooms.

I too had fallen in love with our accidentally discovered old house, partly on account of its views, which were those shown on my treasured post card, and partly because it seemed, it felt, right.

Its immediate character was late Victorian, but there were odd spaces, windows, door frames, that indicated a different, earlier, pattern of living; one slate doorstep worn down by the boots of generations. Listening to Dad's footsteps as he made his way around the two upper floors, I mused on our predecessors and their family events.

Births, marriages, deaths, love, hate, comedy – all taking place within these walls. My feelings on our new home? Curiosity and delight. I do not subscribe to moody atmospheres, if there had been one, I didn't feel it. The house felt fine to me. Dad appeared from his tour.

'Are you sure?' I asked him, '*absolutely* sure?'

'I am. I can see us living here. A few things to be done to the place, nothing fundamental. I can do some of it myself.'

I hugged him. We had found our new home.

The housing agent was unprofessionally sceptical of the wisdom of our choice.

'From *Australia*,' he commented, with raised eyebrows, as if we had just landed from Mars. 'Are you sure you'll feel comfortable here? D'you know what the winters are like in this part of the world?'

'I know what they're like in London' I answered tartly, 'with no central heating. I was born there.'

'Well, there's central heating in this house. And a log burner in that small adjoining section that used to be a barn, or maybe pig sties. The place is a bit remote, though. The village is at least a couple of miles away.'

I laughed at him. 'In Australia that would be considered next door, 'I told him. 'Don't worry about us. We'll be fine in The Cottage.'

The process of purchase took longer than we thought. So many unexpected hitches, odd searches, linked, I suppose to the age and history of the house. So many people and institutions seemed to have a connection of some kind to the place. There were things we would not be allowed to do, things that we would be obliged to do. Manorial rights, what on earth were those? We finally moved in on my thirty-first birthday. We celebrated with Welsh lamb, asparagus and champagne.

Moving was straightforward. A trip to one of Shrewsbury's supermarkets stocked the larder, fridge and freezer with food that seemed unfamiliar, but probably known to us under different names.

Furniture we bought at local auctions and second-hand shops, hoping that the chairs and tables, chests and desk might be local too, and would sit comfortably in our hundred – year-old house.

We watched it come to life as we shopped and ordered and installed. We'd brought essential books with us, and asked a local carpenter to put up the shelves that we would need to accommodate them and the inevitable new acquisitions. Maps were a priority, we wanted to look at the precise location of the meandering and mysterious border that located us in Montgomeryshire rather than Shropshire, with its peculiar postal alternative, Salop.

We moved in as soon as possible after the arrival of the beds, cooker, tables, and chairs, and before the television. A poor reception area, we were told, but new masts were being installed, and we would soon be looking at Britain's view of the world and at those programmes which made it laugh and cry.

Dad laid claim to a couple of upstairs rooms for his own purposes, one to be used as a kitchen where he could experiment without compromising the main one downstairs. The other a place where he would keep his fishing tackle and his trophies, and watch football matches on his own television. I took possession of the small barn adjacent to the house, the one with the log-burner mentioned by the agent. This would be my workshop, office, or study, whichever name seemed appropriate at the time. It had the view towards the Welsh hills that were on my post-card, now framed and in pride of place on my desk by the window. My bedroom looked out over Wales, his faced eastwards towards England.

My typewriter was unpacked and set in its place in the middle of my desk, one day, I thought, to take its place in history. New machines were coming on to the market – electronic typewriters which could make small scale alterations before printing. Goodbye to the correction fluids that repaired mistakes in a typescript. Welcome, 'Brother'.

My father advised patience. These things are still innovations, he said, they'll be getting better and cheaper all the time. No point in buying something that'll be out-of-date in a few months. Not realising, of course, that this would be precisely how we would live as the years went by, permanently trying to catch up with the fast-changing world of technology.

Newly arrived, we were the focus of some curiosity. Most people seemed to have heard of us via the village shop, the postman, and local gossip. They knew that Dad was a retired businessman, and thought I was some kind of teacher. Whatever our occupations might be, they were not as extraordinary and interesting as the fact that we were from Australia. This was mentioned at some point during each conversation with our new neighbours. We were expected to be surprised and delighted with each new experience, each unfamiliar aspect of life. They were a little disappointed to discover that we were in fact English and originally from London.

The vicar called, I was grateful for his welcome, but I told him it was unlikely that he would see me in church. Equally unlikely would be my attendance at any one of the many non-conformist chapels, even if I could differentiate between them. A visit from two Jehovah's Witnesses was productive in that they managed to start a recalcitrant new lawn mower that was giving me trouble. I suggested that they crossed me off their list of possible candidates for conversion, since although I enjoyed our discussion, it was a serious waste of their time. They departed, making way for yet another visitor. A tall, tanned woman, dressed in tattered, slightly muddy jeans.

She introduced herself.

'I'm Bethan Lewis,' she said, 'I've come to welcome you on behalf of our Women's Institute.'

Goodness me, I thought, curiosity is such a driving force, easily disguised if necessary.

'That is very kind of you and the Women's Institute. We didn't have one where I come from. But I have heard of it!'

'As far as the language is concerned,' she said, 'we're half Welsh, half English, but meetings are in English. Border villages like Newfield are very mixed – it's a Welsh village with an English name, but on the other side of the border there are plenty of English villages with Welsh names. We're a diverse community. We would really like to see you at our meetings.'

'I'm Kay', I said, 'It's nice to meet you. But just now I've too many jobs I need to do. Maybe later, when I'm more settled, I'll give the Women's Institute a go. But thank you for calling!'

She laughed, wiping grubby hands on already grubby jeans.

'It's not purely a social courtesy,' she said, 'it's a chance to solve one of my perennial problems. I'm the W.I. speaker finder. Permanently on the lookout for someone willing to give us a talk. Would you be willing to think about this?'

'What topic did you have in mind?' I asked her.

'Oh, Australia, of course, everyone would be fascinated to hear about life there!'

'I promise you I'll bear it in mind, but you must excuse me for the present.'

We chatted for a few minutes, discovering a mutual interest in gardening, one of the obvious areas of ignorance for someone from the southern hemisphere. I gratefully accepted her offer of cuttings and surplus plants from her garden. I imagined her putting down garden tools reluctantly and deciding to visit this new occupant of The Cottage. Wash and change first? Obviously, she had decided it was not necessary.

I'll tell them at the next meeting', she said, departing with a wave of her hand, most of the soil now transferred to her gardening jeans.

I certainly liked the idea of being part of a community, but I wasn't prepared for the instant immersion that was threatening us.

'We're a novelty,' Dad said. 'It'll soon wear off.'

It wasn't long before we learned how to pronounce those local place names that were Welsh, discovering that it was in fact a phonetic language, unlike English. A few of the consonants and vowels were difficult for us to say, but we had a go. One day, I told myself, I'd learn to speak Welsh. The agent who'd sold us our new home had said that it originally had a Welsh name. I intended, in due course, to find out what it was.

SIX

Newfield, 1972

We had been in The Cottage for six months when my father suddenly remembered the batch of envelopes that had been kept by Adam Patel's wife in London. We should contact the couple, they mustn't think that their action had been simply forgotten, unappreciated.

We sent them our address, and the package arrived a few days later. Accompanying the letters was a note. 'Call again if you're in these parts' it said, 'it was good to meet you. We'd like to hear more about life in our house during the war.'

Dad put the bundle on the kitchen table, and we settled down to an examination of its contents. The sun was shining. I glanced through the window; the garden was calling me. But Dad had started on the package.

'Let's get the boring ones over first,' I suggested.

The political communications occasioned us some amusement. Europe? Isn't that where we were? Apparently not, or at least only geographically. Some of our political leaders wished for a closer economic association, with a political one in the offing. Not to worry, though, we would be consulted before any fundamental changes were made to our national status. Our current prime minister, Edward Heath, wept tears of frustration at each failed attempt to join the European Union. We didn't know enough about it to care.

At last, we came to the two envelopes that were personal and handwritten. They were addressed to Mrs. K. Francis, and each contained a short, pencilled message.

'You owe me too months money will you send it now as I cant manage without it
S. Meredith.'

It was dated the first of August 1948.

The other was fiercer:

'If you dont send the money you owe I will come and get it you will have to pay our fares too
S. Meredith'

The shock of a changed past hit us without mercy. Where were we? *Who* were we? Husband and child of a woman we didn't know?

Dad picked up the second missive, handling it delicately, as if it were infectious.

'This one was sent a month later. We were well away on the high seas by then.'

We stared at each other in amazement. What on earth was this all about?

'Well,' Dad said, 'looks like she'd been sending money to someone, on a regular basis.' He got to his feet and fetched a packet of cigarettes, his hand trembling a little as he flicked his lighter. He examined the scrap of lined paper. 'How odd. Why on earth should she be sending money to anyone, without telling me about it?'

'It was obviously something she didn't want you to know about.'

We were stunned, confused. Dad was silent for several minutes, staring in front of him, trying to see through the layers of the passing years that obscured the picture of our London days. What had been going on? A story, a saga, running in parallel with our ordinary, harmless, unmysterious lives – a secret narrative written alongside my father's search for a new job, a new house, my mother's domestic activities, as well as my own ordinary school life. Not the kind of secret you could keep in a corner of your mind, forgetting about it as time passed, but one that didn't let you go, renewed as it must be, every month.

'It explains something,' Dad said.

'Back in London. I could never understand why the housekeeping money went so quickly. We had arguments about it. I supposed she was careless, bought stuff without looking in her purse to see how much cash she'd got left. I offered to help once, sit down with pen and paper and see where she could economise, but she went hysterical and said I didn't love her anymore.'

Dad and I discussed possibilities. Had she borrowed a sum of money and was paying it back in instalments that she couldn't afford? What would she have wanted the money for? Had she bought something expensive, and was paying for it? She had never seriously indicated a wish for anything beyond our means. A darker thought occurred to me, that she'd done something for which she was being blackmailed. I didn't voice this possibility, Dad was upset enough already. He stubbed out his cigarette and lit another. For the first time I felt angry with his habit. A quick and easy way of dealing with stressful moments, I thought. What did I have recourse to? I glanced out of the window. Half-an-hour's fierce weeding might help.

'Cup of tea?' I asked him.

He nodded, third cigarette extinguished. The atmosphere felt rancid, deeply unpleasant. A brief rift between us, a tremor in the foundations of our relationship. You have a shock, your unconscious mind looks round for someone, something, to blame. The moment passed, I felt his distress, went to fill the kettle, anger transferring to my mother.

'Why didn't she talk to me about it?' Dad said. 'I knew the problems of life after the war. Things were more difficult to get after I came home than they were I was away. I knew that if you wanted more and better food and clothes than the rations allowed you, you had to look for the people who sold them on the black market. The stuff wasn't hard to find, but you had to pay over the odds for it. There was absolutely no reason for her to think I wouldn't understand.'

He spoke with some bitterness. I think he felt hurt. The fact that she hadn't turned to him when she was in trouble bothered him more than the nature of whatever her difficulties had been. Not incompetence with household management, as he had supposed, but a real, continuing reason for a habitual shortage of cash. He looked at me, sadly.

'So much for trust.'

I thought of our life in our grotty little basement flat, before Dad came home. A shortage of money? It had always been there. No money for new curtains, no money for presents, unnecessary purchases, treats. I was so used to it that I'd never bothered to wonder why. Mum had been an army wife, she should have had enough.

We spoke little of this matter over the next few days, each of us busy with the new house, making small discoveries that intrigued us – a woman's shoe in the attic, a stone slab in the garden which upon lifting, we found covered a fine brick-lined well. Dad took over the cooking, which had started to interest him before we left Australia, and in the evenings I would drift to the kitchen for a glass of wine at our large wooden table, before he started dishing up. A pleasant end to the day. Much to talk about in the ordinary run of things, but now there was a mystery in our lives. Each of us puzzling over the letters, uncertain how often the matter should be aired.

Behind the chat we were thinking, wondering, going over the strange missives that were now in our possession. From time to time, one of us would voice a new aspect of the revelation. We looked carefully at the words. They seemed deliberately vague, obscure. Had they fallen into the wrong hands, the reader would gather that a Mrs. K. Francis owed money, but would have no idea why. Was this vagueness intended? And what was meant by the final sinister comment that there would be more than one fare to be paid? Someone else would be coming too. As though the writer didn't need to say who it was, my mother would have known.

I was pretty sure that the writer was a woman. 'Why d'you think that?' my father asked me. 'I don't know,' I told him, 'It doesn't sound like a man talking. The idea of not being able to *manage* without enough money. There's a touch of domesticity in the wording. Of how women see their day-to-day problems. *Managing* is what many women's lives consist of. A man usually has a woman to do that for him.'

'Here we go again,' he observed, drily.

I put my arm round him. 'You know I'm not talking about you,' I said. 'You've never taken for granted the organisation that goes on at home. Behind the scenes.' Which was true. Purchases that would make life easier had often been his suggestion, and he would always lend a hand with routine domestic chores. Better behaved in that respect than I used to be.

'You see S. Meredith as a poor woman, then.'

'Yes. Poor and uneducated, obviously. Determined, though.'

I wondered exactly how determined she was, and how things would have panned out if she had been able to confront my mother on the doorstep of our London home. Determined enough to overcome the embarrassment she must have felt in being obliged to call and ask for money? Determined enough to make threats of some kind if the money was not forthcoming? How far was she prepared to go? We had to bear in mind that the wording of the note suggested she might not come alone.

Days passed, with the occasional remark indicating that the subject had not been forgotten.

'I wonder if the writer ever carried out her threat, and went for the money?' Dad commented one day. 'She'd have come to a place either empty or occupied by strangers.'

'Would it have been possible to trace us via the Commonwealth Office, or some such authority?'

'No idea. But why would anyone try? We hardly knew our neighbours, there was no point in telling them we were leaving. Our destination could have been round the corner as far as they were concerned. The writer wouldn't have got any useful information from asking around. Even if someone came up with something like 'Oh, I heard they went to Australia', you would have needed time, energy and resources to investigate at a level that stood any chance of finding us.'

If she – I was now always thinking of the writer as a woman – had made up her mind to come to our home in London's East End, find the place and demand the money, she would have paused to check the house number, descended the area steps, rapped the metal doorknocker. She would have peered through the letterbox, perhaps, and almost certainly tried to look through the basement window. There had been occasions when my mother hadn't wanted to answer a knock at the door. We would hide, silently, in the scullery, till we reckoned the unwanted visitor had gone. Once, I had come out too soon, and saw a man's face at the window. The face had scowled fiercely at me. Then, obscenely, stuck out his tongue, before departing.

' Mum! Who on earth was that?' I reported the incident to my mother.

'Dunno,' she said. Then why didn't she want to answer the door? One more puzzle to add to my list. The image had stayed with me for many years, before being buried beneath the accumulated debris of childhood terrors.

The writer of the messages would have had no success at our basement flat. Perhaps she had tried upstairs, ringing the front doorbell. No luck there, we were uncomplaining tenants, paid our rent, had no other communication with landlords. I don't even know if we gave notice. No goodbyes were said.

She might have tried a neighbour or two. Nothing and no-one could have helped her. She would have stood there in despair, facing the prospect of never having the money that was owed, of the hardships the future would hold, having to 'manage' as best she could. There would have been two of them, at least. What did they do next? Go back, I suppose. Where to? I realised that in the confusion and mystery of the two messages, we had omitted to look at the envelopes, to see if there was a postmark. Retrieving them from a drawer in my desk, we looked. The pale blue circular mark was unreadable on one envelope, on the other we could just make out the name of the town. It was not surprising that the writer would have wanted the cost of train fares, the letter had been posted in Shrewsbury.

Of course. This was the link between our train journey that had made such a vivid impression on my childish self; that long-ago journey that had so much surprised and delighted me that it had brought us, Dad and me, twenty-five years later, to our new home, on to the doorstep of a mystery.

Something had happened at Newfield, in the cottage where Mum and I had stayed the night, that had led to money being dispatched on a regular basis to an address not far from where we live now. Already, in mild curiosity, I had tried to find the cottage where my mother and I had slept for those uncomfortable hours so long ago. The fact that the situation had suddenly assumed a new dimension didn't alter the fact that the house had disappeared, no-one remembered who had lived there, and I could think of nothing more I could do. Did I have the time and the energy to research old maps, ask more people, give the whole project all my attention? I was still coping with settling into a new country, a new life. My typewriter was still silent, I had written little, and that without enthusiasm.

'I wonder', I said to Dad one evening, if the money was ever paid off. Once you'd started earning good money in Melbourne, she could have sent what was due in a single final payment, maybe without making a noticeable dent in the housekeeping finances. I imagine any offer would have been accepted. A better option than waiting for the unreliable arrival of cash.

'As soon as I could,' he said, I set up her own bank account, so she could manage expenses herself. She was not extravagant, there had never been any problem of that kind in Melbourne. Don't think I ever bothered to look at past bank statements. Even when I had to take over management of her money after she got ill.'

He became reluctant to pursue the matter. 'Let it lie,' he had said to me, after one of our puzzled conversations. 'Nothing has changed for us.' It had, of course. For him, the memory of the woman he had married, for me a new angle on my recollections of my mother's attitudes and behaviour. But not one that enlightened me or explained anything at all.

SEVEN

Winter 1972

Frost. I was up early, and walked down to my little paddock, picked a leaf of grass, and saw microscopic six-petalled flowers of ice covering the blade. They disappeared in the warmth of my breath. The fields were white along the riverbank. I kicked through the leaves that were gathering in sheltered hollows.

'Cold morning' Dad observed on my return. 'Misty. Time to turn up the heating.'

That wasn't the idea that occurred to Keats in October, Dad. Crab apple harvest was more likely on his mind. There's a few empty jars waiting to be filled.'

Gathering, sorting, washing the little jewels that dropped from the crab apple tree kept us warm for a while, but I wanted a fire, a visible and sensual ritual for welcoming the stranger I had lived without for most of my life. Winter, a distant memory of the London days. Woollen gloves, scarves, chilblains. Runny noses, handkerchiefs to be washed and rewashed. Mum telling me not to complain. No warm arm around me.

Firewood must be sourced for the log-burner in my study. A notice in the village shop window indicated that Dafydd Jones, Pen-y-Pentre, could supply timber, so I made a phone call. Yes, Mr. Jones would sell and deliver a trailerful, but I should call and see the logs first, to make sure they were the right size. Mostly ash, he had said, but with some beech mixed in, I'd better have a look before I ordered any.

I located the farm, and with some difficulty, Mr. Jones. There seemed no-one at home in the house. Peering into the cowhouse I found a young man cleaning the stalls.

'Good morning' I said, 'I'm Kay Francis. I've come to look at your firewood logs.'

The young man continued to wash down the stalls with his hosepipe, directing the jets of water perilously close to me. Hastily I stepped to one side.

'It's Dad you want. He's up in the wood behind the house.'
'How do I…'

He sighed. I'll show you.' He turned off the water and removed his cap. Water dripped from his nose and ears. I did not feel welcome.

We made our way silently through a couple of fields to an area where a considerable amount of tree felling had been done. The climb was steep, my guide showing no sign of pausing to give me time to catch up. The lungfuls of air I was obliged to take up smelled sweetly of freshly cut wood.

Logs were piled everywhere, all shapes and sizes. The young man pointed to his father who was operating a circular saw.

'That's who you want,' he said.

The noise stopped and Mr. Jones senior greeted me; he indicated the logs that he was selling for firewood. They looked ideal to me.

'Gareth can deliver them on Monday,' he said, 'O.K. Gareth?'

The young man grunted assent. To my inexperienced eye, the wood seemed perfectly fine, and having looked at offers from other sources, appeared very reasonably priced. Yes, they knew where the Cottage was, and had heard that it was now in English hands.

'Well, I suppose so,' I said, 'though it's Australia we've recently come from. We left England when I was a child.'

'So you're not used to dealing with fires in cold weather.'

'No,' I said, 'that's something I have to learn.' I picked up a log and examined it. 'Seems quite heavy.'

The younger man said something to his father in Welsh. He was answered sharply, Gareth did not reply, looked sullen, kicking at a log that had escaped from a nearby pile. There were problems between the two of them, I thought, Gareth exuded dissatisfaction.

'I'll see you with the logs on Monday, then?' I asked.

A muttered O.K. from Gareth was the only recognition I received that the logs would be delivered as his father had suggested.

I said goodbye and turned to go. Not a chatty couple, I thought, but no matter. However, Mr. Jones senior called after me.

'When are you going to use the logs?'

I stopped and turned. 'Well, as soon as it gets cold enough, I suppose.'

Funny question.

'They should be left for a year before you use them.'

'Why?'

'They're not properly seasoned yet.

Hastily dismissing visions of salt and pepper pots, I wondered what I was supposed to do about the condition of the wood.

'Where can I get some that are ready to use *now*?' I asked him.

'A timber merchant's. There's plenty of them. Don't you want these, then?'

'Yes of course. As long as I know to leave them for a year. That's perfectly all right. Thank you for telling me.'

A second brief goodbye and I left. I heard the torrent of Welsh behind me as I walked away. It sounded angry. My next stop was a timber merchant's yard.

I was shown the firewood that was ready for use. It looked the same to me as the logs I had just left, though they were more expensive. I picked one up, it was significantly lighter. Monday saw the delivery of both lots. Dad had built an open sided shed to house them and was busy transferring the unseasoned ones from the pile that Gareth had dumped in front of the house. Stacked in their new home, they were a comforting sight. The ready-to-use logs were piled up nearer the house. How quicky would I get through them, I wondered.

I would know soon enough, winter came early. I lit my fire with the kindling wood I'd collected at odd times during the summer, chopped into suitable sizes and bundled nicely into usable batches. One log placed lovingly on to the small flames. I'd have a cup of tea and watch it burn. I put on the kettle, two minutes later, carrying the warm cup in my cold hands, I went back to my study to enjoy the flames. There were none, just charred wood and a few wisps of smoke.

What can have happened? I dismantled the bits of blackened wood and started again. First lesson learned, don't leave the fire alone for a second after applying the match. Stand by, watch for signs of distress, another match at the ready. The first stages of a long and hard learning experience. You cannot start a fire with one log. It needs company. Two, three or four. You had to get a good large, hot fire to start with. Get the whole cast-iron construction feeling hot to the touch, the long chimney-pipe hot too. Then you could sit back a bit, and start feeding it one log at a time. Ah, but for how long a time? The days got colder, the evenings longer, the new logs were disappearing at an alarming rate.

'That lot aren't going to last the winter,' I told my father, and it's hard work, too. That fire eats logs like there's no tomorrow.'

We ordered more, twice the previous quantity. Dad extended the woodshed.

Our first Christmas was quiet, a few cards arriving from Melbourne, and one or two from our new neighbours in Newfield.

We watched the Queen on television, and thought of Christmases past.

Thought of wartime Christmases, Dad's in Germany, mine and my mother's in London. These had involved little in the way of celebration, no Santa Claus for me as a young child, no stockings hung at the end of the bed on Christmas Eve, Mum disliked all feasts of the imagination. There would be a token present which was invariably something I needed in the way of clothing. There was no money for games or toys, she said, purchases had to be useful and to last. I thought of Christmases in Melbourne. There had been two or three with Brad, one split between my life with him and my increasingly incapacitated mother.

'Why are you lighting candles?' she had asked. 'Is it an air raid? Is there another power cut?'

Brad had spent that Christmas day with us. We all did our best, but the turkey and Christmas pudding were a formality. In addition to which it was just about the hottest day of the year.

I'd not seen clean snow before. So white it was almost blue. Not grey, as it used to be in London. Dirty grey stuff that had to be scraped off my boots before I came into the house. There'd been grey snowmen built in the streets I'd passed through on the way to school, grey snowballs thrown at me by the neighbours' kids. I'd come home crying with fear and discomfort.

'You should throw snowballs back at them,' my mother had commented, not understanding that you didn't know how to do things that weren't part of your childhood culture.

Dad and I watched the snowflakes whirling in spirals outside our windows, driven by the random whims of the wind, round corners, under the barn roof, through an open window in the kitchen.

In the house, the burning fire, the white world outside my study window, was a delight interrupted only by the fact that the fire needed another log on it.

'This can't go on,' I said, I've no *time* to write.' I'm looking after the fire every hour of the day.'

The problem was solved, with a compromise of sorts. The fire was a dual-purpose one, designed, once you had mastered the controls, to burn smokeless fuel as well as wood. And once loaded with a bucketful, it lasted for hours. Not with the living beauty and movement of flames, but with a dependable and continuous output of heat. You could go out and leave it, it would be black, but with tiny glimpses of red if you looked hard, and which would respond with a cheerful glow if you turned up the appropriate controls. Logs were a treat if you had visitors and the time to enjoy both.

The run up to Christmas amazed us both. Decorative lights appeared everywhere, strings of them in the most unlikely places. No fairy lights on the church, however, but there were signs of activity and a glow from inside.

How can you pass by a church on a cold day at Christmas time, brightly lit from within, and with an organ quietly tempting you inside? We couldn't, feeling the pull of the church at its most powerful at the year's turn – a celebration for the faithful, a bonanza for commerce, and nostalgia for the lovers of tradition for tradition's sake. We entered.

We felt uncomfortable visiting the church simply to look and listen. We looked at the Christmas decorations and the crib made by children. We read the leaflet that told us the church's history. We admired the old building and appreciated the efforts of the church members to celebrate the occasion that was the reason for its existence. However, we distanced ourselves, as we always did, from the worship for which it had been built and used for generations. Both of us had long ago abandoned all religious belief, but with a sneaking respect for what the church was trying to do for the community. The right things for the wrong reasons.

We fished in our pockets for some money to help pay for our pleasure, and assuage our guilt, knowing that money was not a solution to the church's true problems.

'Come to the Plygain!' we had been invited by neighbours and friends. 'You'll love it.'

This was a traditional service of Welsh carols, sung, without accompaniment, by members of the congregation – as solos, or in twos, threes, any number. No prayers, no sermon, and strictly no applause, this was not a concert, but a form of Christmas worship, practised by generations of local families. We looked for familiar faces among the participants and found one. Gareth Jones, our log delivery man. Singing with two other men, a glorious tenor soaring above the two bass baritones. Five minutes of amazement and sheer joy. Returning to his seat at the back of the church, he walked past me, with no acknowledgement. Perhaps that too was customary, I thought, the rituals at this occasion seemed quite strict.

Looking round the church after this traditional and moving occasion, I encountered the vicar who had called on us shortly after our arrival. He smiled.

'You were wrong,' he said, 'you said it was unlikely that I should see you in church. And here you are!'

'For the wrong reasons, sadly,' I answered him. 'For the history that it holds inside its walls.'

'Yes,' he said, 'The building and the institution, two very different things. Their relationship is changing, the congregation is changing, beliefs are changing. I have two parishes under my care now. My opposite number in the non-conformist tradition has five chapels to look after. Thank goodness I shall soon be retired, before the church finds more parishes to add to my collection.'

The Rev. Powell looked old and tired. I wondered how many of his parishioners he remembered. In particular, I wondered if he had ever come across one S. Meredith. I asked him. He thought for a moment. 'A common name,' he observed. 'I'm sure I've come across it somewhere, but I can't be sure. I could have a look through some of our records. Is it important?'

'Could be,' I said. 'Or maybe not. I don't really know at the moment.'

'I'll have a quick glance through some of the parish records. That is, if you're not in a hurry.'

'No,' I assured him. 'But please don't go to too much trouble.'

A long shot, I thought, but worth trying. If we ever found S. Meredith, what on earth would we *do*? But I didn't see the solution to this mystery as a goal I was desperately anxious to achieve. Merely one of many puzzles I considered when I had nothing more pressing to think about.

Winter passed, days lengthened, wild daffodils showed their heads on the fringes of forest and woodland. The Rev. Powell called again, accompanied this time by a young woman; they were holding hands. Her thick chestnut hair was tied back in a ponytail, her soft brown eyes unfocussed.

'This is Melanie', he said, 'My daughter. Melanie is very fond of birds. She likes to put up nesting boxes for them in all sorts of places.'

'I put up boxes for the birds.' Melanie said, 'then I clean them out ready for the next ones.'

'The birds are very lucky, 'I said, 'to have someone to look after their homes for them. Do you have special boxes for the different kinds of birds?'

Melanie brightened. 'I got boxes for robins, and boxes for tits, and boxes for woodpeckers and boxes… '

The vicar interrupted gently. 'Such a long list of bird homes. You can tell Miss Francis about them all later.'

'Not Miss Francis, please, Kay is my name.'

Melanie fell silent.

'You wanted to know' the vicar said, 'if I knew someone of the name Meredith. I've been looking through my records, such as they are. Quite an interesting search, I hadn't realised how much things had changed over the years. Such a drop in church attendance, such a proliferation of church-related activities today, people are too busy raising money for good causes to actually come to church for Sunday *worship*.'

'Write it all down, Mr. Powell, an interesting project for your retirement. Did you come across the name I mentioned?'

'Well, there was a Susan Meredith there. 1951, I think it was, on a list of people in the parish we distributed Christmas hampers to. Mostly the elderly, who couldn't easily get out to do shopping. We also included those we thought were needy for one reason or another. Susan Meredith was on the list for that year. The name didn't appear again. Where she is now, I have no idea.'

'Thank you for going to so much trouble. It's only a matter of curiosity. You know how small puzzles niggle you unmercifully. But I'll try to forget this one for now. Thank you for your help.'

I turned to Melanie, in a world far away from our conversation.

'Will you be putting up boxes on your way home?'

She brightened. 'Can't carry them all.'

'If we're distributing them,' the vicar said, 'we usually do it by car. But inspection jobs Melanie usually does by herself. She likes to know which ones are being used.'

'Of course.'

Melanie volunteered no further part on the discussion. Her range of topics for conversation was obviously limited, I wasn't immediately sure to what extent. However, it was clear she had a world of her own, one that she enjoyed, and maybe in terms of names of bird species, location of the boxes she fixed, and how many had been occupied, her interest in the life of birds rewarded her well. They left, and a whisper from the Rev. Powell elicited a reluctant 'Goodbye' from his daughter.

It was April. I heard the first cuckoo. Was Melanie expecting it? How much she expected, hoped for, feared, I didn't know. Maybe she just dealt with events as they happened.

I thought about this iconic bird, spending our winters far away in Africa. Spring was arriving here early this year, but she wasn't to know that. Sitting on a branch of her sub-Saharan tree, she would have felt an emptiness in her small stomach. Breakfast was meagre this morning, the usual menu of berries and insects becoming scarcer day by day. Somewhere, far away, her genes would tell her, sap was rising in the trees, leaf buds swelling on their twigs... She'd feel a tingle in her wingtips, a northward urge in her tiny brain. Time to go. She would set out on her long annual journey, star-guided, hungry, impelled by the lives of her ancestors built into her mind and body. Set out on her usual date, to arrive here on her usual day, April 18th, to find spring well on the way. Oh well, I thought on her behalf, you can't get it right every time.

EIGHT

Summer 1974

Two homes or one? I had considered the question, and we had decided to start off with one. We had settled in quite happily in the Cottage, it was spacious and comfortable. With all the complications of the move, we certainly didn't feel like starting another house-hunt. But for me there was another aspect – the bond between Dad and me was not simply that of parent and child, it was a genuine companionship His own parents had divorced. He'd been brought up by his grandmother who had taken over their child, and raised him, with kindness but with no desire to keep in touch with either of his parents. They were irresponsible, she had decided, not fit to raise a child, he would be better off without them. His grandmother had died before he was twenty. I had no family but him, not even a remote cousin or two that I was aware of. Dad was the only family I had, my lucky accident, my refuge from my mother's lack of love.

I used to wonder, what if he had not returned from the war? How would my mother and I have lived? What would my life have been like? Burdened with my mother's indifference, what route would I have chosen? Almost certainly to leave home at the earliest possible opportunity, and then, a diversity of choices. Some of these might have been risky, and none which would have brought me to my present comfortable circumstances. Dad would stay with me so long as he wanted to, and I would care for him as he grew old, whether or not I ever had a family of my own.

He took up fishing, found mates in the pub in Newfield, developed his cooking skills, a real bonus for me. We made acquaintances here and there, found professional expertise in Shrewsbury where we located a dentist, an accountant and a solicitor, Alex Pritchard. The latter lived in Newfield, so knew our area well, and had already become one of Dad's good friends. I had already consulted him on a matter of copyright, about which he said he knew nothing at all, but would point me in the right direction.

We visited the cinema in Shrewsbury, wandered around the town, took in the traditional tourist sites, argued about the existence of Falstaff's famous clock.

Back home, Dad would set to work on the garden. I wrote one or two articles for a literary magazine, tutored an adult education course in Bridgnorth. Time passed quickly enough, immersed in our new life in Wales, we had no desire to return to Australia; we barely even considered it.

However, today I fancied a change of scene, a new perspective. I wrote one or two first chapters of a possible new novel.

These continued to be consigned to the uncomplaining log-burner as I grappled with the topic of the story I'd been thinking about, the idea of exploring the relationship between characters who found themselves in the environment of a new mindset, away from the family and social ties that had moulded their childhood and early adolescent years. One or two contemporary characters were beginning to take shape, these seemed hopeful prospects.

I still fancied a break. Dad was sympathetic.

'With the best will in the world, Kay, I can't take on as many of the jobs as you are doing. This is your home, and if you choose to stay here, it will be yours when I have gone. There's a lot of work still to be done and decisions to be made, ones that you must make. I worry that you're not getting on with your writing.'

'Then you worry about it more than I do! I'm absolutely fine,' I reassured him, feeling less assured myself. I'd never before had any difficulty in telling a story – in fact there had always been more in my head that I could cope with at any one time. They were still there, but in a mindset that was still struggling to leave the southern hemisphere. They didn't fit in this place. Here we were, settled in Wales, in a life that was new, interesting, one that occupied my mind to the extent that I didn't feel like putting it aside yet, and start bringing to life all the stories that were waiting to be told. However, Dad had been saying that I needed a change of scene, and had suggested we take time off and have a look at what Europe had to offer. Florence, perhaps, or Rome, to see what the Renaissance had to show us. Or Egypt to look at older civilisations. Or, he had said, 'Why not go off somewhere on your own?'

'I've got plenty to do here, and a small project in mind for your birthday. Go and look at Stonehenge, or somewhere that takes your fancy. You don't need to be trailing round with an old bloke all the time!'

I thought about it and decided to go south, have a look at Stonehenge on the way, spend a few days in London, visit the National Library. If there's time, I'll visit the Patels too – have another look at our old home. Feeling, inexplicably, that there were answers there, if only I could find them, to all those problems between my mother and me.

I viewed the famous stones from a distance, thought of the early British people who raised and transported them long before the Roman occupation and the arrival of the English. Yet another story idea evolving in my head. Wish I could get at least one of them down. I went on to London.

A day at Chelsea to visit the Physic Garden satisfied my horticultural yearnings. Lunch with an old friend from Melbourne enabled me to catch up with some of the events there. The National Library engulfed me, but I couldn't concentrate.

I had contacted the present occupants of our old home, Dr. Adam Patel and his wife, inviting them out for a meal, a small gesture in recognition of their many years' custody of a few old envelopes. I didn't propose to talk about the contents of two of them.

I was glad to see Adam Patel again, and meet his wife Laila, both still happy in their East London house, – their home, and my birthplace.

'Rather too big for just the two of us,' said Laila, so we are anxious to produce one or two more occupants!'

I had seen that she was in the later stages of pregnancy, and congratulated them. I asked Adam if his appellation of 'Doctor' indicated an academic qualification or a medical one.

'We are both medical practitioners, I am a paediatrician at St. Thomas's Hospital, Laila is in general practice.'

'You will have access to excellent care, Laila, when your time comes.'

'I shall, Kay, but perhaps not where you might expect. I am going back to my parents In Yorkshire for the birth.'

She laughed. 'Partly in support of Adam's book! He's writing up his research into the effects of birth trauma. It often has unforeseen consequences.'

'Could you tell me more? Or would you prefer not to talk shop?'

Adam intervened. 'That's O.K.- only too glad to find someone who can put up with shop. The implications are interesting, and sometimes counter intuitive. I'm looking at the factors that affect maternal bonding.'

So was I, but didn't propose to tell them my reasons. Adam launched enthusiastically into an account of his work.

We put people into hospital with the best of intentions. For their health and well-being. But in the research I've been doing – and I hope that a book will come of it – the outcome of hospitalization is not always what we intend. I'm looking at the effect it has on mother and child. Bonding happens most successfully where a woman gives birth in the context of an extended family and community, each providing support. Where we take the mother out of that background, the bonding is sometimes less successful. Which offers the surprising conclusion that those who can afford the benefits of expert monitoring of childbirth in a hospital run a marginally greater risk of lessening – or even losing – the normal strong bond between mother and child. The risk is even greater where there has been birth trauma. We dare not withhold our expertise, but we must be aware of possible negative consequences, though these are rare.'

I asked him what forms of birth trauma he was thinking about.

'Complications of any kind. A caesarean section, problems with the presence or absence of the baby's father, anything that prevented the mother from doing exactly as she wished during the birth process. The psychology of childbirth is underrated.'

'That's certainly very interesting,' I commented. More so than Adam could have realised. He went on.

'Both of us speak from personal knowledge of traditional communities and their attitudes to pregnancy and birth. Unsuccessful bonding is rare, certainly in those places that we know well. Hospital births eliminate some risks, introduce others. In modern times there has been such a rush to eliminate every factor that threatens us, or simply that we do not like.'

Laila interrupted, with a smile.

'Like getting old!'

I smiled, in agreement.

'I say this not only in the context of medicine, but in relation to many other areas of life. We may need to take a more thoughtful approach in the future. It may be better for our species to learn to live with certain factors that we see as unpleasant or risky, rather than automatically setting out to remove them.'

Laila turned to me.

'You've got him going on his favourite topic, Kay.'

I thought that maybe Laila was anxious to ease Adam away from his passionate exposition of current attitudes to life and its hurdles. I gently changed the subject.

'It's certainly an interesting one. You'll be the centre of attention among all your family, Laila, spoilt rotten. Everything just as you want it to be. Sounds a good idea. But the expertise will still be there if you need it.'

'Yes. I am privileged, I know.'

The conversation moved on to the other aspect of Adam's research, the effects on children of their mass evacuation from London during the Blitz.

'Didn't your mother consider sending you too, Kay?'

'I don't really know. She had never mentioned the possibility, though if she had, I hardly know what my reaction would have been. I was not a sociable child, the constant threat of air raids meant that I spent most of my time at home. I wasn't used to meeting new people. I guess I'd have been homesick. Dad once told me that my mother had considered sending me away with all the other evacuees, and had written to him on the subject. His view was that I should stay at home with my mother, that we were company for each other, the only family we had, apart from him, and he was too far away to give us support. But the letters were so irregular, I really don't know how much they were able to talk about everyday matters.'

'A difficult decision for your mother. Did you discuss it with her when you were older?'

I didn't tell Laila that conversation with my mother on any topic at all was a rare event, there were times when discussion with the Patels veered towards topics that were too close for comfort.

Adam had provided a new train of thought and I couldn't let it go. Sleep didn't come, with his information that birth trauma was one reason for a lack of maternal bonding. What did I know of my own birth? Absolutely nothing, but here was a new angle for speculation.

My mother, as far as I knew, had been on her own. With no close friends, no family, the pregnancy must have been a lonely experience. There would have been check-ups, I supposed, and visits to the doctor, none of them on the scale we have today. I wondered about air raids on London. I needed to find out whether these were happening at the time of my birth.

Imagining the worst, that always had to happen before a more sensible conclusion was reached. All might have gone well, there had been holidays from the nightly raids. I could surely find out. Was I born during an air raid on London?

I considered talking freely to Adam and Laila about my experience of the lack of bonding between my mother and me, but decided that this bordered on a consultation, inappropriate to a simple friendship. Nor did I know how I would cope with such a revelation. Sometimes I felt little more than puzzlement and curiosity, occasionally a sharper hurt surfaced. I had talked to my father about it all, but to no-one else. I didn't know what I would say, how much of my life I'd reveal. I had a strange feeling that somehow the couple had a key to my puzzle, if only I knew how to access it. We said goodbye, promising to keep in touch. New unexpected friends, custodians of my old house. We got on well together.

Immeasurably glad to be home, I found Dad putting together a new greenhouse in the garden. It was to have been a surprise, he said for my birthday, he had not expected me back so soon. I told him of my meeting with the Patels, of our pleasant dinner, and of Adam's thoughts on birth trauma. A few days later I raised the subject with him.

'Dad, did Mum ever talk to you about the occasion of my birth? Did she manage O.K., being on her own?'

'She didn't say there was any problem. She was booked in at the local hospital on July 5th, 1940, and if the baby hadn't appeared before then, it would be induced on that day. Things were difficult and unpredictable enough for a hospital without waiting for late arrivals. She packed a few things and walked, probably waddled, into the maternity ward. You were born within a few hours. Quick and easy, she said the birth was. She was kept in the hospital for a couple of weeks, a customary length of time in those days.'

'Yes,' I said, 'Women must have almost lost the use of their legs after such a long stay in bed! Female physiology was considered a great deal more delicate than people consider today. I wonder if she had any help after she came home from hospital with a new baby.'

'I think something or other was arranged, and I remember her telling me that after a few weeks she'd have to manage on her own. As for the birth itself, it was me that had the worries, waiting day after day for a letter. I think this was the only occasion in my life that I wept, as I did when it finally came, telling me that I had a daughter. Tears of joy, of course, and relief. Kath wrote as regularly as she could, but I had nearly five years of only bits and pieces of news. I can't tell you how much I longed for more detail. All the news I had of you was always out of date. By the time I knew that you were uttering your first words, you were probably reading them!'

There was no indication from my father that my birth had been difficult, or that there had been any air raids at the time, but who knows what my mother had truly felt. The prospect of being alone at the onset of labour must have been worrying, though. 'Let it be daytime,' she must have prayed.

I wondered at my own tendency to grab at possible reasons for her behaviour towards me, her lack of love. I would have liked to accept it simply as a fact of life, put it behind me as we put behind us the war, the loss of life, the personal tragedies. Could I ever let it go?

NINE

Newfield, 1972 – 1974

A year went by, a third person obtained a foothold in our household. Only for one day a week, but she changed the dynamic of our lives.

I acquired a cleaner. This was not part of the life I'd envisaged, but each day seemed to provide a new and unexpected problem that required my attention. I found it hard to find the time to make a start on writing any of the stories that occupied my mind. It would be nice, I thought, to have some of the routine housework taken over by someone else. I would try and find a local person to come to The Cottage on a regular basis.

An odd set of circumstances brought about a knock at the door. Opening it, I was surprised to find on my doorstep a woman I had come across a few days previously.

My first meeting with Ellen had not been propitious. I'd been walking by the river, contemplating what I'd read of its history, and promising myself that one day I would explore its source in the mountains of Mid-Wales.

Severn, Hafren, Sabrina, its three names making a song in my head. I would try and find ways of seeing the bore, too, but knew the timing and location would be distracting.

"There twice a day the Severn fills.
The salt sea-water passes by,
And hushes half the babbling Wye,
And makes a silence in the hills."

He was teasing me, Tennyson was, in writing those strange, evocative, lines.

I thought about the quietening effect of a wall of water surging up from the Bristol Channel. I must see it and listen for myself I supposed that small obstructions which interfered with the flow would now be under the surface, unheard. Bury those persistent distracting sounds, the poet had said, and you won't hear them anymore. A psychological metaphor, I thought, how much did he know? Poetry shouldn't raise matters of science to distract the curious, wondering reader. It wasn't fair.

Grappling with the complexities of water flowing down to the sea meeting up with water coming in the opposite direction, I trod the riverside path blind to the details that normally brought me to pause, and look. A clutch of newly hatched ducklings, a patrolling dragonfly, a flash of blue that had to be a passing kingfisher, so brief that it felt subliminal. I berated myself for too frequent excursions into the past, into the abstract, missing the delights of the present. So, making a conscious decision to look around me and take notice, I glanced ahead. A small figure was approaching, and as it drew near, I could see how extremely small it was.

A little girl, no more than two or three years old, and apparently alone. This will not do, I thought. I stopped, smiled at the child, and spoke to her.

'Hello', I said, hoping that being addressed by a stranger would not frighten her.

The child looked at me, saying nothing. Was she talking yet?

'Are you having a nice walk?' Still no reply.

'Where is your Mummy?' The child whispered something. I squatted in front of her. 'Where's Mummy?'

'Mummy sleepy'

I tried again. 'Where is your house?' No answer.

'You've had a lovely walk, haven't you, but I think it's time you went back home. Mummy will be wondering where you are. Will you show me where you live?'

The child pointed back along the path. 'I'll walk with you' I said, 'and you can show me the right way to go.'

We set off together in the direction from which the child had come. I tried a few simple questions, and she was soon confident enough to reply. She pointed with delight at a group of ducks.

'I give breakfast for ducks' she explained.

'With Mummy?' I queried.

'No. Me an' Tony', she said, 'we give them breakfast.'

The path joined a small road, and I could see, not too far away, a caravan park, with a cluster of buildings near the main entrance. The site sloped gently down to the river, terraced to provide standing for a diverse collection of mobile homes.

The little girl turned confidently towards the site, and I followed her. Did she live here, or was she just visiting?

We moved between the terraces towards the river, the vans at this point less well maintained than the higher ones, many looking far from the "luxury homes" advertised at the entrance. One was situated apart from the others, dilapidated and uncared for, awaiting refurbishment, perhaps. It soon became obvious that this was where the child was heading. She climbed the wooden steps and pushed at the half-open door. I followed, hoping that this was the right place, and saw, to my dismay, a dishevelled figure sprawled on a narrow bed.

Mummy?' I asked, the child nodded. The figure coughed, woke, reached for a cigarette, saw the child, and spoke, angrily.

'You've been out! I told you, you're *not* to. I *told* you.' Looking up, she saw me.

'What d'you want? What you doin' here?'

'Your little girl was down by the river. I was worried she might be lost – she seemed so small to be by herself. I just wanted to make sure she knew where she was and could get home safely.'

I glanced round the caravan and shuddered. It was not clean; it smelt of stale food, of stale clothes, cigarette smoke, and an underlying sweetness that took me back to student days.

'She's bin out before. Knows 'er way home.' I wondered whether I should suggest that she was too young to be wandering alone by a river...but decided that people didn't want to be told what they knew already. It would not help the little girl. I uttered a few conventional remarks in praise of the child, her apparent common sense, her pleasure in the riverside.

The young woman muttered something, glancing at her watch.

'God, it's nearly five. Mum'll be back any minute, she'll kill me...for Chris' sake get out of here!' It was too late. The van door opened, an older woman came in, took one look at the scene, and turned to the younger. 'What's going on?' She turned to me. 'Who are you?'

The young woman started 'She were lost and called in to ask the way...'

'That's a lie'. The woman looked at me and stared.

'You from Social Services?'

'No, I'm not. Please don't worry – I found the little girl down by the river and thought she might not know her way home. I just wanted to make sure she got back safely.'

The woman continued to fix her eyes on me. 'What's your name?'

Why should she care what my name is?

'My name is Kay Francis. I live down the road at The Cottage.'

'Kay Francis.'

'Yes.'

The woman was silent for so long that I thought it was time for me to leave. I was moving towards the door when she started to speak again.

'I heard someone with that name had bought the place. Where'r you from?'

'I've moved recently from Australia.'

'You're Australian then?'

'Not really. I was born in London.'

I found myself growing increasingly uncomfortable. I don't have to put up with this intrusive inquisition, the child's back home, I can't do any more. These people might at least say thank you.

I wanted to leave, but the woman was blocking the doorway, I felt trapped. 'Well,' I said, if everything's O.K. now, I'll be getting along'. I went towards the door. The older woman did not move.

'You can see as well as I can that it's *not* O.K. Laura got out as usual and went off.' She seemed to debate with herself for a moment, then, looking at the younger woman, 'I don't suppose *she* said thank you. You'd better have a cup of tea, as you've come all the way from the Cottage.' She seemed oddly reluctant for me to depart, though equally reluctant to speak with minimal politeness, let alone gratitude. She moved to the sink, as if to start washing the pile of mugs and plates. But she stared into the debris and remained motionless, her back to me. I tried to make sense of the painful scene, wondering if there was anything I could say that would defuse the situation. A wind had risen, the van felt unstable, I felt odd, a little sick. I needed to sit down. I propped myself against a wall and took a deep breath. The little girl was clinging to the older woman's jeans, and looking up, asked her -

'Gran'ma, teatime soon?'

A cup of tea was the last thing I wanted from this unsavoury set-up, but it might help the odd, uncomfortable, shaky feeling that I was experiencing. Hoped I wasn't getting 'flu.

In addition, it occurred to me that a refusal might be taken badly. This woman would have known my name from local gossip and would have been briefed in full. To be able to buy a nice house, run a car, live comfortably without needing a job… to refuse a cup of tea might indicate that this incomer was toffee-nosed as well. I would go through with it. Mugs were retrieved from the unwashed collection in the sink, rinsed and placed on a small table. It was clear that any cleaning or tidying wasn't done by the younger woman, who seemed in danger of falling asleep again. The child stayed close to the older one, ignoring her mother.

It was not an easy occasion. The older woman spoke. 'Her,' indicating the figure on the bed, '*She's* my daughter. I can't do nothing with her. I've told her, time and time again, this can't go on. She's got to give up the booze, get herself a job, we'd manage the child between us, somehow.'

She shot a quick glance at the little girl, and the love in it was unmistakable.

'It's me that's got to do everything. The money's got to come from somewhere, an' I don't want the social services here, they'll see what it's like an' take the child away. I don't want that. Any family is better than no family, an' I should know. I had a husband once an' he buggered off, an' hers did the same. She looked bitter. 'Can't say I blame either of 'em'.

She was silent for a moment, staring at me.

I struggled to find words. 'I'm sorry. A sad story.'

'My life's not been worth living. But I've got Laura now. There's nothing I wouldn't do to get her a better life than the one I've had. She's got a *right* to it. No-one knows that better than me.'

The woman looked at me, angrily. Her behaviour was extremely odd, to say the least. She seemed confused, aggressive at one moment, demanding pity at the next. One hand was clenched over the other, so tight that the knuckle bones shone white through the skin.

I finished my unwanted tea. The older woman had taken the child on her knee, seemed quieter, and kissed her 'Poor little mite' she said, 'she don't deserve a mother like *her*'. Puzzling at the woman's attitude, distinctly unpleasant, but with a seeming reluctance to let me go. I wondered, did she want more from me?

I felt moved. I could at least make a small gesture. Nervously I fished a couple of notes from my purse and held them towards the woman. 'I'm truly sorry', I said. 'Life is hard for you. It's not much really, but it may help a bit.'

The woman stared at me, took the notes, and put them in her pocket. Turning away from me, back at the dirty sink, her voice was strange and harsh.

'There must be plenty more where those came from, if you can afford to throw 'em around like that.'

The bitterness in her voice and her rudeness was insupportable. I glanced towards the child, who, for the first time, gave me a shy smile. 'Goodbye Laura,' I said, making my way carefully down the rickety steps. Looking back, I saw a small pale face at the caravan window. I waved.

An odd, unsettling episode, one that briefly clouded the next couple of days. I thought about it, and concluded that the poor woman's hopeless inability to deal with her situation, combined with her obvious love for the child, had rendered her incapable of ordinary behaviour. Defensive aggression, perhaps, was her only weapon against life as she knew it.

Putting the incident out of my mind, I settled down that evening to the matter of my new book. I'd been contemplating the idea of an individual in a new location, and the extent that they would have to change, and the degree to which their new community would have to change as a result. A new and more interesting variation had come into my mind. The context might not be geographical, but cultural. The protagonist would find herself in a new environment, one to which she was attracted, but hindered by her cultural history. An intellectual joining the peasants' revolt, the Tory impelled to support the miners' strike.

I tapped out a potential opening sentence. Read it five times. Pulled the paper out of the machine, screwed it up and threw it in the wastepaper basket. A not uncommon start.

Finding the woman from the caravan on my doorstep a few days later, was an odd and unwelcome surprise. She made no reference to our earlier meeting.

'I need some more work,' she said. 'Don't suppose you could do with a cleaner. Don't mind what I do.'

Well, well, here was my cleaner. Offering her services, and as I took in the possible implications, it seemed a quick and easy solution. Our new home necessitated a routine I hadn't established yet; it was a house that seemed to resent attempts at minimal alterations and provided problems wherever it could. Trying the patience of its new owners.

I knew I was pushed for time to get on with my writing. I didn't pretend to call it earning my living – Dad's investments were more than enough to provide for our needs. But I still thought of writing as my job, and loved it in spite of all the false starts.

Of course, the extra time would be a blessing.

The woman spoke again. 'My name is Ellen Parry. I can get references if you want them.'

'I -I'll think about it,' I said. 'Come back next week.

TEN

Dad thought it a good idea. I had told him of the odd and rather unpleasant circumstances of my encounter with Ellen, and he pointed out that at the time I'd been moved enough to offer money. A job would give her a modicum of help that she could rely on. I contacted the people she had named as willing to give references, they had pronounced her work as perfectly satisfactory, though said that she herself was unfriendly and prickly in her manner. They were aware of her problems, but thought she was doing her best in difficult circumstances.

I took her on. She had asked if she might occasionally bring her grandchild, at times when things were particularly difficult at home in the caravan. I could see that leaving Laura in the care of her mother was a worry, so readily agreed. In a moment of unaccustomed candour, she told me that she was permanently terrified of a visit from the Social Services, and a verdict that the child should be taken into care.

I tried to reassure her, saying that a loving grandmother could make up for much that was missing in Laura's life. She would look beyond me, as if towards a distant landscape.

'I *will* get her better life. It's all I've got to live for. It'll happen, somehow or other. She's got a *right* to it. There's … other people in the story.'

She was thinking, no doubt, of the man who had married her daughter, and fathered the child, and I wondered if any attempt had been made through the courts to extract maintenance from him. Easy enough for a man to disappear, though, if circumstances became inconvenient.

What sort of right did Laura have? Over and above what any child under British law was entitled to? She could be placed in an institution where her material well-being would be a great deal better than was apparent under her present circumstances. But if Ellen could struggle through the early years, and keep out of trouble with the authorities, the close bond between the two might be more rewarding for Laura than removal to a cleaner, safer place.

She came with Ellen, more often than not, and we had our coffee – break at the kitchen table, where Laura put her few tattered picture books and toys, donated, I discovered later, by some of Ellen's other employers. Conversation was not easy, Ellen volunteered little more than I knew already about her unfortunate history. I found some of her questions about mine intrusive and inappropriate, focussing on the differences in our circumstances. I tried to direct her attention to Laura, who was beginning to open up a little, becoming more confident in her weekly visits. I asked her grandmother 'Aren't there any other kids on the site? It would be nice if she could have someone to play with from time to time.'

'No one would let any kid near our van. She hasn't got any friends.'

Laura whispered a few words.

'I got Tony.'

'Who's Tony?' I asked her, interested.

'It's no-one,' Ellen commented. 'It's all in her imagination. She pretends she's got someone to play with. Don't know if she really believes it.'

I remembered Laura's comment about Tony and the ducks, recalling the imaginary characters that peopled my own early childhood.

'That's quite a common feature of loneliness in children. Best to go along with it if it keeps them happy. I had an imaginary playmate when I was little. I remember her even today.' A brief flashback of Nellie blocked the image of Laura's grandmother. 'She'll soon forget about them all when she goes to school.'

Tony was mentioned once or twice during Laura's visits. Apparently, it was he who was responsible for Laura's occasional excursions while her mother was asleep. He wanted to go for a walk along the river, she said, and feed the ducks with bits of bread. I remembered trying, as a four-year-old, to tell such little stories to my mother. It took time for my childish self to realise that she was only interested in things that had actually taken place, all else was Nonsense, or in extreme cases, Lies. Bad enough that I should tell stories to *her*, but on one occasion I had made the mistake of telling them to a neighbour. My mother had hit me, calling me a liar, sat down and cried.

What had I said that provoked this outburst? Some little story about me and Nellie going to the shops, as harmless as Laura's tale of her Sunday duck–feeding jaunts with the imaginary Tony.

The episode had not been referred to again. I'd felt confused. I thought I knew what a lie was, it was something you said to avoid punishment or a telling-off. What I had been saying was just fun. Not meant to be anything to do with what anyone had actually been doing. Didn't people know the difference? At least Laura was permitted a few flights of fancy. I could not imagine Ellen inflicting punishment on the child.

Laura's mother would sometimes lock the door to keep the child inside, Ellen said, but that meant that the spare key had to be kept in some hiding place outside the van. Ellen was anxious that the van could always be accessed from the outside, in case of emergency. The location of keys was a permanent feature of an unsatisfactory situation, and probably always on her mind while she was away from the van.

I tried not to take the unfortunate family's problems into my study. I wanted to keep it a place where I could work without external worries. I'd got used to the self-discipline necessary to dismiss them from my mind and had got quite good at it. The room was a later addition to the house, stone-walled to match the rest, and with a recess for my log-burning fire. This was lit daily during the winter weather, and its welcoming warmth was a constant blessing. The logistics of keeping it supplied with seasoned wood and solid fuel, the daily emptying of the ashes were chores willingly undertaken, a small payment for the bright welcome of its glowing morning embers, and its obliging acceptance of my wearily discarded chapters. I loved it.

ELEVEN

Newfield 1974 – 1976

It was time to meet my publisher face-to-face. Jonathan's firm was English, I had used it for my writing in Australia. The address was in Birmingham, no more than an hour's drive from Newfield. I'd always spoken to Jonathan on the phone, he'd seemed pleasant if somewhat formal.

We shook hands. A friendly welcome, with elements of humour that I hadn't expected. His persona was Dickensian, with sideburns, Micawber- like. Waiting for something to turn up, I thought, but unlike the original, he knew exactly what he was waiting for – my next book.

I explained that progress on the long-delayed new novel he had been promised was slow. I couldn't concentrate, I told him, with all the problems associated with family loss, change of country, the complications of settling down into a new environment. He had accepted what I told him on the phone, somewhat gloomily. 'We must think of our readers,' he'd said, 'we may lose them if they have to wait too long. Transfer their loyalties elsewhere. '

Buy from another publisher was what he meant. I'd not seen the ironic smile that would have accompanied these remarks. But the affectionate grasp of my arm told me that he was sympathetic to the problems that beset my writing progress.

'I'm not usually as patient with my other writers. But your last book went well, readers are hoping for another.'

I sighed. 'We may have to change our relationship, Jonathan. No longer publisher and author. Just a couple of good friends. Till I can write again.'

'No need for anything so drastic! But you're not to worry, Kay, just keep in touch, let me know how things are going.'

I'd spoken many times on the phone to Jonathan, a formal friendliness had come through, but not his joviality, the kindly smile that went with it, his expansive persona, his optimism, discovered at last at this meeting.

We parted, glad on both sides that we had now met. I liked him, thinking that much of our assessment of people depended on our means of communication with them. Letters allowed you second thoughts. You could rewrite them, they could remain unposted. On the phone thoughts were unedited, but feelings censored by the speaker. Pretence much harder face-to-face.

I drove home, glad at the way the meeting had gone, but still with the worry that I couldn't settle down to the book that was still churning away in my head.

My father pottered around the garden and was absorbed in creating a vegetable patch from which he produced far too much for the two of us to eat. He'd had a bad winter though, with a chest infection that left him tired. He decided to sort all his old photos and get them properly organised in an album. This activity was convenient for me, as I had been approached again by Bethan, asking if I felt like filling a gap she had in her schedule of speakers at the W.I. meetings. She had a projector, she said, and hoped I had a few slides, people liked to have something to look at as well as listen to. It was Australia they wanted to know about.

So, Melbourne it would be, one or two essential facts of history and geography, but with the emphasis on daily life.

I used some of Dad's collection of photographs to go with what I'd decided to say, went along to the village hall one evening and did my best. The president welcomed me and managed to quieten the constant murmur of chat so that I could make a start. It all took a little longer than I had expected, the audience was lively and seemed to enjoy questioning me on aspects of life in Australia that I knew nothing about. Tell us about the W.I. there, they had asked.

'Doesn't exist, as far as I know,' I replied, 'but I think they have it in New Zealand. You'd better send some missionaries.'

From the back of the hall a disapproving voice made itself heard above the laughter.

'The Women's Institute is not a religion.'

'I apologise. Just a joke.'

A few more questions, and I had finished. it was a new experience, it was fun. I enjoyed myself. The feast of tea, sandwiches and cakes was impressive.

There was a consequence, though, one that I did not enjoy. A couple of days later there was a knock at the door.

'Good morning, Miss Francis.'

I had heard that voice before.

'I'm a member of the Women's Institute in the village. I was at the meeting you spoke to the other day. My name is Mrs. Dorothy Hayleigh. L,E,I,G,H. Spelling is so important, don't you think? As a writer yourself, you must be constantly dealing with its peculiarities.'

'Well, it's certainly an interesting aspect of words and their history, but I can't say it's at the top of my list of priorities. Please come in, I'll put the kettle on.'

She entered the house, a sharp-featured woman, with black curled hair meticulously emerging from a fashionable hat, secured by a pearl-topped hatpin. She removed her gloves, looking for the proper piece of hall furniture upon which to lay them. I remembered that my mother would refer to 'the hallstand' – an ungainly free-standing contraption with large hooks to receive visitors' hats and coats. Should I try to locate one? Together with spelling – bottom of my list of priorities.

'May I take your coat?' I asked her. She handed it to me, and I deposited it on the back of a chair. My visitor looked around the large empty hall with a frown and located the mirror. Would the hat be removed as well? This was obviously a step too far; it remained in position.

She preceded me into the kitchen, her eyes resting upon each item in turn. She looked carefully at the cooker, the cupboards and working surfaces, took in the Aga, touched the large central table, peered through the door that led to the utility room. All was being assessed. She spoke.

'You haven't changed the old place much. In fact, it's almost exactly as I remember it.'

'You know the house, then?'

'Oh yes. You can say that I was a regular visitor here when it belonged to Madge Evans. Madge was sister to our member of parliament, Barry Evans. But you wouldn't know any of that, being from,' she paused, '*abroad*.'

She managed to invest the word with dark, undesirable, untrustworthy implications.

'That is true. I'm looking forward to learning about the history of the area.'

'I can help you with that. Although I say it myself, my knowledge of the district and its people is considerable.' She spoke with modest pride.

A picture flashed into my mind of Mrs. Hayleigh, dictionary in hand, telling me of things, places and people I had never heard of, and how to spell them.

'I enjoyed your talk on Wednesday, Miss Francis.'

'Please call me Kay,' I said. 'I'm glad you liked it. I've never given a talk about Australia before.'

'Really? But I haven't come to speak about that, Miss Francis.'

She stood a little straighter, lowered her eyes for a moment, an internal battle was being fought, and I was to be made aware of it. Taking a deep breath, she spoke.

'I must tell you why I'm here this morning. It isn't something I could mention the other night. It would not have been appropriate.'

She paused, with an air of solemnity, then in a hushed tone, made her announcement.

'It has been brought to my attention that you employ a cleaning woman.'

Why on earth someone would be bothered to bring that to anyone's attention I couldn't imagine.

'Yes. It's not a secret.'

She looked at me suspiciously. I poured the tea.

'Sugar?'

'Yes please, and just a very little milk. You employ Ellen Parry, from the caravan site.'

'I do.'

'I suspect that you don't know about her.'

'I'm not sure what you mean.'

'Did you know that she has living with her a daughter who's usually…intoxicated, and that – you won't believe this – there's a child there.'

'I know there's a child there. She's Ellen's granddaughter. She sometimes brings her to work.'

'I am extremely worried, Miss Francis. It's not right, I'm sure you'll agree, for a young child to be brought up in such a situation, and I'm sure you don't know that the place where they live is filthy and disgusting.'

'How do you know? Have you been there?'

'Certainly not. I wouldn't dream of setting foot in a place like that. But I know of one or two people who have. I thought that if someone informed you of all this, you might prefer not to employ a person who lived in such conditions.' She sipped her tea and took a biscuit, examining it closely.

I was shocked at her words. What an appalling woman. I hoped she would leave as soon as possible.

'What are you suggesting? That I sack her?'

'There is a child to consider, Miss Francis. It is disgraceful that a child should be brought up in conditions of dirt and neglect.'

'If it is avoidable, yes. But if I dismissed Ellen it would make things worse, not better. She needs the money. They have no other source of income other than what she can earn from her cleaning jobs.'

Mrs Hayleigh looked at the ceiling, whether in exasperation or renewed assessment of the kitchen I was not sure.

'The important thing here, Miss Francis, is the child. It should be in care. By employing that woman, you are contributing to keeping it in that filthy caravan, in the custody of a drunken mother, who sometimes goes out and leaves the child alone in the van. It is a serious case of child neglect. By supporting Ellen Parry, you are prolonging the situation. You are new here, I was sure you had no idea of the circumstances, so I thought you might be glad to be told.'

I knew what would make me glad, which would be to tell her she was an ignorant interfering bitch, to mind her own business and go away. I also realised that she could be dangerous, I must be careful.

'Mrs. Hayleigh, I can't agree with all your conclusions. I know of Ellen's circumstances, and I'm sorry for them. She is devoted to the little girl and does her best to keep the family together as far as she can. I am not prepared to make things worse for the three of them.'

'And *I* have to do what *I* think is right, Miss Francis. I am not willing to stand by and see that poor child abandoned, left alone in the caravan, often with the door open, so she can wander off by herself. There are dangers, Miss Francis, I'm sure you'll agree. It is my duty to report the matter to the Social Services. I was hoping that, now that you know the facts, you might support me in this.'

I was aware of a dilemma. I was angry and upset, and just wanted her to go. But I was also aware that it was possible that she would do what she threatened. I didn't want to see Laura in care. I wanted the fragile balance of the three lives to be sustained for as long as possible, in the hope that somehow or other Ellen would battle through. I would have to be careful, to compromise.

'Mrs. Hayleigh, I appreciate that it must have been difficult for you to call this morning and talk to me about all this. It's a sad and sorry situation, and I agree with you that the chief priority must be the child. But I can't see that being looked after in an institution would necessarily be better for Laura than her life as it is. The one thing she has now is her grandmother's love. Ellen's determination to make a better life for her grandchild can't be questioned. Would you be prepared to delay any decision to report the matter? We can think it over and I promise to keep a close eye on the little girl when Ellen brings her. What do you think?'

Her face reddened. I guessed that her first reaction was anger at being openly defied. I'd refused to do what she wanted.

'Well, I must say I'm disappointed that you don't see the full seriousness of the situation. I had hoped you would be as shocked as I was to learn about the conditions that this child is being brought up in.'

Mrs Hayleigh would be even more shocked to know that I had personal experience of those circumstances, and wasn't prepared to dismiss the unfortunate woman who lived in them. Some serious buttering up was required.

'Thank you for coming, Mrs. Hayleigh. But we mustn't rush things. I suggest that we do nothing for the time being, and see how the situation develops. I promise you that I'll get in touch the minute I think that something needs to be done.'

'Very well Miss Francis. I must confess that I'm surprised and disappointed. It seems that there's no more that I can say to you. I can only hope that you'll think about what I've told you this morning.'

I assured her that I would. That at least was true.

'I'll be getting along then. I have a busy day in front of me.'

With alacrity, I fetched her coat and gloves. She put them on, slowly, silently, turning to look in the mirror for final adjustments. Neither of us spoke.

She moved towards the door, with a final assessing glance round the hall and what she could see of a dwelling that had once housed a person of some standing in the community. 'Goodbye Miss Francis,' she uttered coldly, and left. No doubt to continue her mission to put the world to rights, as unpleasantly as she could, exuding virtue without compassion. I hoped I would never see her again, but felt apprehensive.

I reported the visit and conversation to Dad, who was feeling tired this morning, hadn't slept well, he said, this wretched cough keeping him awake.

'You're upset, Kay. She won't do it. She's all bluster and righteous indignation.'

I hoped he was right. I heard no more from Mrs Hayleigh.

I did, though, hear from Bethan, the W.I. speaker finder, who called with
an armful of greenery, pots, and cuttings of plants that did well in her garden, and that she hoped would flourish in mine. She thanked me for the talk, especially since I had refused payment. I pointed out to her that I was inexperienced as a speaker on other than literary topics, and that it should count as practice.

'I hope we'll see you again as a member, Kay.'

'One day, I hope. I am enjoying my new life here, but I must admit I hadn't realised how busy I would be settling all sorts of matters that have cropped up. But I find it all interesting. Noticing the small differences in life here, the unexpected similarities too, almost too small to comment on, but adding up to small differences in the way of seeing things.'

'I'm so glad. By the way, don't take too much notice of that woman who commented from the back of the room during your talk. She a bit of a menace, actually. Very disruptive, causes trouble. Thinks our branch should do more to right the world's wrongs. But since she's often got a point in some of her criticisms, it's hard to know what to say. She does manage to be quite aggressive while holding forth on whatever her pet moan is at the time.'

I decided that I would not mention Mrs Hayleigh's visit.

'It's surprising,' I said, 'how much damage can be done from the moral high ground.'

My visitor nodded sadly.

'I'm anxious that you shouldn't be put off joining us on her account. We still hope to see you as a member when you feel ready.'

I thought of Mrs Hayleigh's current target. If Ellen could talk about her life, her difficulties, her fears, talk freely without the emotional and social baggage she always carried with her

– the jealousy, the bitterness, the dislike – maybe together we could find a way out of it all. I had decided that her attitude was simply a means of focussing the myriad of circumstances that had led to her present position on to a single person – me. I was someone who had everything that she lacked, Including the time and attention I was able to give to Laura during her visits.

Occasionally I asked after her daughter, about problems in the caravan that I knew troubled her. Her replies were dismissive. 'Same as usual,' was the only reply I had.

There were other things to worry about. As time went by, it became clear that my father was not well. We had a battle about the necessity for a visit to the doctor, for, he said, something that was nothing more than a touch of bronchitis which would clear up when the weather improved in the spring. When he finally consented to an appointment, the news was not good. The years of smoking had caught up with him, and his lungs were in a poor state. Treatment provided only a temporary improvement, his health failing to inspire a vain hope that a cure was possible.

TWELVE

Newfield 1974 – 1976

What can I say of my father's death? He faced it with equanimity, we talked of it freely. There was no pretence between us, his life was coming to an end. 'A little sooner than I had anticipated,' he commented, 'but I have found a good place to die in. I'm so glad we came across it in time.'

There were jokes on his good days, weariness on the bad ones, but he never lost touch with reality. 'There's to be no grieving after I've gone,' he announced on one of his better days, 'won't do me any good, nor you either. Waste of time. Feed the birds. Dig the nettles out of the rose borders. Think of the fun we used to have. I've had a lucky life.'

He died on a sunny day in October. His funeral was tiny, with one or two people he'd met regularly at the pub, a farmer, Selwyn Hughes, whose land adjoined ours, Alex, our solicitor, and Bethan Lewis. Dad had already told me, unnecessarily, for I knew it already, that there were to be no references to God or an afterlife. 'One life is plenty,' he'd said, don't want another one.'

Bethan had said that it was customary for people to assemble afterwards for light refreshments and to talk of their recollections of the departed. They had all known him for such a short time, I thought, they knew nothing of the man he was, only as a kindly English incomer.

Obediently, I tried not to grieve. It was not easy. Beside my bed I had always kept the photograph that used to be on the mantelpiece of our London home. The serious face of a young man, self-conscious in his new army uniform, but, I guessed, trying to suppress the smile that was always waiting to emerge. Photographs were a serious matter in those days, spontaneity not the virtue it is today. I had other pictures, of course, many from Melbourne, and a few from here. I put these away for the time being, they were too close to today. You get on with your daily tasks as best you can until those acts which had become automatic in your life with the other person suddenly become redundant, and you are brought up sharply with this new aspect of being. Coming across the now unused sugar in its bowl brought the first tears of grief that I wept.

To say I missed my father is to omit any account of strange unfamiliar periods of time, some passing in flashes of pain and sorrow, some long, tedious and boring, with no point, nothing to look forward to but bed and oblivion. But day comes after day, jobs get themselves done because there is nothing else to do.

Later, after the weeks of looking after an increasingly incapacitated man, my responsibilities shifted to dealing with the usual consequences of a death. Letters to be written, calls to be made, mostly to Australia, where there were still remnants of his life. Tax requirements to be complied with, legal matters to be sorted. Some of these surprised me, I hadn't fully realised how large his assets were. Gradually, life recovered its balance, my still unwritten book shifting its shape arbitrarily in my mind. Would it ever come to heel, fully under control? Did it even matter? I didn't need to work; I had inherited more than enough to live on for a single woman with no family. I was on my own now, with no responsibilities other than ones I chose.

Ellen had been coming as usual during my father's illness, but now that he had died there was not a great deal for her to do. I said that I would pay her more for the extra work she had been doing during his last weeks of life, but that a fortnightly visit would be more suitable now that I was on my own. A friend in the village was looking for a new domestic help. If Ellen wanted to make up the hours lost with me, she was welcome to apply. She had made no comment on Dad's death. There was little to say, but most people observe the formalities. Her silence on the subject made me angry, but I knew that there were those who found it difficult to utter words of sympathy. She didn't even try.

'I'll come here every other Wednesday, then,' she said flatly. Whether the change in arrangements was agreeable to her or not, I couldn't tell, she made me feel guilty whatever I said or did. I hoped that her new employer would make no objection to Laura's occasional presence, most of her employers didn't, the child was little trouble.

Seeing that I was dealing with the death of my father without support of family or old friends, Bethan Lewis called once or twice.

'How's the garden doing, Kay?' she asked.

'I've not been outside much, actually, Bethan, November's not my favourite month.'

'Not mine, either.' She looked a little pale, I thought. A teacher at the local primary school, she'd been putting in a lot of work in a school that was suffering from lack of pupils, a not uncommon situation in a country whose rural population was noticeably declining, year by year.

'Still fighting for the future of your school, Bethan?'

'I am. It doesn't get any easier. I've had to put my course on hold.'

'You're doing a course as well? What's your field?'

'History. A love of mine, but I simply haven't time to do the research as diligently as I should.' She sighed, looking despondent.

'What period?'

'Fifth and sixth centuries, particularly in the areas still held by the British. The borders fluctuated amazingly, there were countless battles whose result could have gone either way.'

'But, ultimately – the political geography settled down. The invaders won.'

'Yes, but the war is still being fought. Today the battlefields are cultural.'

I thought about what Bethan was telling me, and wondered, what if the final result, the map of Britain that we see today, had evolved differently? If the invaders from northern Europe had been driven back by the native British, if the Welsh Marches were much, much further east…

What would the place where I live have looked like? How would the inhabitants have seen themselves? I filed these questions in my mind, looking forward to retrieving them later.

She left, leaving me with new ideas, the best gifts anyone could have.

THIRTEEN

Shrewsbury Hospital 1980

Sunshine. From the mists of childhood to the fog of the present a voice chided me.

'Get your hat, Kay. You know you mustn't go out without a hat.'

Wearily, I answered my long-dead mother.

'O.K. Mum'.

I awoke slowly, bright sunshine falling across my face. I closed my eyes against its painful brilliance. How fiercely my head ached – what had I been doing last night? I tried the routine checklist of returning consciousness: day of the week? jobs to be done, problems to be addressed, pleasures to look forward to… why should such ordinary daily matters be so elusive?

Something is wrong, something is strange, something which does not fit into that lifetime of awakenings, at different times, in different rooms, in beds, on bare ground, on beaches, at sea, with a friend, with a lover, or alone – momentarily disorientated, perhaps, but with location and continuity soon established. Too tired for the effort of thought, I felt myself slipping back into sleep, but, wrenching myself painfully back into the sunlit room, suddenly I knew what was wrong. *Sunshine.*

My bedroom faces north-west, its windows looking towards the long, low line of the Welsh hills, touched with gold in the morning sun, featureless and dark as the sun sets behind them. The back of the house looks over the wide Severn valley, strips of silver clearly visible on a bright day and shining wonderfully on a moonlit night. For a few weeks in high summer the rays of the rising sun slip past the corner of the barn, illuminating the rough texture of the white plastered wall opposite my bed, but never reaching my face. This place could not be home, for I never woke up touched by the rays of the morning sun. I put up a hand to cover my eyes. No, this was not my room, nor a normal awakening. Here were smells and sounds that belonged to a more public place.

Yes. I knew where I must be, and began the struggle to remember why.

'What is your name?' I opened my eyes to see a friendly, worried face. The young nurse bending over me looked relieved, and repeated the question.

'Kay Francis'. My voice sounded odd, croaky.

'So you're back with us again. That's good.' She smiled.

'What happened to me?'

'An accident, sort of…you're not to worry. You're doing fine. Doctor will be round quite soon. He'll talk to you about it.'

I didn't want to be *told* what had happened. I wanted to *remember*. An accident? I moved my legs, my arms, my limbs seemed undamaged, must be concussion, that was why my head ached so badly, the thumping inside it bringing back the sound of bombs over London when I was a child. I closed my eyes, the illusion persisted, a voice drifted over the years, 'That was a close one.'

Waking again, some immeasurable time later, it was a man's voice I heard.

'Feeling better?' White coat, doctor, I supposed.

'My name is Doctor Bhatia. I saw you when you first came in.'

'Why am I here?'

'You are here because someone called at your house and found you unconscious. They called the ambulance straight away. Carbon monoxide poisoning it was, lucky you were found in time.'

'Who was it?'

'I don't know, a neighbour perhaps.'

He paused, waiting for a response.

'I've got a sore throat.'

'That doesn't surprise me. But you're recovering nicely, and we don't think there'll be any long-term damage. But I'd like you to stay for a couple more days for checks, and as soon as all is clear you can go home. Can you remember feeling unwell? A headache? Very sleepy? Trying to stay awake?'

'I don't remember anything. I don't know what day it is. When did I come here?'

'The day before yesterday. Don't worry too much just now, everything will be much clearer soon. We'll have another chat tomorrow.'

He disappeared, no time to answer any more questions, even if I could gather my thoughts together well enough to ask them. The rest of the day passed in an uneasy amalgam of efforts to recall recent events and lapsing into periods of weary sleep, compounded by sounds, impressions, tiny flashes of consciousness, attempts by a fuddled brain to make sense of what had happened to me.

I was aware of the tea trolley, the newspaper delivery, of routine hospital procedures. The taking of temperatures, the measuring of blood pressure, porters with bodies to take away for x-rays, porters with bodies to be rolled back expertly on to their beds, whispered conferences behind closed curtains, the laughter of nurses. A different world, with its own priorities, its own rituals, its own language. Not a peaceful place, but busy with its own life. What am I doing here? I struggled to sit up, experiencing a familiar discomfort. I needed a pee. 'Can you manage?' The occupant of the next bed watched anxiously. 'The loo's just round the corner.'

'Thanks. I'll be fine.' I stood up carefully on hospital socks. I suppose one should always have contingency plans for unexpected hospital admittance – clean pyjamas, slippers, toothbrush. How much should one prepare for one's unknown future? What would such a life be like? I smiled at the thought. I felt a steadying hand on my arm.

'O.K.? need any help?'

'Thank you, I'm sure I can manage. I'll take it slowly. First time on my feet for a couple of days and don't know my way about this place!'

'Haven't lost yer Aussie accent yet! The ridiculously young ward cleaner grinned. 'You sound just like my Mum. She's from Sydney.'

I laughed. 'I'm as English as you are. Just happened to grow up in Melbourne! Nice to meet you, excuse me if I rush off, I'm desperate!'

Excursion successfully completed, I navigated my way back, smiled at the occupant of my neighbouring bed, and sank back gratefully into the pillows. Just in time, as the outside world suddenly erupted into mine. People in shoes, coats, carrying handbags, books, flowers. Animated, anxious, they'd navigated the corridors, followed the directions, lost themselves in labyrinthine passages, found the ward, located their loved ones and flushed with success, were collapsing into bedside chairs. Relieved greetings, muted conversations, loud whispers, bursts of laughter filled the room as the ward re-organised itself into public mode.

There were visitors for most patients, none, of course, for me. Who would I most like to see? My father, of course, but he is no longer here. My one-time friend Cherry, but of course that cannot happen – she is ten thousand miles away and will never forgive me.

My publisher, Jonathan Parfitt? Malfunctioning bodies matter to him in the context of a novel, deadlines are what interest him. He would be concerned about my presence here, but his sympathy would focus on when the new book would be finished. Must get the title sorted. It would be nice to see Bethan, but how would she know I'm in hospital? I might, of course be visited by the Rev. Powell, perhaps, doing his traditional round of visiting the sick, and giving such comfort as the church can provide.

Selwyn Hughes? That would be nice, but he would be embarrassed and awkward. Not socially comfortable in my kitchen, let alone a hospital ward. I thought back to the occasion of our first meeting.

I had opened the door to a tall, black-haired stranger, in the standard torn and well-worn clothes of a working farmer.

'My name is Selwyn Hughes. I'm your neighbour. Your paddock shares a boundary hedge with one of my fields.'

I introduced myself. 'Kay Francis. Will you come in for a moment? I'm pleased to meet you.'

My visitor hesitated.

'This isn't really a social call. A branch has fallen across the hedge. My ewes can get through to your paddock. I'm just coming round to ask if it's all right for me to do some repair work from your side.'

'Of course. If you like, we'll go and have a look. See what wants doing.'

I grabbed my boots and a jacket. My visitor didn't say much, which was a pity, I thought, for the Welsh accent was becoming more familiar to me and sounded like music.

We, or rather, I, chatted as we picked our way over the long grass in the little paddock that went with the Cottage. Thistles were growing there, and a rogue hawthorn seedling, foolhardy pioneer of the forest that would one day reclaim the area, if radical new thinking prevailed. However current opinion required me to *manage* the land I had acquired, to let it go wild would be a waste of resources. In the company of a farmer, I felt guilty of neglect.

A big branch had fallen across the hedge and smashed the wire fence that reinforced it, leaving a gap through which an enterprising ewe could make her way. Was the grass greener on my side?

My neighbour made some temporary repairs, threw the offending branch over into his property, and departed over the wire. 'Needs a bit more work,' he observed, 'I'll finish it as soon as I can.'

I wondered if I would see him again. It would be nice, I had decided, to get to know my farming neighbours better. A gateway to the culture of the small country I had come to live in, a way of life and a language still completely unknown to me. Yes, it would be nice to have a visit from him, but this is obviously out of the question while I am hospitalised.

Wrong again. Opening my eyes again, there he was, beside my hospital bed. I looked at him, speechless. Was I dreaming?

'May I sit down?'

I indicated the vacant chair. He was carrying a bunch of small, pale daffodils.

'Are these for me?'

'Yes.'

'They are beautiful.' Which they were. Small, delicate,

and pale. Little resemblance to the large, brash, eye-catching blooms that dominated many gardens at this time of the year. Not for the first time I wished that commercial plant breeders would leave our native plants alone. They were breeding double daffodils now, and *pink* ones.

'I phoned the hospital first before I came. They said you were doing well.'

'It is very kind of you …' my voice trailed off, I felt incapable of commenting that it was rather strange to make a hospital visit to a person that you had met only once before.

'You must be wondering why I've come.'

'Well, I …'

'It was me that phoned the ambulance that brought you here. I'd come by, and knocked at your door. There was no response. I thought you must be at home; your car was there. I couldn't find you in the garden, so I looked through your study window. You were fast asleep at your desk, so I tapped on the glass. You didn't wake. It was then I began to worry. I went into the house and realised what was wrong. It was the smell. Not the real culprit, carbon monoxide, that has no smell, but the fumes that usually go with it, the result of poor combustion of fuel.'

He paused, waiting, perhaps, for some comment on the story so far. I pictured his immediate recognition of a crisis, my shocked neighbour moving fast.

'I couldn't wake you, so I called an ambulance. I explained that I was a neighbour, and told them what little I know about you. That you were from abroad, hadn't been here long, that you had lost your father and I didn't know of any relatives. They whisked you off pretty quick.'

'You saved my life.'

'It was lucky I had a reason to call. Nothing important really. Just about your little field. Everything's fine, we'll have a chat about it when you're home again.'

'I should say thank you, but it seems such a feeble offering to someone who has given me the rest of my life.'

'I only did what anyone else would have done... it was a stroke of luck that I'd decided to call at that particular moment. No virtue on my part.' He was clearly embarrassed, one of those people who cannot cope with being thanked.

'The nurse told me you'll be home soon. That's good.'

'Tomorrow. Please say thank you from me to your wife, for the lovely flowers.'

'I don't have one. I did once, but we're not together now.'

'Oh, I'm sorry. A foolish assumption.'

'A natural one. I felt I couldn't visit without bringing a small token, they are from one of my fields, a patch of wild daffodils that I haven't the heart to get rid of. In Welsh we call them St Peter's Leek. Cennin Sant Pedr.

I sighed. 'What a lot I have to learn.'

He stood up, preparing to depart.

'I'll leave you alone now. I'll call when you're back home.'

With his first smile, he stood up and walked towards the exit. Glad to have this embarrassing interview over, no doubt. I lay back on my pillows and considered the whole episode. Did I really owe my life to this man? If he had not called by, would I have succumbed to those wretched fumes? Presumably, without replenishment, the fire would have burnt itself out. Before I had done the same? Ellen would have found me on her next visit. One more black mark to support her disapproval of my lifestyle.

My reaction to Selwyn's bedside visit does me no credit. Dopey and unattractive, my hair a mess, clad in standard hospital gown, not an impression I would have wanted to make. 'Appearances matter, Kay,' my mother always admonished me, after some failing on my part to match her own meticulous grooming. I would mutter crossly that there were more important things in life, and we would finish up, as usual, in angry silence.

It was obvious that I was not myself, I did not normally worry about such things. This is what hospital does to you, I thought. It shrinks your world, small unimportant issues filling it to the exclusion of the world of things that matter. I shall be so glad to be home. Back to my usual routine, clearing up the infinite number of small complications that have followed, even years after, a change of country, the loss of my father, a new house, a malfunctioning log-burner, and writer's block.

The white coat returned. He read his notes and looked satisfied.

'Signs are all good. I think we can discharge you tomorrow.'

'Thank you. I'm grateful for your care.'

'And I'm sure you're grateful to the person who found you. Now you have one more obligation. It's imperative that you get your heating arrangements checked straight away. It must be a question of ventilation. A blocked flue pipe perhaps. Problems like this are usually due to birds or squirrels. Is there anyone else in the house?'

'I live alone'.

'Then you must get in a heating engineer to find out exactly what happened. I cannot put this too strongly.'

I felt scolded, and for the first time, was aware of a few incipient tears. I do not need to be told where to place my gratitude. I thought of my house, becoming increasingly loved as each day passed. How could it have done this to me? Had I had been negligent? Did everyone used to living through cold winters regularly examine their heating arrangements? Probably not, just took them for granted. It was late spring, and I'd been lighting the study fire only intermittently, allowing, I suppose, windows of opportunity for birds to investigate possible nest-building sites. A fine 'thank you' for my conscientious feeding of them during the winter months. I closed my eyes, and watched the pageant of perching, fluttering, swooping birds that visited the feeding station outside the kitchen window. Patiently, identification book in hand, I'd been trying to learn their names. Which one was the culprit? Maybe Selwyn would know. I would ask him, but don't suppose there'll be much opportunity.

Between dozing, waking, sleeping, observing and listening, the jumble of thoughts in my head began to arrange themselves in some sort of order. There were things to be done at home. The first was to arrange a visit from a heating engineer. Then I must decide what to do about the paddock, I needed advice about that. And, importantly, a decision about my ageing typewriter.

I remembered thinking that I would replace it with an electronic one. Small mistakes repaired so much more easily, the final draft sheet looking, well, almost respectable. However, there are always second thoughts on the document you are working on. There would always be passages to be moved, redrafted, deleted. I'd read accounts of a machine that was even more magical. A computer, it was called, already used in universities, research institutions and large commercial enterprises. Huge, room-sized constructions, capable of handling data on a scale and time that you could scarcely conceive. A breakthrough had occurred recently, which meant that all these operations could now be done on a scale small enough to fit into a device that could sit on your desk. A whole page of text would appear on a screen in front of you. A version that could be altered as much as you wanted, and whenever you chose. Your changes would be saved and appear on the screen next time you opened it up. I fell asleep in happy contemplation of the paradise that was on the horizon.

One more day, and I was ready to leave. Dressed again in the now repugnant clothes I had been wearing on admittance, and thinking that they would be disposed of as soon as I arrived home, I said goodbyes and thankyous, carefully wrapped my daffodils, and left the hospital. Selwyn had located the house keys, locked up, and left them with me in hospital.

Deposited outside my own front door, I assured the ambulance driver that I was perfectly fine, and there would be someone at home to look after me. Just one of the lies I felt would be advisable to tell, in case my discharge should be delayed. I had invented an old friend who had dropped everything to come and stay for a while. I knew quite a lot about her, as she was a character in one of my stories. A sculptor, living in Cornwall, as far as I remember. I was almost disappointed not to find her on the doorstep, waiting for me.

I unlocked the door of The Cottage, and made for the kitchen, where I put the daffodils in a bright glass vase, and placed them on the large wooden table. They joined a cup and saucer, a packet of biscuits and a bottle of milk that had been put there in my absence. Had Ellen heard of my misfortune and uncharacteristically tried to welcome me home? I didn't think so.

FOURTEEN

Newfield, May, 1980

I was up early next morning, watering my houseplants, and tidying away the remnants of the day I had so unceremoniously left.

I went into my study, examined the suspect log-burner, and cleaned the glass-fronted door which was black with soot. Hadn't I noticed that the fire hadn't been burning clear and bright? Too dopey, I supposed, by then.

I looked at the logs that were piled up beside the black cast iron stove. Picked up one, examined it closely. It had a lovely smell. Sticky, where the resin had started to ooze. A rogue cut of pine, it shouldn't have been there.

I thought about the wood that I'd bought. I ought to know more about the different trees that were used, and how long they should be seasoned for. Maybe I should look into these things more carefully before revisiting the timber merchant. There were gadgets, I'd been told, for measuring the humidity of logs cut for firewood. I'll ask Selwyn about these if he calls again.

I wondered what he had wanted to say about my paddock. I hoped it wouldn't take long; I'd like more from a conversation than a discussion of practicalities. What exactly did I want? Anything he could tell me about this small country I had settled in, inadvertently, I suppose, for like most people from abroad, the distinction between England and Wales had been blurred, no different from the variation between any two British counties. I was keen to find out what my neighbour had to tell me of the history of the Welsh Marches.

Any new acquaintance provoked anticipation that perhaps I would be lucky enough to discover something new, exciting and important about the world and its people. Sometimes this happened, though not always in the way the person would have chosen. Well, Selwyn Hughes was going to call again… some time.

Meanwhile there was the problem of my log-burner. The need for extra heating would be diminishing daily, though I was getting used to the vagaries of a British spring. I ought to get the fire looked at as soon as possible. I fished out the phone book's list of local tradesmen and arranged an appointment. The engineer arrived the next day.

'Hello', I said, 'come in. I'm doing as I've been told by everyone. Looking for an expert to examine my fire. I've just had a spell in hospital with carbon monoxide poisoning.'

The engineer raised an eyebrow.

'I've not come across a case as bad as that before,' he said, 'it certainly needs a thorough investigation. You'd not noticed anything unusual about the fire? Being slow to get going? Smoking more than usual?'

'No. It's always been perfectly alright.'

'Well, we'll see. Most likely there's a fault with the fire, or a blockage in the flue pipe. You've got a lot of trees around the house. Could be a build-up of dead leaves.'

He poked around inside the fire box, removed one or two detachable items, examined and replaced them. Lay on his back, the better to view the components that determined the route of the smoke and gases produced. Pronounced himself satisfied with the examination.

'I can't *see* anything wrong in the grate,' he said. 'Before I dismantle it properly, I'd better have a look outside.

I left him to his investigations, but only five minutes later he came to find me. He looked nervous.

'I've found the cause of the problem' he said, 'not one I have come across before. You're not going to like it.'

'Expensive to deal with?'

'No. It's done. Look at this.' He held out a handful of screwed up newspaper.

'It was in your flue pipe. I had expected a bird's nest.'

The implications hit me like a physical assault. I said nothing for a few moments. He went on.

'The pipe is easily accessible from outside the house, and there's a ladder just across the yard.'

A picture started to form in my mind's eye. I watched the event that the engineer's words had crudely depicted. I saw the movements of a figure crossing the yard, placing the ladder against the wall, mounting it step by step. Not far to go above the ground, the extension was only one storey high. I watched him taking the paper from his pocket, screwing it up in his free hand, stuffing it into the flue pipe. Mesmerised by the scene, I waited for the figure to descend to the ground, to turn round so that I could see his face.

I felt cold and shaken. What was happening to my day? This was not the world I had woken up to. Something had gone profoundly wrong – had I misunderstood what he was telling me? I looked at him, we held each other's gaze for a moment. He looked tense, but I was drowning.

'You're saying, then, that someone tried to kill me. Is that what you mean?'

'I'm sure it's not as bad as that. Some stupid prank probably. It's not my job to advise you about what you should do. But I suggest you have a good think about it. Talk to friends and family. They may say you should report the matter to the police.'

'Could the paper have just blown in?'

'No. It was tightly packed.'

I was finding the conversation almost beyond belief, bordering on the ridiculous.

The engineer was standing in my study. He put down the crumpled paper on my desk, his job done, quickly and easily. He could tell me nothing more, I wanted him to go.

'Well, you have done what you came to do. How much do I owe you?'

He shifted awkwardly. 'I'd rather not take anything. A five-minute job and I can see that it's one that's upset you. I'm really sorry. I'll go now. Let me know if you have any other issues with the fire. Don't worry, I'm sure things will sort themselves out.

'I'll go now…unless you can think of anything else I could do. Is there someone you'd like me to phone?'

'No thank you.'

I walked over to the window. I felt myself shaking, profoundly angry, with the departed engineer for what he had told me, with myself for believing it. I was angry with my bright, pleasant little study, for its being the setting of this hurtful, obscene little drama. I was angry with the spring sunshine, with the view across the fields to that sharp outline of hills that signalled the gateway to a remoter, grander landscape.

I picked up the screwed-up sections of newspaper that had been left on my desk, and walked over to the window. I straightened and smoothed them out, reading, for something to do, the pages I was holding. They were from a local newspaper, dated two or three weeks back, the eighth of April, 1980. There were three double pages, one devoted to adverts, another to market prices and job vacancies. I skimmed them and read on. The rest contained announcements of local events, small misdemeanours, one or two more serious ones. Births, marriages and deaths were there, and the usual corny, heart-rending little poems of grief and loss. No mention, as far as I could see, of anyone I knew. No mention of my village. None of it of any interest to me. That had not been its purpose.

I needed to talk to someone. There were one or two people who knew I had been in hospital, only one who knew why. Selwyn Hughes, who had taken me there. I phoned him in the evening, asked if he could possibly spare the time to look in, I had a problem.

'I'll come now.'

Out of his daytime farming gear, his constant exposure to wind, rain and whatever nature threw at him seemed more obvious. Black-haired without the blue eyes that indicated the Celtic ancestry of so many Welsh and Irish, I wondered if the dark skin and brown eyes indicated a later, Mediterranean origin. The Celtic realms had included Spain. A handsome, strong-featured man, not given to unnecessary words.

He walked to the window, looking at the dark silhouette of the hills, outlined against the setting sun.

'That was the view I fell in love with,' I said. 'One of the reasons we decided to buy this house. It's a view I'd seen once before, as a small child.'

'Those hills are where I'm from. They are called the Berwyns. Not a tourist hotspot, they're unspoiled. I was born among them, on our family farm. As my father and grandfather were. The first of the family to own the land they had rented and worked on for as long as anyone knew. My father had felled all the trees on the farm to help pay for it. I was sorry to leave.'

'Why did you?'

He paused for a moment.

'Circumstances.'

'Selwyn, something rather unpleasant has happened. I called in a heating engineer to have a look at the fire and see what caused its failure to burn properly. He looked in the outside flue pipe.'

'He found a bird's nest I suppose,'

'No, he found this.'

I handed him the newspaper.

He took it silently.

'This was in your flue pipe?' he asked eventually.

'Yes. Just now I don't know what I should do.'

'It was either a stupid prank, or a deliberate attempt to … cause you harm.'

'To kill me. Whoever did that, knew what they were doing.'

'I must ask you, because someone will, sooner or later… is there anyone you don't get on with? Anyone at all? Even small things can upset some people, they think about their… resentments, until they grow huge.'

Melbourne flashed briefly before me.

'No.'

In a voice that was not quite steady, I spoke.

'I almost wish I smoked. You need something tangible to help with things like this, a cigarette, or a whisky.'

'I wish I could help you.'

I went to a cupboard and took out a bottle.

'A Christmas present I've not opened yet, You?'

'O.K.' I poured some for both of us.

'Your visits to the Cottage have not been very propitious.

First, to investigate a fallen tree, second to find an unconscious woman, third, to investigate an attempted ...murder.'

He looked shocked.

'It probably isn't as bad as that. My own feeling is that it was some drunken idiot.'

'That's what the engineer said. Doesn't ring true, though. Drunken idiots need other drunken idiots to show off to.'

'You should tell the police.'

There was a long silence. I drank my whisky, Selwyn sipped his. Slowly, appreciatively.

'You're right of course. I suppose I must go to the police. They will lecture me about security and say I should have alarms fitted. I shall hate having to live like that.'

'Yes. But you'll get used to it – it's routine for lots of people. Do you know anyone who would come and stay with you for a few days?'

Unfocussed anger surfaced again. It found my visitor. I snapped at him.

'I'm not a child. I shall manage.'

That was rudeness. I was not behaving well. What would good behaviour look like? At least I had not gone to pieces, externally at least. Selwyn stood up, expressionless.

'I'm very sorry that this has happened. I think you'll probably want to be on your own for a bit. I'll go now, unless – unless you want me to stay for a while.' He looked at me diffidently. 'Can you think of anything I could do to help?'

'Thank you, I'll be all right. You have been kind, and I owe you ...more than I can ever say. I *am* grateful, believe me, but I'm not showing it very well just now. I'll phone you after I've done some thinking about it all, and I'd like it ...if we can have another talk. Please.' I felt strangely diminished.

'Give me a call when you're ready. But look, I think you ought to speak to someone else about this. You're badly upset.

I don't like leaving you alone. Without family or a close friend to talk to.'

'As you know, my old friends are thousands of miles away, and I have no family, now. But don't feel sorry for me – I just need time to find the right people. It will happen.' Tears were threatening, but I would not cry in front of him. He stood there, a tall, weather-beaten farmer, out of his depth, I imagined, but trying to do what he could to help, trying to say the right things.

He left, and I moved back into the study, with no desire to work, and the desire to weep gone for the time being. What to do now? I asked myself, noticing Selwyn's barely touched glass of whisky. I picked it up and finished it.

It gave me no relief from horror… I poured another.

The rest of the evening passed in a whisky-fuelled stupor. When I awoke it was past midnight. I crawled into bed.

I woke late, with an aching head. Realising, with relief, that it wasn't Ellen's day, I spent the morning getting on with jobs that needed – or didn't need – doing. I had to incorporate the new situation into my understanding of my day-to-day activities. The world had changed since yesterday, and I must change with it. The lack of an old friend at this moment felt raw. I had to *do* something. Call on Bethan, perhaps, but I didn't feel like inflicting my personal troubles on such a new friend, relationships must grow and find their own level.

I lifted my jacket off its hook, changed my shoes and, without glancing back, set off, walking fast, along a footpath towards the hills. New emotions were presenting themselves, not just the anger and horror at the news the engineer had brought me, but also the grief from my father's death two years ago, and the sadness and guilt from my final Melbourne years. All this, and the loss of my one talent, my writing, was beginning to feel more than I could cope with. A fleeting confrontation with oblivion. It passed.

I sat down on the wet grass and let the tears come. The minutes passed, ten, maybe sixty. I felt the rain and the cold seeping through my clothes. I looked up. I was not alone.

A brown hare held my gaze for nearly a minute, before making its way past me, along the track I'd been following. Its goals were simple, I guessed, sex, food, shelter. It was on its way to satisfying one of them. What were mine? What good was I doing sitting here, weeping, in the rain? Feeding my ego with the self-indulgence of misery?

Just getting on with its life was what the brown hare was doing, and so must I. With a brief impulse of gratitude to the departing animal, I got stiffly to my feet and started my long walk home.

Indoors, I looked through the kitchen window at the broad river plain, I wondered, should I move? It is one option; I must at least think about it. I knew the answer, of course.

I love my house. My father had been happy here, there were so many memories of him in the brief time we had shared it. There were plans, too, a garden already on the way, a gentle fusion of the landscape and informal planting – how much I'd been looking forward to watching it grow. Move house again? I dismissed the idea of leaving. I will not run away at the first hurdle. I'll be sensible, take advice, get on with my life. Make friends and learn new things. Explore my new country of Wales, climb a mountain, learn to make bara brith.

Later, tired but quieter, I made a cup of tea, sat down, and examined my situation. You could be perfectly content, I had long ago decided, living alone. Most people, though, had family, close or distant, which linked them to the rest of humanity. It was this that I often missed. Then I thought about a different kind of relationship.

Love. Was that possible for me? I wasn't a young girl anymore. There'd been the odd affair back in Melbourne, motivated by curiosity and the urge to find out what I wanted from life. There'd been Brad. I didn't know what love would be like, if I would recognise it if I saw it.

I was almost forty. Most women had settled down at this age, some of them for the second time. Love? Was it something you found, or did you have to make it happen? I was beginning to feel sorry for myself again, but heard the echo of my mother's voice, telling me how lucky I was. So much luckier than other people she had known. She had been right, of course. I lived, where I could have died.

FIFTEEN

Newfield, May, 1980

Reluctantly, and after some days of thought, I went to the police. Questions were asked, notes made, forms filled in. But once established, the fact that no-one had been hurt, nobody accused, and nothing more had happened, seemed to provide the authorities with little incentive to pursue the matter. Just a prank, had been the verdict of the uninterested but polite young woman who had taken down the details. 'However,' she had added 'for your own peace of mind you should install some security.'

I had anticipated this advice but wondered if my mind could achieve the promised peace quite so easily.

Back home, as I let myself into the house, I picked up a letter, recognising the envelope with a sigh. My publisher, Jonathan Parfitt, asking – in connection with the new novel – how was it going? He'd tried to phone once or twice, but there'd been no answer. Had I been on holiday? How far was the book from completion? Very far, I thought, not more than a first draft of a first chapter, and that had now gone into the bin. Possibly the first chapter of the wrong book. My brain was feeling like a battleground.

I would ring him and explain that I had had an accident and had been in hospital for a few days, but would start work as soon as possible. That should keep him quiet for a bit.

A knock at the door made me jump. I ought to get a doorbell, I thought, not for the first time. Put a bit of technology between me and unexpected callers. Knocking always sounds so peremptory. A bell announces, a knock commands.

The caller greeted me by name and proffered an identity card.

'Huw Penry Jones', he announced. 'Police'.

He didn't look like a policeman.

'Goodness me. Surely you haven't discovered the culprit already! I've only just returned from reporting the incident!'

'What incident?'

A visit from a policeman that had nothing to do with my visit to *them?*

'We are obviously talking at cross purposes. Why have you come?'

'I'm off duty, and this is an unofficial call. I'm here at the suggestion of a friend of mine, Selwyn Hughes. He mentioned that you'd been troubled by intruders, and suggested that maybe I could assist.'

Still trying to help me, Selwyn was, in spite of my behaviour.

'Come in and tell me what you've got in mind. I suspect that you're going to say I should have a proper alarm system.'

He smiled. 'Yes, you're right, but not exactly the kind that you're probably thinking of. The system *I've* got in mind' he said, 'is in the car. It's a dog.'

This was certainly an unexpected suggestion. My first reaction was to instantly reject the idea, so far-fetched did it seem. Dogs were what other people kept, I had never for one moment thought of having one myself.

'Goodness me. Come in and tell me more.'

Hugh Penry Jones came through into the kitchen. I wondered if it was wise for a member of the police force to be in possession of quite so much charm, the bluest eyes I had ever seen, and a shy, disarming smile. Well, he wasn't on duty, perhaps he managed to keep some of these attributes under cover while he was working.

He was a police dog handler, he told me, and had just finished training a batch of young dogs for a variety of work. The one in the car had failed the discipline trials. A good, intelligent dog in many ways, first class at sniffing out drugs, but with a hopeless tendency to chase cats. One had appeared during a trial when his main job was to stay on guard over a suspect package, and the episode had caused much hilarity among the dog handlers and considerable severity from the judges. Poor concentration on his work, they had said, and failed him for the second time. He would have to go.

'I was really sorry about this. I'd tried so hard with him, but it was no good. It's absolutely essential that a police dog should be able to concentrate on the job in hand. It's not enough that he comes back when he's called, he should be able to be relied upon to stay put and finish the task as instructed. He shouldn't even *think* about cats when he's working. Selwyn thought a good dog might make you feel more comfortable and be a deterrent to possible villains. Jack does have an impressive growl if strangers are about. Do you like dogs?'

'Well, I'm not what you'd call a doggy person, but I don't *dis*like them. I've never given them much thought.'

In fact, the only thought I remember having about dogs was a distinct wish that people would shut up about them, a view that I wasn't going to articulate at this point.

'I've never kept a dog before; I'd be a bit nervous of a new responsibility like that.'

'Well, it's a good thing that you see it as a responsibility. That's one box ticked.'

I laughed. 'Are you interviewing me?'

'Of course. I wouldn't leave him with anyone unsuitable. But I think you'd get on with each other just fine. He needs a daily walk, though. Are you O.K. with that?'

'It would be good to have a reason for getting out every day. It's too easy to chicken out if it's raining.'

'I must warn you that as well as a fearsome growl, he does have a very loud bark. But his reaction to strangers is no more than noisy. Basically, he's a gentle, friendly creature, if no great beauty. Would you like to meet him?'

'Well, as I'm not ruling out the idea, I suppose I should'.

Would it be wiser to think about it before inspecting the animal? I remembered the advice that you should never go to look at a puppy for sale, you will always come home with it. Too late. My policeman friend had disappeared through the door. I followed him to the yard, and watched as he opened the car door. The animal that emerged was large, dark, and intimidating. It looked around for a moment, taking in the layout of the yard and buildings, possible escape routes for an intruding cat? It quietly accompanied its handler into the house.

'You might like to try making a fuss of him' Hugh Penry Jones said, 'he's perfectly safe.' I offered a few tentative pats, which were ignored.

'He's thinking about you. At the moment he's taking his cues from me. He doesn't know what's expected of him in connection with a new person and unfamiliar surroundings. His name, by the way, is Jack.'

'I really don't know what to say. It's a question of whether I can cope with a dog, – I've never had one before, but I can always learn. I would need to think about it. Why don't you have a coffee, while I recover from this unexpected suggestion?'

Huw Penry Jones assented happily, while I carefully stepped round the animal who was taking up a large part of the kitchen floor, and switched on the kettle. Another Welshman, my new human visitor. Since arriving in eastern Wales I had learned to recognise the dialect and the words used by my neighbours and acquaintances. Now I was recognising more subtle differences between Welsh speech and the sound of English as I knew it. Aware of the small hesitation between the syllables of a word, and the conscientious acknowledgment of final consonants, so often dropped by English speakers. I really must reign in this habit of listening to how people spoke rather than to what they were saying. I switched my attention to the reason for his call.

He was suggesting that it would be a good idea for me to have a dog.

A dog! Whatever next? How much would a dog change my life? I'd never contemplated such a happening. Dogs were a tie, of course, but could be left, I supposed, for short periods. You couldn't decide upon a life without ties, – to people, places, events. And as I have no people, I can choose to have my life restricted by a dog. A family substitute, perhaps, someone other than myself to consider. And it would surely make unwelcome visitors think twice. Selwyn's idea was probably a good one. I wondered how well they knew each other, Huw Penry Jones, and my neighbour.

'Has Selwyn Hughes had a dog trained by you?'

Huw laughed. 'No, he trains his own! But I've known him for years. We went to the same school, played rugby together. A good chap, clever, too. Could have gone far.

'Well, Mr.Jones…'

He interrupted me. 'No-one calls me that. There'd be no

point, it's the name of over half the population in this area. I answer to Huw.'

'Well, Huw, what ought I to do?'

'The sensible thing for me to do is to leave Jack here for tonight, and see how you get on together. Think about it.'

'Can you come back tomorrow? If I do decide to take him, I can promise you I'll do my very best to make a good home for him. Has he been living with you?'

'Yes. There are volunteers who take the dogs out most days, to get them socialised, but I do the formal training.'

'He would miss you.'

'That will soon pass.'

'You're speaking as if his future is settled.'

The policeman smiled, a huge devastating smile. I tried to remain undevastated.

'I hope it is.'

I looked at the large dog. One eye was open. I thought of his lupine genes, more visible here than in many others of his species. What have we done to the wolf, I wondered, that we have produced from it both a Great Dane and a Chihuahua? A status symbol for the carriage-owning aristocracy and a pretty little toy for their wives.

'I'm glad,' Huw said, 'that you're willing to give him a trial. I have a feeling that you'll suit each other very well. I've brought something for his dinner. And I've written out some commands that he understands, and you may like to practice. But don't bother too much about all that – the main thing is to get to know each other. I'll be back tomorrow, probably in the afternoon. 'Bye Jack. Behave yourself. Bye …Miss Francis.'

'Kay,' I said, returning his dismissal of 'Mr. Jones'.

He left with a cheerful wave, and was gone. I looked at the animal. There were so many good reasons why I should keep him, none that should cause me to decide against it. Except that I was not used to owning a dog, and was not sure how I would feel about it as the days went by. It was all so sudden.

'So here we are,' I said, realising that articulating my thoughts could not now be dismissed as talking to myself, since I could now address them to Jack. He spent an hour or so sitting by the front door through which Huw Penry Jones had exited, then proceeded to investigate the ground floor of the house, settling eventually in the study, on my best rug. I looked at him guardedly. Had the policeman not reassured me, I might have been a little nervous. More than just intimidating, he looked like a creature from that distant, prehistoric age, before our ancestors had domesticated many of the wild animals that shared the world with us. He was licking his paws; I had a glimpse of large white teeth. What could I do to make him feel at home? I found a ball that Laura had left behind, and rolled it across the floor. He looked at it contemptuously. I spoke a few words of sympathy for his change of home, and explained that I was his likely new owner and mistress. Just getting him used to the sound of my voice, I thought, that's how he's going to hear his instructions from now on.

Leaving him to get to know his new surroundings, I sat down at my desk and tried to write. I was aware of a loud moan issuing from the wide-open mouth of my companion, but was relieved to find that it was simply a yawn. He rolled over and went to sleep. I turned back to my typescript.

I thought of the last conversation I'd had with Bethan, a few comments we'd made about the history of Britain after the departure of the Romans. So many battles fought to advance or defend land occupied by native British against invaders from the continent of Europe. How those who lived and farmed in these areas must have dreaded each confrontation, drawn into political and geographical changes that destabilised the local economy and brought death to those caught up in the conflicts. Could I write about these people? Could I tell a story about the individuals who lived through these events? I made some notes. Much research to be done, I was not a historian, I was a story-teller. My typewriter jammed, I swore at it and wearily picked up pen and paper to jot down a few ideas.

It will all be so much easier and quicker when I get my electronic typewriter, – at least the mechanics of writing will – no guarantee that my brain will co-operate. I thought of famous writers who had never given up pen and paper, the closest physical contact between brain and recorded thought.

My father and I had bought the Cottage with the hope and promise of a quiet and peaceful life. Too much had been happening, I had written nothing of any worth since arriving here. Writer's block I suppose, though it sometimes seemed to me that the real block lay somewhere else in my life, but what it was, and how I could remove it, was another matter.

The phone rang.

'Jonathan! You got my message? That I'd been in hospital for a few days?'

'I'm so sorry Kay. But you sound O.K., so no doubt you're back at work. Mustn't let the grass grow under out feet, must we?'

Master of the tired cliché, my publisher.

'The last couple of years haven't been easy, Jonathan. Nor have the last couple of weeks. Or the last couple of days. Just lay off for a while, will you?'

'Sorry. I was just getting in touch, to see how you were.'

'Of course, thank you. Sorry for being so ungrateful and bad-tempered. But can you put the book on hold for a while? I'm really not in the mood for writing, and in any case I'm planning to get one of these new electronic typewriting machines.'

'Excellent idea. You'll be pleased as Punch with it.'

'Hope it comes with instructions.'

'It will, but I'll be glad to help if there are any difficulties. I look forward to seeing the first draft from it. There's one other thing, though, that I must mention. Someone was here the other day, wanting your address or phone number. Pleasant lady. From Australia, she said, an old friend of yours. She'd read one of your books and as she was coming to Britain she thought it would be nice to get in touch. She didn't have your address or phone number, so she looked for the publisher's details. It's a coincidence that she's staying here in Birmingham. Just around the corner, as it happens. I thought I'd better check with you before handing out your number.'

'Quite right Jonathan. Did she leave a name?'

'I've written it down somewhere.'

There was a sound of scrabbling among papers.

'Here it is. Cherry Martin. Name mean anything to you?'

Two names. Now linked together. It meant, of course, a great deal. Old, part-buried flashes of shame, regret, sadness, re-surfaced. I needed time to take in this news.

'Jonathan. I don't want to sound unfriendly, but I just can't cope with a visitor just now. Can you put her off somehow? And please don't give her my address. Later, perhaps, when things have settled down a bit. Could you tell her I've been in hospital and am still a bit fragile.'

'You don't sound fragile. Couldn't you at least speak on the phone to her?'

'No.'

He sighed. 'I'll tell her.'

Cherry, the last person I ever expected to hear from again. But the one thing that stood out from this revelation, was, of course, that she was now Cherry Martin. She must have forgiven Chris, and he must have re-discovered what had drawn him to her in the first place. They were married. I was surprised and enormously relieved; I had not brought about the split between her and Chris that she claimed had ruined her life.

She was wanting contact with me. I didn't feel like reciprocating. This is always the way with a person you've wronged. Their presence reminds you of your bad behaviour. I remembered thinking about Cherry while I was in hospital, and how three stupid people could manage to mess up a good relationship. Chris had not behaved well, I had not behaved well, and Cherry should have given us both the chance to talk, and to think more clearly about everything that had happened. She had always been kind to me, as an awkward teenager, someone who needed steering carefully through the rocky waters of the teenage years. My God, I'm beginning to sound like Jonathan. I went to bed, leaving the dog to choose a comfortable sleeping place.

The blocked flue pipe and its contents had been coming into my mind whenever ordinary problems were dismissed or solved. Alone in the house, thoughts of an intruder somewhere around had grown more frequent and more believable. When you're feeling nervous normal sounds lose their ordinariness and became significant. The crack of a door frame recovering from a hot day becomes the creak of a stair, the movement of a foot. Jack would know the difference, and respond only if sounds meant strangers. Tonight, we both slept soundly, Selwyn had been right.

I awoke to rain. Must let the dog out, thank goodness the yard's securely fenced, though this had been more to keep livestock out, than to keep anything in. Must make sure the gate is always shut, warning notices put up for visitors, I suppose. I must check the gate to the paddock, the fence there is surely negotiable for an intelligent dog. I'll keep him, of course. Huw Penry Jones knew perfectly well I would!

Jack was waiting at the foot of the stairs, tail in furious motion. Well, that's a good sign, I thought, trying another friendly and more confident rub behind the ears. Poor chap, he must wonder where he's landed himself.

SIXTEEN

Newfield May, 1980

I had promised Selwyn that I would get in touch with him when I'd recovered my balance, come to terms with the fact that someone had either played a dangerous practical joke on a harmless incomer, or put baldly, had tried to kill me. So ridiculously impossible this last scenario seemed, that I had more or less dismissed it. Why choose the least likely of all explanations?

Chance had made us neighbours, luck had brought him round for a routine chat, and the Fates had decided that I was not to die. I imagined the three of them, laughing and asking each other – what will she do now?

I had to decide. And my first job was to speak to Selwyn again, to apologise for my incivility and apparent ingratitude in the light of all he had done for me and try to re-establish normal neighbourly relations. Though I suspected that events had been too unusual for that to happen.

I had not behaved well on that last occasion. But then – nor had life.

I decided that I would ask him to supper, apologise properly, thank him for suggesting the dog, and talk about how I felt about my brush with death. My other agenda was to get to know him a bit better. See if I can get round his social awkwardness, his shyness, if that's what it was.

I had not expected an enthusiastic response to my invitation and had to be satisfied with a polite acceptance. I spent the afternoon washing my hair and preparing a meal. Duck bought from the supermarket with fresh cep mushrooms I'd found under an oak tree that was part of our shared hedge. Apple pie and cream to follow, traditional and safe, what man could resist that?

The kitchen was not modern in the glitzy streamlined style that is standard in many houses of all ages. I had what I wanted, plenty of cupboards, warmth from an Aga cooker, a comfortable chair or two nearby, and a large table, big enough to re-pot the geraniums, re-assemble the vacuum cleaner, fill in my tax returns and hold an informal dinner party. In short, it should serve every possible function that I could throw at it. Occasionally, a picture came into my head. There were children seated at that table. They were doing a jig-saw puzzle, or opening a box of Christmas decorations, maybe doing their homework, or rolling the pastry we had just made. Who was their father? A door closed behind a departing figure… In my mind, I spoke to these dream children.

'Hi kids! I need to start supper! Will you clear your stuff away or take it into the playroom.'

Tonight, the kitchen was empty, awaiting my dinner guest.

A phone and a small television completed a comfortable place for most current occasions, and as a concession to this evening's event I had placed on the table a bowl of wild ox-eye daisies, cow parsley and honeysuckle, picked at the last minute as my hair was drying.

I wondered if my visitor would arrive on foot – the official route would take him about twenty minutes, or he could cross the fields to the gap in the hedge. This, I noted, had still not been properly repaired. Or he could cut the time to ten minutes in the car. I heard it arrive, the familiar sounds of a gate being opened, scraping the gravel beneath it, the car driven in, parked, footsteps, gate closed. Jack barked and growled; I quietened him.

I opened the front door to welcome my guest. Dressed with conventional anonymity he was holding a small bunch – no more than four or five – stems of pink flowers. we shook hands.

It was up to him I thought, to instigate less formal physical contact. Hugs between friends were just beginning to become the new greeting. He looked embarrassed, ours was such an unusual relationship, reflected on this occasion by mutual awkwardness.

'How are you, Kay?'

'Better, thank you, than when you saw me last. I am glad to see you, please come in.'

The flowers were offered to me, I took them with curiosity, noting the scattering of small black spots over the leaves.

'From your farmland?'

'No, from yours. They're orchids, growing by the damaged hedge. I finished mending it today, and thought you might not know that there were early purples in your field.'

'I didn't know orchids grew in Britain at all! Come into the kitchen and tell me more!'

I placed the flowers in the vase with their commoner hedgerow acquaintances, where they looked, I thought, uncomfortable. I indicated a chair for my guest.

I never liked leaving visitors on their own while I was cooking, waste of good chatting time. Selwyn looked on as

I threw a splash of wine from my glass to the gravy. 'Adds a personal touch' I explained.

He laughed, the first proper relaxation of tension.

I was pleased with the meal, pointing out the source of the mushrooms.

'D'you cook for yourself, Selwyn?'

'Rarely. I enjoy being taken pity on by kind neighbours!'

'And what do the kind neighbours get in return?'

'Odd jobs. They can always call on me if needs be.'

'What you have done for me will take a lifetime of dinners to repay.'

He smiled. I shall look forward to them!'

Selwyn told me a little of our other neighbours, mostly farmers, of the different kinds of sheep they kept, their cattle, the geography of their farms, of their history in the area. Away from the topic of ourselves, he spoke with kindness and humour.

Supper over, we picked up our glasses and the remainder of the wine and made our way into my study. I had moved my desk from its place by the window, fine for light but fatal for concentration. Easy chairs now faced the distant hills, no need for a clock on a fine evening, I could always tell the time with a glance at the angle of the rays of the setting sun as it sank below the dark silhouette of the Berwyn hills.

I started the conversation that I'd decided was the purpose of the occasion. The acknowledged one.

'Selwyn, I want to say how sorry I am for my ungracious behaviour on your last visit. You have been immensely kind and thoughtful since my…well, my accident. I don't really know what to call it. I'm also very grateful for your suggestion that brought Huw Penry Jones to the house, with Jack.'

My new watchdog twitched an ear as he heard his name mentioned.

'I'm glad you decided to keep him. I was pretty sure you would. Huw's an old friend, we were at school together. A good chap and an excellent rugby player.'

'That's exactly what he said about you!'

'Did he say anything else?'

There's a something else, then, that he's wondering if I know about. A pause, and the cautious revelation -

'The cupboard has a few skeletons in it.'

I laughed. 'So do most people's! He told me only that you were passionate about Welsh history and politics. Which interested me. I know nothing about either. Back in Australia we have barely heard of this small country attached to England.'

He frowned, putting aside the glass of wine he'd been holding.

'I don't care for that description. I suggest you say it differently. Tell me instead that in Australia you had hardly heard of this small country *annexed* by England.'

How was I supposed to know these turns of phrase? I felt cross. I'd made a perfectly innocent remark. There was no need to reproach me for it.

'I used the wrong language, but I know so little about how such things are seen.'

'Sorry, Kay. It's unreasonable of me to expect you to think and speak as I do. Especially as a newcomer to Wales.'

I forgave him instantly.

'We were talking about Huw. I wanted you to know what a loyal friend he's been to me. Some things he has done have gone beyond the call of friendship.'

I decided to proceed cautiously.

'Do you want to tell me?'

'People will drop hints sooner or later. I have done things, some years ago, that have caused trouble. I'm telling you this because you will certainly hear versions, sympathetic or otherwise, from people who live here.'

'What things have you done?'

'There used to be a joke, sort of. "Like a good fire? Come home to your Welsh cottage!"'

'I don't understand.'

'*Arson* is what I'm talking about. I went about with groups of people who were determined that Wales should not be overrun by hordes of English incomers buying up old places to come to during holidays and occasional weekends. Not only were locals being squeezed out of the housing market, but our culture was being displaced too. Local populations distorted by an influx of the wealthy and retired. Welsh children disappearing from the area. To say nothing of the language.'

His words were coming faster, he tensed, rose from his chair, gazing through the window at the foothills of the Berwyns, his homeland hidden in the darkness of the shadows cast by the setting sun.

'Imagine what it feels like to have your country, your language, your history – not so much being taken from you, but being *smothered* by an alien invasion.'

He spoke passionately – barely speaking to me but addressing a distant, wider audience. He turned again to me.

'It had to be stopped, somehow or other. Violent action we saw as the only answer. We set fire to properties while their English owners were absent. No-one was hurt and the publicity was excellent.'

I was shocked. Forgot to be cautious, and blurted out

'Is that one of the ways you justify what you did?'

He returned to his chair, finished his glass of wine, and didn't reply.

I was silent with shock. One or two discrepancies fell into place. I recalled the odd rapid change of subject during conversations with neighbours. A nervousness when speaking to me, a preference for thinking of us as Australian rather than English. An occasional coolness, a rare but observable unfriendly response. I thought of Gareth. I looked at Selwyn.

I breathed a sigh of relief as he spoke once more to me.

'Huw has never kept away from me because of these activities. He is a policeman, after all. I think his superiors had a word with him about his choice of friends, the people he associated with. People like me. He laughed at them.'

The bonds that hold people together, I thought. How strong they can be, and in some cases, how fragile. Nothing could break the friendship between Selwyn and Huw. I thought of Cherry, my best friend, who I believed to be lost.

Selwyn was looking at me, questioningly.

'I hardly know what to say, Selwyn. I know so little about you, I cannot make judgments. I need to know so much more. About you, and what drives you – your history? Your farm? Your family? And why you have chosen to tell me about all this. Did you plan to?'

'You would have known it all sooner or later. I thought I'd get my oar in first.'

A long pause in the conversation. He'd have known he'd given me a lot to think about. I decided to change the subject.

'I'd like to know more about the history of Wales. Can you recommend a book for me to start with?'

'Yes, of course. There are plenty. I'll look on my bookshelves. And…as you're a writer, you might like to read some poetry from Wales. To get the feel of the place.'

'I've heard of Wilfrid Owen.'

'From Oswestry. Not far from here. It's in England but its culture is Welsh. And R. S. Thomas is writing now, in Manafon, where he's the vicar, in a burning rage that he was not brought up to speak and write in the language of his forebears. He blames his mother for this, in a vitriolic poem. He learned Welsh, became a fluent speaker, but I suppose that when it comes to poetry, it is in the language of your birth that the heart speaks, and for him that is English. Poor man, he is obliged to write his poems in the words of his enemy.'

'That must be hard. Is speaking English as painful for you?'

'There is nothing I would like more than to speak to you in Welsh, but you wouldn't understand.'

'Of course not. But I could learn. I've thought about it several times.'

'I mean that this is not simply a linguistic problem. We are not standing in the same place.'

I felt cross. Again. This was just another way of saying "*You wouldn't understand.*" So often said, a cop-out. One of the commonest excuses for not bothering to explain something. Or for being disinclined to discuss things that you might be wrong about. Leaving the other person with the responsibility for making all the effort. Explanation and understanding are reciprocal activities, they need equal contributions from both sides. I scowled at him.

'Give me the chance to move!'

He burst out laughing. You are a persistent woman, Kay, and I'm sorry for the way I am putting my difficulty in saying what I feel. I speak from experience, from so many failed attempts to communicate with English people. You are different. Your mind works differently. I'll try and do better.'

A move in the right direction, I thought, and he knows that our understanding of each other is precarious.

'*I* have a passion too; it is about the words we use to talk to each other. It is all we have, to express the truth of things.'

Selwyn was silent for a moment.

'There are some things that are better left unsaid, however true.'

'Then obviously I can't possibly ask you what they are! But let me tell you why I wanted to talk to you tonight. Words that must be said. I cannot rest until I've said them.

I want to try and thank you properly once more, and I promise you, for the last time, not only for saving my life – as you say, any other person would no doubt have done what you did – but also for other unobtrusive kindnesses, which you might think I hadn't noticed when I came home from hospital. I shan't speak of these things again, but don't think I haven't noticed them.'

He started to speak, an embarrassed dismissal, I knew, of all he had done for me. I stopped him.

'Accept my gratitude graciously, Selwyn. A burden you must bear for my sake!'

His laughter was full of fun, as he rose from his chair and wandered round the room, as if impelled to action, but not knowing what it should be. Or knowing what it could be, but not daring to implement it. A moment to marvel at – it could always be like this, and more. But it passed. He returned to his chair.

What next?

'Another glass of wine?' I suggested. He smiled and accepted.

'Do you sleep better, now you have a dog in the house and the alarms?'

'I do. I think less about those strange days, in hospital and afterwards, and they often seem like a dream. I forget about it all for hours at a time. I still feel that somewhere or other, waiting to be discovered, is a perfectly ordinary explanation.'

'I'm sure you're right.'

But the picture I still carried in my mind was of the ladder, the figure mounting it, stuffing the newspaper into the chimney pipe, descending, turning round, faceless. Putting this persistent vision into words, I spoke them. Selwyn listened.

'You have a way with words, Kay. You bring things to life with them.'

'Thank you. But I have a problem now. I have the words, but not the ideas. Writer's block, it's called. It's strange, Selwyn, that I feel at home here, yet cannot write.'

'I think, Kay, that perhaps you underestimate the effect on your life of a move to a new country, the loss of your father, a spell in hospital and the mystery that surrounds it – the bird's nest that never was.'

He paused for a moment, his expression softened.

'And speaking of birds' nests reminds me of Melanie Powell.'

'Melanie? The vicar's daughter? The young woman who lives for birds?'

'I was wondering if you've come across her.'

'I have. You're not suggesting *she* had anything to do with – my blocked flue pipe?'

'No. She's not mischievous. But she's always up trees, with or without ladders. She doesn't care whose property she's on. You come across her in all sorts of unexpected places. It might be worth having a careful word with her. She could have seen something, you never know. A strange soul, Melanie – away with the skylarks much of the time. Sometimes she seems rude, dismissive. You have to see past that. She speaks of what matters to her, she doesn't bother with greetings and ordinary thanks, goodbyes and so on. By our standards, her life is limited, but she manages her small world remarkably well. What you have to remember is that what other people think and feel is unknown territory to her. I saw her in your little paddock once. She wouldn't have understood that she was trespassing, that she should ask permission before going on to other people's property.'

He doesn't need to defend Melanie to *me*, I thought. But he will be her defender and friend if ever she needs one.

His dark eyes focussed on my old typewriter. Sitting patiently, not much used, on my desk.

'Get rid of that thing,' he said, it's not helping you.' It's keeping you in Australia, chaining you to your old life. Stopping the ideas from coming. There's a new world out there, knocking at all our doors. Get yourself a new machine. To fill in the gap before we can afford to have our own computers, with grateful thanks to the silicon chip.'

He glanced at his watch.

'Thank you for dinner, Kay, and the talk. A welcome change for me. I should leave pretty soon, there are jobs still to be done before bedtime.'

I held my breath. This was the moment that could invite a suggestion of another meeting. I waited; it didn't come. He rose from his chair, thanked me again. I walked with him to the door, opened it, he stepped outside. A last chance, perhaps, for a return invitation. He made a few polite comments, said goodbye, and left.

I had been too argumentative, perhaps, a gentle massage of his ego might have been more appropriate. How much would I have to change to elicit some interest? Why did I want his interest so much that I was prepared to go to so much trouble to arouse it? This had not happened before, affairs had come and gone without taking over my thoughts as this one appeared to be doing. Was I simply suffering from damaged pride?

Give him time, I thought, there are hurdles to be overcome, cultural differences, two worlds, two histories, two personalities. I considered the evening that had passed. Not one hundred per cent successful – we had both managed to irritate each other – but I felt an attraction that went further than mere curiosity. I recognised the symptoms, it had happened before, more than once.

SEVENTEEN

Newfield, May 1980

It was Ellen's day. She arrived with Laura, clutching a book which she held out for me to see.

'I got it from a car boot sale' Ellen said. 'I don't want her to start school an' be the only one who's never seen a proper book before.'

'What a good idea,' I said. 'It's a lovely book. Look, Laura, here is a little girl with red hair just like yours. I used to have hair that colour when I was little, my Dad used to call me Carrots.'

'The boy next door calls me Ginger," Laura said. "Gran'ma don't like it, she gets cross with him.' I wondered if the 'boy next door' was in a neighbouring caravan, or if he was the mythical Tony.

'This little girl is called Alice,' I told her. 'One day, when she was sitting with her sister in a field, she fell asleep and had a wonderful dream. All about animals that could talk and do everything that people can do. When you're older you'll be able to read about them.'

'I want to read it now,' she said.

'You'll have to wait till you go to school,' Ellen told her.

'I want to read it *now*,' she repeated, close to tears, 'you can show me how.'

Some intervention was required. I tried to explain.

'Well, it's rather difficult for a little girl of four to read a book like this. But I've got an idea. Let's start with an easier book, written specially for people about your age, – a book that you can use for learning to read by yourself. If you like, I'll bring a book for you to start with, and I'll show you how all these letters make words, and the words make a story. Would you like that?'

She nodded. Ellen turned her head away. I had a feeling that she too was close to tears.

The weekly reading sessions started. I had to admit to myself that time with Laura was becoming enjoyable to me too. I had no training as a teacher but was confident that I could spot any signs of boredom.

She had formed an instant and reciprocal friendship with Jack, so one day, with her arm around him, she asked for a story about a dog. I thought of tales from myths and oral tradition, and wondered whether she would encounter these in school, would they appeal to today's children? They had served countless generations well. I told her the story of Gelert, the brave Welsh dog who was wrongly killed. I hoped the story wouldn't upset her, but the legend was widely told in many countries, in many languages, and children must learn that the world is more than Janet and John. She loved the story; I was to re-tell it many times.

I had supposed that the reading sessions would continue in much the same pattern as they had started. I was not prepared for Laura's rapid recognition of the words on the page. Within three months she was reading the books I had bought for her. I had not been prepared for this change, like someone conscientiously watering a plant each week, and being surprised to find that it actually grows.

I was as amazed at my own success in teaching her. It seemed a miraculous event, I had made a difference – had this ever happened before? This was not the child I'd been reading with last week. This was a child on the threshold of a new world. A world that she'd be able to visit on her own, making new friends, seeing new places, all from her stool at the kitchen table. If Anything was magic, surely this was!

I was unsure of Ellen's reaction to our sessions. I had concluded that her pointed unfriendliness was a consequence of a smouldering resentment of my situation compared with hers. She hadn't the time or the energy to provide fun for her granddaughter, however much she might want to. Laura's obvious delight in having someone to devote time to her did not go down well. I had made some remark – I barely remembered what it was – that I hoped Laura enjoyed her visits to the Cottage.

'I suppose you think she should be grateful' Ellen said furiously. Let me tell you she's as much right here as you have!'

'What are you talking about?'

'As much right… to a decent home an' a comfortable life!'

My self-control, often at risk in Ellen's company, nearly slipped. 'If I knew what a right was', I answered quietly, 'I might say that I have a right to be spoken to politely.' I drew a deep breath, 'but let's not quarrel, for her sake. I know that life's not been easy for you, Ellen, but you can't blame me for that. Life isn't fair, life isn't interested in fairness and justice.'

'If I had the chance to get a decent life for Laura, I'd take it, no matter what I had to do to get it.'

I didn't know –and dared not ask – about the condition of Laura's mother. There was obviously a degree of neglect in

Laura's home life, and it wouldn't be surprising if, in addition to Mrs. Hayleigh's proposed intervention, a caravan dweller or visitor decided that the situation should be reported. It was likely that the possibility was rarely out of Ellen's mind.

Such little conversation as we had together usually finished with some direct or implied criticism, dismissive of my competence, my friends, my work. She reminds me of my mother, I thought, in the way she speaks to me…in the way she looks at me. I don't have to employ this woman. I can get another cleaner. But it was a decision I put off, from week to week, unable to make up my mind. And there was Laura.

Huw Penry Jones (Why could I only think of him in terms of his full name?) had been making one or two visits, ostensibly to check on Jack. I suspected that he had another undisclosed agenda. He mentioned that he was making his police presence felt in case the relative isolation of the Cottage might tempt another intrusion, but I was beginning to feel that Jack's simple presence was sufficient. But here he was again, sitting comfortably in the kitchen, Jack at his feet.

'Seen Selwyn lately?'

'No,' I said. 'He said he was going to call to talk about my little paddock. Don't know what he wants to say.'

'Probably he doesn't either. "The heart has its reasons of which reason knows nothing."'

'Pascal.'

'Yes.'

I wasn't going to query the relevance of the famous quote. But the implications were interesting.

'Not many people drop a mathematical philosopher into everyday conversation.'

'I read some philosophy from time to time. I have to fill the evenings somehow.'

'Are you married, Huw?'

'Good question. The answer is yes, I am. But exactly where my spouse is just now, is difficult to say. Somewhere in Berkshire I believe.'

'Has she left you?'

'Well, she's not at home now, but she did turn up one day last week. I don't think she has left our marriage, but there are things she believes are more important.'

'What things?'

'Peace, for one. She's joined the Campaign for Nuclear Disarmament, and gone off to a women's peace camp somewhere or other.'

'That's interesting. Do you support her in this kind of direct action?'

'I'm not sure. I just don't know how long it will go on for. She says she'll stay with the camp just as long as is necessary. She says that some things must be sacrificed for the greater good of humanity. Does that include our marriage, I asked her. 'If that's what it takes, she said.'

He got up from the table, wandered over to the rack of bookshelves. Nothing of importance or greatness there, no philosophy, just Mrs Beeton (present from Dad), Elizaeth David and other newly popular cookery writers. A Welsh/English Dictionary for learners, a bird identification manual and a book about dog-training. Some gardening books, a trade directory, a book about Offa's Dyke. He picked up one or two of them. I let him be silent for a bit, sensing his embarrassment.

I had read about the actions of these women who were joining the Peace Camps. It had all started as a response to rumours about the possible sites for the location of Cruise missiles, a deterrent, said the British and American governments, to possible hostile action on the part of the Soviet Union. One or two places had been selected, some abandoned for logistical reasons, some on account of local feeling. Others had been the focus of organised Peace Camps. Groups of women had set up camp on proposed sites, refusing to move in the face of the tree felling, the levelling, the construction of access roads, the disruption of agriculture and the blocking of traditional hedgehog routes.

The camps were causing delays to the programme. In one area the authorities had lost patience and had built an impenetrable perimeter fence, to which the women were doing as much damage as they could.

'In terms of publicity,' I said, 'the camps have been very successful. They've attracted support from most unlikely sources.'

I had a flashback of my conversation with Selwyn about his belief in the value of publicity for his ideology of protest. Inconsistency, or a change of mind on my part? Oh dear.

Huw nodded. 'Their morale is high. There's no way that Ffion will give this up, in fact I think she's thoroughly enjoying herself.'

I wondered if enjoyment were part of the attraction of the movement. A break from the daily household chores that were beginning to bore and frustrate women who had their eye on more interesting activities, but had been obliged to put their lives on hold for their child-rearing years. However, strategies were evolving for having your cake and eating it.

I looked at Huw. He looked weary and a little lost.

'Motivation is rarely a simple matter. It must vary from woman to woman. I'm sorry, Huw. I can offer you no advice.'

'When she first told me that she was leaving, she said that she had to go away and find herself.'

'Which is what we're all doing, I suppose. You don't necessarily have to leave home to do it. For some people it's an internal quest. Does she keep in touch?'

'I get the occasional scribbled note. Just says she's all right.

Sometimes I write long letters to her. They never get posted. I wouldn't know how to get them to her anyway. It gives me something to do in the evenings.'

'You must miss her, Huw.'

'I miss having someone at home, in the house. Someone to talk to. Don't you?'

I considered his question. There's a difference between the presence of a particular person and the simple fact of human company. I suppose I had always imagined a future with a man to grow old with, but I couldn't say that on a daily basis I felt lonely. Without books to think about and, hopefully, to write, things might have looked different. I changed tack.

'What do you do in the evenings, then, when the last letter is finished?'

'Go for a pint. Read.'

'Which brings us back to Pascal! What else d'you read in the field of philosophy?'

'Bit of Plato. I don't understand an awful lot of it.' Huw looked at me hopefully, I thought.

'Not my field, I'm afraid.'

'And I don't like fiction, Kay, so we must both try and go it alone.'

'Not necessarily. There are other ways. I'll give it some thought.'

He smiled. 'Thanks for listening, anyway'.

He finished his tea, said affectionate farewells to Jack, a friendly one to me, and departed.

After he left, I thought about the peace camps. They were unusual in their composition, attracting women from diverse backgrounds, education, politics. I wondered about the dynamics of the groups; it would be interesting to explore this. But not possible without joining them.

The phone rang. I picked it up.

'Kay, Jonathan here. Any news?'

'By which you mean am I getting on with the book. Only in my head, I'm afraid Jon. You'll have to continue to wait patiently.'

'Since I hadn't heard from you, I was afraid you'd say something like that. And I've had another visit from your Australian friend. She still wants to contact you.'

'God, is she still here? I'd have thought she'd have gone back by now.'

'She's not in a hurry, she said. In fact, she's not going back for two or three months. Got some kind of temporary job in Birmingham with a theatre company. Is she an actress?'

'Probably. But I'm sorry I just can't manage a visit from her just now. I've got too much on my plate. Will you please tell her?'

'I will. But she'll be disappointed.'

I wondered if Chris was with Cherry in Birmingham. All the more reason to avoid direct contact. Why did she want to get in touch with me? To show that she had won the competition for one particular man? She would surely get fed up with her unsuccessful attempts to try to prise my address from Jonathan. I thought for the hundredth time of our university days, the days on the beach, the gatherings I hadn't been confident enough to attend alone, the times she had rescued me from situations where I was uncomfortable, keeping an eye out for me, an older sister, although we were the same age.

I thought of her parting words 'I hate you.'

Said in anger and misery, I think now, but out of character. An understandable message to someone who, she believed, had spoiled her life, but the feeling, would that stay with her? Knowing Cherry, I guessed it would have resolved into sorrow, disappointment, resentment at the most.

Of course – I *would* like to see her again. My present refusal wasn't prompted by any lack of fondness for my old friend, but a result, I recognised, of embarrassment and guilt. Should I respond to her invitation?

One more problem to be pushed to the back of my mind. It was getting crowded there.

I wandered to my study, for another glance at the distant hills. No sign of them today. The skies were black with the promise of rain. I wondered if Huw was hopeful of a date. A nice man, but the wrong one.

EIGHTEEN

Newfield, June 1980

Today's walk with Jack had taken me, once again, along the half-remembered route over the bridge and towards the spot where, after much calculation, I'd decided was the location of the cottage where my mother and I had spent the night when I was a young child. The shop where I'd bought the postcard had been replaced by a row of modern bungalows, but there was no sign of anything that might account for the small black dot on the map, which may have represented the house. It had acquired extra significance now, as I was pretty sure that this was the place where one S. Meredith had lived, the woman who had written those two accusing letters to my mother. I sat on a stone wall opposite the place where I imagined so much had happened. No cottage now, just a picture in my head, and in front of me, a black dog investigating where it had once stood. Decades ago, I had slept there.

My mother had thought it necessary for some reason to make the long journey from London, with me in tow. I suppose she couldn't find anyone to leave me with; she had made it clear that she hadn't wanted me around. Her mission, whatever it was, must have been important. She had certainly been silent on the journey back to London but that was not unusual.

My temporary squat was getting uncomfortable, Jack was getting restless, a few drops of rain falling on his shiny black coat. We started for home, passing the row of bungalows on the way. I was startled to hear my name called.

'Good afternoon, Miss Francis!' There was only one person who insisted on addressing me in that way. She was working in her front garden as we passed.

'Hello Mrs. Hayleigh. I didn't know you lived here.'

'I've been here for twenty years now. A very nice place. Quiet, like your house.'

Twenty years. Perhaps she remembered something – or someone. I recalled her offer of help with local history. Worth a try.

'Mrs. Hayleigh, I wonder if you knew this area before your bungalow was built. I'm trying to locate a cottage, quite an old one I think, that once existed just a little way back along the road. I once stayed there as a child.'

'Oh yes, there was a rather small place there, – occupied by some woman from England, I think. There used to be a heap of stones behind the hedge, they were all that were left after the fire.'

'I didn't know there'd been a fire. The stones must be well hidden. I didn't spot them.'

'Oh they've nearly all gone now. I managed to get hold of a few for my rockery.' She pointed with pride at the symmetrical arrangement of dressed building stones placed alongside the path to the house. Some of them were blackened.

'When was the fire?'

'I don't know the exact date. You'd better ask your friend.'

'My friend? Who do you mean?'

'Oh, the farmer. Mr. Hughes. I'm sure he'll remember the date. Him and his friends.' Mrs Hayleigh offered the cold smile I remembered so well, betraying her pleasure in conveying unasked for information that the recipient might find upsetting. There was no need for her to say more, I understood what she was implying. Selwyn had warned me that I would hear references to his involvement in such episodes, but I did find it upsetting, my first encounter with the consequences of a fire, deliberately started, on a place I knew, and where I had once stayed. I was not going to compound her satisfaction by reacting in any way. I didn't reply. I wondered if she was still proposing to contact the authorities over Laura's situation. She answered my unspoken question.

'With reference to my visit to you, Miss Francis, you may be interested to know that I dropped a word where it mattered to someone I know in the Child Protection department of Social Services. They thanked me very much for my interest in the matter, and would take notice of what I had told them. I had the impression that they were very grateful for the information I was able to give them.'

'I'm *sure* they were, Mrs Hayleigh'. My heavy sarcasm passing unnoticed.

I wondered what the reaction had really been. But I was alarmed. Presumably no action would be taken without a visit to check on what Mrs. Hayleigh had said. I would have to wait and see if there would be any mention on Ellen's part of an official visit from the child protection people, any noticeable change in her behaviour, any obvious distress.

I had no desire for further chat, and started to walk away, but was temporarily halted by a shrill scream. I turned to look back and saw Jack in determined pursuit of a large tabby cat.

'My Toodles!' she yelled, that dog'll kill her!'

I shouted the one word he generally responded to.

'No!'

To my relief, he paused, but Toodles didn't make a quick getaway. She stood in the porch, back arched, spitting and hissing, hairs on her patterned body erect, defence mechanisms fully functioning, claws at the ready. I called Jack, who reluctantly but wisely left his victim and came back to me.

'So sorry Mrs. Hayleigh,' I called, 'But your Toodles is well able to look after herself!'

She stood and glared at me, and I left her to her righteous weeding.

By now I knew enough about Selwyn to gather that he had been part of the movement against the English who bought cottages that seemed cheap for their budgets, mostly as holiday homes. I found it difficult to reconcile the person I knew with actions that led to arson, but we make so many mistakes before we are properly grown up. And maybe it wasn't a mistake on his terms. Publicity was what the group wanted and that was what they got.

It was obvious also from Mrs Hayleigh's remarks that Selwyn had not visited me unobserved. Conclusions had been drawn, at least by her. Exactly what the conclusions were I wasn't sure, but I regretted that they were probably wrong.

Jack and I quickened our pace, it was raining again. He ran in front of me, too far, I thought, and I called him back. He stopped, turned to look at me, but something had caught his interest ahead, and he hesitated. Disobedience was on the cards.

I called again. He looked at me and compromised. He didn't come back, but sat on the spot, looking eagerly ahead. I caught up with him, attached his lead and looked for whatever had attracted his attention. It was now raining hard, and I spotted a man sheltering under the heavy branches of a tree.

'Hi Kay!'

'Huw! I wondered what on earth was the matter with Jack! Come back with us and get yourself warm and dry!'

It was summer but I switched on the central heating. Thought a coffee would not be a sufficient remedy for our discomfort. We hung coats up to dry and put shoes on the radiators. Steaming gently, we sat back, sipped our whiskies, and commiserated.

'Only out for a walk' Huw said, 'as I guess you were too.'

'I came across the last person in the world I wanted to see,' I told him, 'and then one other that I am always glad to see, but Jack saw you first!'

'I've got the afternoon off. Thought I'd do a bit of reading and have another go at some chap called Hegel. I couldn't understand a word and decided to have a walk instead. A much better outcome, as it's turned out!'

I've been thinking about your academic difficulties, Huw. I admire your persistence in keeping at it. I'd help if I could, but I'd have to read so much, and I simply don't have the time. However, I would like to suggest a much better alternative.'

'Which is…?'

'A course. These days lots of people are doing some form of distance learning. The Open University is probably the best. Why don't you drop them a line and see what's on offer? There's bound to be some philosophy courses, though you'd probably have to do some kind of foundation level first, to get you into the hang of academic study. You'd at least get some guidance from people who know what they're talking about.'

Huw considered for a few moments. I feared an automatic rejection of the idea, many people were afraid, not just of failing to reach the level demanded, but also of the discipline necessary to follow a rigorous course of study.

'I suppose it'd be expensive.'

'You'd probably get help with that. The government are anxious for this new university to be a success, and don't want people put off on grounds of cost. I'll make some enquiries about it if you like. But it's only an idea. Don't let me push you into doing something that doesn't appeal to you.'

Huw sat up straighter in his chair.

'It would give me something to do, Kay. All that stuff out there that is strange and new that I can't get to grips with. D'you think I could cope? I rather fancy the idea.'

I felt pleased. He had the ideal qualities for someone venturing into higher education – he was aware he knew very little. A good start, I thought, not always the attitude of learners, and would be quickly remedied.

I gave Jack his evening meal, and examined our discarded garments. Shoes dry enough to be put on; coats still dampish but they would do.

'Where did you leave the car?'

'In the pub car park.'

'I'll give you a lift there.'

Huw hesitated. 'Must I go?'

'You must.'

'Oh well, thanks, for the drink, and…the chat.'

He ruffled Jack's damp coat. 'You're a lucky old chap. Keep her safe.'

I have never felt so near to changing my mind. But Huw didn't know that and gathered his clothes. We ran to the car and in a few minutes were at the Cross Keys.

Declining an offer of a pint, I said goodbye to Huw at the car park, picked up some fish and chips for supper, and drove home thinking of other ways the evening might have ended.

Arriving back at the Cottage, I opened today's post. I knew that business envelope, it was from Jonathan. What on earth was he writing about? We dealt with practically everything on the phone. Inside, was another smaller one, and a covering note.

'Cherry Martin wanted you to have this.'

It was brief.

'Dear Kay,

Your publisher said you had been in hospital, but that you seemed O.K. now. I don't want to let slip this opportunity of meeting up with you again. A lot has happened since those days in Melbourne, and I've missed you. Please let me visit.

Love, Cherry'

A straightforward request, no apologies, no excuses, no recriminations. A simple statement of how she felt. It was so welcome, a chance to banish the sadness, the regret, the remorse that always shadowed memories of those parts of my life in Australia. With a simple gesture she had cut through the complexities of our relationship and held out a hand. I quickly wrote a reply.

I thanked her for getting in touch, and that we could meet in Jonathan's office, and go for lunch somewhere nearby. If things did not go well, I didn't want the scene to be played out in my home. I settled down in my study, hoping that some sort of order would emerge from my disordered brain. But I thought instead of Ffion trying to find herself, and Huw, too, doing the same thing, differently. And of me, as lost as both of them.

NINETEEN

Birmingham, June 1980

I embarked upon the drive to Birmingham with apprehension, unsure of how well I could manage my behaviour. I wanted to say that I was sorry, but was afraid of sounding insincere, making an apology that was just a formality for the sake of the occasion. Apologies come in so many forms; there are so many ways in which the words you use could be ill-chosen. At all costs you had to avoid the inclusion of that traitorous little word 'if'.

I parked and made my way up to Jonathan's office. I recognised the same frozen-faced receptionist, excused by him on the grounds that she believed maximum formality indicated maximum competence. She picked up the telephone.

'Miss Francis has arrived.'

Mr Parfitt would see me now, she told me. I opened the door to his office. Cherry stood by the window.

The same smile, the same lovely face. A few more lines, perhaps, her expression an acceptance of all that had passed between us. She made a movement towards me. We hugged. It didn't seem strange. Nearly overwhelmed with delight, I whispered to her.

'I am *so* happy.'

For the moment, nothing else mattered. So much put right, restored, forgiven in one brief moment of encounter. A piece of my life given back to me. I didn't deserve such good fortune.

My arm around her, I turned to Jonathan.

'Can't thank you enough, Jonathan. We've a lot to talk about, Cherry and me. It may well take longer than one lunchtime.'

He looked relieved and a little puzzled. He must think it strange that I had tried so hard to put off this meeting.

'Have you found a place for us to eat?'

'I have, and booked a table. Have a good time.' He turned to Cherry.

'It's been nice meeting you, Mrs. Martin.' I flinched at his use of her official marital title, but told myself that I must get used to it.

We started talking straight away, breaking off only to park the car and settle down at the small restaurant Jonathan had found for us. My pleasure at finding my old friend once more was overwhelming, and we both found it hard to know where to begin. She must have known that my mother had died – our circles of acquaintance overlapped – I knew nothing of Cherry's life since we parted on that day in Fitzroy Gardens. I didn't want to bring Chris into the conversation at this point. It would be difficult enough when the time came.

'Yes, yes,' I said hurriedly to the waiter who was trying to take an order for drinks. 'Two glasses of white wine.' Remembering what we used to have with lunch in Melbourne, and not wanting to waste a second of our meeting with trivial decisions. I continued my disorganised flood of information about my life since leaving Australia.

'I went back to Uni for a couple of years. Got a job, moved in with the boss. Then Mum's dementia started taking over. It was hard on all of us.

There were a couple of difficult years – these were tedious and sad. Dad and I did our best for her, otherwise I didn't do much of any interest. We felt relief when Mum died. Dementia takes people away from you long before death arrives. Her loss was the main reason, I suppose, that Dad and I decided to come to Britain. There was another I'd suspected. He'd been homesick for years. We had a chat, and decided we needed to kick-start a new life. But you probably don't know that Dad died only a couple of years after we made the move. Lung cancer, after a lifetime of smoking.'

I paused, the strains of 'Shadow Dancing' covering the gaps in my story.

'Oh Kay. I am so sorry. I didn't know you had lost him too. I know how close you were.'

'True. I owe him all the benefits I have today. And not just the material ones.'

'He was so proud of you, Kay, and spoke of you constantly. You made him very happy, that should be a comfort.'

'It was. It is. There's so much to say, Cherry. Strange things have happened. Jonathan told you I'd been in hospital?'

'Yes. I could understand that you weren't keen on visitors at that point.'

'That wasn't the only reason, Cherry. But we can't go into everything now, there's so much to say, it'll take time. More than one session. Your turn now. So, you are Mrs. Martin. Which means that you forgave Chris. Is everything O.K. now?'

Cherry's reaction was not what I expected. A burst of laughter, a slug of wine, more laughter, contemptuous.

'Oh Kay, I've been such an idiot! Forgive him! *That* was the biggest mistake I made. Why he bothered to say how sorry he was and swear that it would never happen again is a mystery. On second thoughts perhaps it isn't. People say that serial philanderers like being married. It gives them a safe base from which they can play the field. The forgiveness lasted until the next episode.'

I began to feel a glimmer of understanding.

'There were other episodes? After you were married?'

'Yes. The first after only six months. I was as devastated as I was after his flirtation with you. The next one went much further. I was beginning to see the light. "Sorry," he said. "I'm a bastard. Forgive me and I promise it won't happen again." It did, of course, but by then I had ceased to care. I'm getting a divorce. Can't come too soon.'

The waiter was trying to take our order. Difficult to wrench one's focus from affairs of the heart to that of the stomach. However, we managed to spend several happy minutes considering the relative merits of the varieties of Chinese delicacies on offer. We suspended our chat for a minute or two, so that we could try them all.

Shadow Dancing lyrics drifted across the room. 'There ain't nothing come between us in the end…'

I had made up my mind to offer Cherry a proper apology for the thoughtless way I'd behaved in Melbourne. Of course, the emphasis might be different now, the collapse of their marriage and its reason shifted some of the guilt on to the shoulders of Chris. It hadn't been *all* my fault. But the apology must be made, I wasn't going to use new information to wriggle out of it.

'I'm truly sorry, Cherry, for the way things have turned out. And sorry for the part I played. I was very young and extremely naïve. As well as being in a permanent muddle. My mother was furious, wouldn't speak to me for weeks. She was very fond of you.'

'Yes. Oddly so. She once said that I was the daughter she never had. I thought that rather unkind. She had one already, but it wasn't hard to see that you and she didn't get on all that well.'

'She never liked me, Cherry, let alone loved me. Something went wrong somewhere, the normal bonding just never happened.'

'Yes. I can see that. And I remember how puzzled I was when I came to your house. How keen she seemed to hear about how I was doing, how uninterested in any conversation that turned to you. I was sorry for you.'

'Things got better after she became ill. She forgot who I was, and became quite pleasant. Dad and I looked after her, and she was grateful, in her own way. I missed her after she died. That is, I missed the woman who had forgotten who I was, not the one I'd known all my life. I felt disoriented, at a loose end, unsure how to get our lives going again, and in what direction. I talked to my current boyfriend, who had already proposed marriage! I was quite shocked. Poor Brad, I hope he's found a nice girl to take my place in the shop and in his bed. When Dad let on that he wanted to come back to Britain I jumped at the chance. Seemed the right decision for both of us.'

'So here you are. A good choice?'

'Yes. It made Dad's last years happy ones. And I have been so busy since we moved here that I've barely had time to ask myself if I'm truly settled. I just wish I could get down to my old patterns of writing. The ideas haven't been coming, Cherry. It's called writer's block.'

I could hardly believe how easily our old relationship was restored. There was no embarrassment, no awkwardness. I told her the story of my mild infatuation with Chris – not the first I'd experienced with tutors at Uni. Almost anyone older than me, cleverer, and charming was a likely victim, especially if he chose to notice me. Delayed teenage crushes, I suppose. I had taken an awful long time to grow up.

We recalled old friends, acquaintances, happenings, laughed at them all, at ourselves, at our ignorance, at our belief that we were the first people in the world to have such amazingly enlightened views of life. Cherry asked the question that I knew would come sooner or later.

'No special man at the moment, Kay?'

'Well, there is, I suppose, but I'm afraid he's not interested. At least, sometimes I think he is, but then he backs off. The trouble is, I've got a serious competitor!'

'A rival?'

'Sort of. It's Wales. She grabbed him first, and won't let go.'

Cherry looked nonplussed. 'I've never heard of that before.'

'It's a complicated situation. I can't explain it all now. I'm not even sure I understand it all myself. We don't always get on well together.'

'I'm sorry Kay.' A pause, then falling back into teasing mode, 'but you always were a bloody awkward customer!'

'I know, I know. But I'm working on it. I will be a better person, Cherry, I promise you.'

My voice faltered, I had never spoken of Selwyn before, to anyone. Cherry took my hand.

'We'll look out for each other again, Kay.'

The waiter cleared the table, and I made a mental note to thank Jonathan for bringing about our reunion in this fine restaurant, which we had been unable to appreciate fully. What we had to say to each other was all we were interested in, our conversation jumping randomly backwards and forwards until we were dizzy with reminiscence.

I asked Cherry about her plans.

'I really don't have any,' she said. 'I can get jobs in a theatre, but not the ones I had dreamed of once! I'm still interested, though, and perfectly happy dealing with costumes and make-up. And an occasional minor part. Back home a friend told me of a vacancy here in Birmingham, so I thought I'd have a go, for a while. I'm still intending to go back to Melbourne.'

I nearly invited her for a visit, but hesitated. Elements of an idea had been buzzing around my head, I wanted to get them down on paper. I already felt so much better now. This old mistake in my life put right. I felt that I'd been put back on track again.

'I've a feeling, Cherry, that my writing problems may be receding. Not sure, as I've had the feeling before. This time seems different. Maybe the book is kicking, like an unborn child!'

'When it's done,' I told her, I'll have a break. We could go on holiday together. Somewhere completely new and unknown to both of us.'

We rose to go, still talking, gathered our belongings, paid, and went back to the car, still talking. Much left unsaid, but we both knew that further meetings would take care of that.

The occasion I'd been dreading had resolved into a day replete with joy and interest. I thought of our friendship in Melbourne. She had been the confident, successful one, and looked out for me in many ways that I didn't realise at the time. We were good friends again, though I suspected that the dynamics of the relationship would be changed. That didn't matter. I knew that she felt like family, and would always be there for me, whatever happened.

Back in Jonathan's office, we thanked him, and promised that next time Cherry and I met for lunch, he would be a welcome addition.

'A celebration, perhaps,' he said hopefully, 'for the completion of the new book!'

Next morning, I set out for Shrewsbury. I was finally going to buy the new electronic typewriter I'd been promising myself. Hoping that I remembered all the advice I had been given, the machine was bought with much trepidation. Suppose I just couldn't come to terms with it? Suppose the muse, this mythological creature we all knew but had never seen or heard, just didn't take to it, and refused to perform? Suppose *I* didn't take to it? I had smiled at stories of authors who simply could not abandon their fountain pens, even for a change to ball-points. Maybe today's purchase would be my sticking point. I envisaged addresses to literary groups, the amazement.

'Is it true, Miss Francis, that you still use your old typewriter?' My confirmation of this rumour would simply enhance the aura of the quaint eccentricity of a working author.

I unpacked the machine. All I must do now is get it to work. I started reading the manual.

A knock at the door, a muted 'woof' from Jack indicated the identity of my caller.

'Selwyn, you've came at exactly the right time. Come in and show me how this thing works!'

Selwyn had already spotted it and sat down at the table. He pressed a few keys, and words appeared on a tiny white space. I wrote down, with pen and paper, the sequence of key operations that would take me to a small blank screen. I repeated these operations and felt confident that I could perform them alone. I was rewarded by a page of typescript with no mistakes, no alterations, but looking pretty near perfect. I was pleased with the result.

'It'll do for the time being. Ten years on you'll have your own computer. That'll be something worth waiting for. You won't have to keep printing pages, the machine will keep and save everything for you, all your corrections, alterations and revisions done and kept safe until you want them. Hitch everything up to a printer, and you'll have whichever version you choose in print.'

'Thank you, I look forward to it. Coffee, or a beer as it's a hot day? Tell me what you've been doing on the farm.'

'I came to talk to you about the paddock.'

'Well,' I said, 'I've given up hoping for a purely social call. A friendly chat about politics, the state of the world and its ultimate destiny.'

He laughed. A small breakthrough, but it cheered me.

'We discuss these things by implication,' he said. But I've called to talk to you on the subject of your little field. I've used it for nearly a year now. I'd like to put it on an official basis, pay you an appropriate rent, and have an annual contract.' He paused, with the ghost of a smile, and ventured a joke. 'If you prefer, we can use this as a basis for a discussion on the morality of ownership of property!'

'I've brought the draft of a contract.' He shoved a printed sheet in front of me. I shoved it back.

'You have a gift,' I told him, 'for ruining any civilised conversation between friends. I've told you, I'm not taking any rent from you. Just as I'm beginning to enjoy myself you start talking business. If that's what you want, I'd rather get myself lunch and start work.'

'That's a dismissal, I suppose. I may have to think about putting cash in an envelope and putting it into your hand.'

'In that case, we'll have to compromise with a mutually acceptable charity. I won't take rent from you, Selwyn. I mean it.'

We were standing close. I had an impulse to provoke some kind of reaction to the situation. What I said next was contemptuous, patronising, rude, and true.

'You need the money more than I do.'

There was a silence that lasted long enough for me to regret what I'd said.

'I didn't know you could be ridiculous, Kay.'

He turned his back on me, and walked out of the house.

I had offended him. Which is not what I had wanted to do. Offence is a cold, rather formal response. Anger, a change of colour, a slap in the face – would have been a more welcome reaction to my discourtesy. But he was gone now, leaving me cross, childish, and ashamed.

It's no good pretending I don't care. I do, and it gets in the way of my daily life, my small pleasures. The view from my study window, the company of Jack, my reading sessions with Laura, my garden, the river. I hope the writing doesn't succumb as well, it's so good to have it back. I have so much to be thankful for. Love, as well, may be asking too much.

TWENTY

Newfield, July 1980

'Have you seen Melanie?' It was the Rev. Powell on the phone, early next morning. Too early for a social call. I answered with trepidation.

'No, I haven't. Should I have seen her? Where is she?'

'We don't know where she is. She didn't come home last night. We've spent most of the night looking for her. The places we knew she went to, the trees where she kept her bird boxes. This has never happened before. We are dreadfully worried. I'm phoning people just to find out who saw her last, where she was, what she was doing.'

'Oh, Mr. Powell, I am so sorry. This is bad news. Have you contacted the police?'

'I have. They took details, but told us not to worry. She'll turn up, they said, young women are always going missing for one reason or another. They suggested she's probably staying with a friend somewhere. They wanted to know if she had a job. I told them she wasn't able to cope with the things that most young people do. I explained that she didn't understand much of what was said to her, unless it related to the things she was interested in. I told them about her birds.'

His voice broke; he was deeply distressed. I didn't know what to say, not knowing whether comfort or advice would help him best.

'I'll come over straight away. We'll talk about the best thing to do. Have you spoken to anyone else?'

'I've phoned Selwyn Hughes. He said he'll come as soon as he can.'

He would, of course. Nothing would stop him responding to a call for help. I couldn't stop a moment's tremor in my stomach as I recalled our last encounter.

'I'll be over straight after Jack's walk, Bill.' I put the phone down.

I was inclined to agree with the police view that she would turn up in due course, they were used to disappearances of young girls who'd had a row with their parents and left home in a huff. This wouldn't be the case in Melanie's family, of course, but it was early days for serious concern. I guessed she'd been on some bird-related matter and dropped off to sleep in some shelter, barn or haystack perhaps.

She knew intimately the area around Abbotsbury, probably better than most, she knew the remote unvisited spots, places where she had put her nest-boxes. She could have had an accident, fallen perhaps, calls for help too far away to be heard, if she had called at all. However, at the moment the vicar and his wife needed support.

I let Jack out briefly, gave him breakfast and put him back into the house. His walk would have to wait. I set off for the Vicarage. Selwyn's car was already there, together with a couple of others. I rang the bell. It was a neighbour who let me in. In the kitchen, a group were poring over a map spread out over the table. Selwyn raised his head, saw me, and nodded. He wasn't going to let personal feelings distract him from getting on with what he had come to do. Seeing him again, apparently unmoved by my appearance, was hard.

Returning to the map, he was tracing out routes with his finger, looking at places where he'd seen Melanie.

'What I'll do, Bill, is notify as many farms in the area as I can, explain the situation, and ask them to look in their barns, any derelict building, anywhere they can think of, where she might be. Look for any signs of trodden grass, disturbance of any kind. Not to miss the unlikely places.'

The vicar spoke. 'Some of the farmers know her, have been kind to her.'

'She lightens the day, Bill, with her boxes, and her passion for things we take too much for granted. Something she does for me.'

The room fell silent. I moved to the office, where I could see Mrs. Powell sitting by the telephone.

'All I can do,' she said, eyes red and weary with waiting.

I put my arm round her.

'People say it has not been long,' she said, 'but it's a lifetime for me. I want her back so much.'

'Of course,' I whispered,' we all do, and when we have her back we'll all rejoice with you.'

'Please let me know if there's anything I can do to help' I told Bill, 'I can come any time, but I don't want to get in the way.' I glanced at Selwyn, who saw I was on the point of leaving. He knew exactly what I was thinking.

'We'll send for you, Kay, if we need help and have decided what must be done.'

I left the house, one or two other people were turning up, church members, I supposed, who would surely take charge of practical matters. They would know what needed to be done there. They spoke the language of comfort.

Back home, I felt useless, but resolved to be particularly vigilant during Jack's walk by the river. I thought of Melanie. Did the Vicar and his wife worry during her hours' long absences from home? Had they ever thought of restricting her activities? I couldn't see how that could have been done, even if they had wanted to. That she should be as happy as she could, would have been their goal. They would have discussed this, I'm sure, and decided that her happiness was worth the risk. The strategy had been successful, up till now.

I took Jack for his daily walk. He found a duck to chase, earning disapproving scowls from other dog-walkers. No sign of Melanie, save for a couple of bird-boxes she had put up in a beech tree. I had watched her do this one day, amazed at her grace and agility up the tree, and quick competent descent to the ground.

'Big boxes, Melanie, I had said. 'Are they for eagles?', teasing her a bit. She'd looked at me wonderingly. I guessed that contempt was not in her emotional cupboard, just surprise and puzzlement that anyone could be so stupid.

'The boxes are for woodpeckers,' she had told me.

'The ducks must be quite jealous,' I said, that you put boxes for other birds in the trees, but not for them, down on the ground.'

Her reply had surprised me.

'Mandarin ducks have their nests in trees,' she said, and the baby ducks fall out before they've learned to fly.'

'I've never seen a Mandarin duck,' I observed. 'What are they like?'

Her face shone with delight.

'The drakes are orange and red and blue and green! The female ducks are just brown. But their eyes are different, so you can tell they are Mandarins. They don't like my boxes, so I don't put any up in the trees for them.'

I had learned something. If what Melanie had said was accurate. I had never seen a duck as colourful as the ones she had described to me.

She had talked more than usual. I wondered precisely what lay behind that impenetrable exterior. But she had left our brief discussion and was walking on. No more conversation, no parting words. And now, today, still with no goodbye, could she have gone from us all?

Jack and I finished our walk, I wondered if there had been any news. I didn't want to distract the people who were helping, by asking questions. I would know soon enough. The day dragged on, I couldn't write. I made supper, didn't feel like eating it. Went to bed with a book, couldn't sleep for thinking, worrying. The urge to get out of bed, no matter what the hour, and search for her, was powerful. I had to restrain myself, it was not a sensible idea.

Waking early I watched the clock moving sluggishly towards a civilised hour. I phoned Selwyn.

'Any news?'

'No, afraid not.'

'I feel so useless Selwyn. Afraid of getting in the way.'

'I'm thinking now of organising parties of searchers, who will cover the ground area by area. Up to now the search has been a bit random. Would you like to take a group to some place, preferably out of the way, that you know well?'

'Of course. I'd be glad to be of any use. It'd save me moping around at home.'

Something to do at last, I felt a sense of relief.

'Go over to the Vicarage, Kay, people are meeting there.'

I went. They were quieter today. Less hopeful chatter. A cloud was forming over Abbotsbury, I had one of my own.

Someone had stuffed newspaper into my log-burner's flue pipe. Now a young, vulnerable woman was missing. Could there be a connection? How could there be? But here were two unpleasant occurrences, the first known only to a couple of people, the second by now known to most of the village and surrounding farms. A coincidence, of course, but sinister if you believed in dark forces that affect human lives. I didn't, but took a deep breath, the air seemed thick, stale. I needed to get out.

A few of us decided to comb an area where I had once come across Melanie. We were joined at the last minute by Gareth, my log supplier. He responded to my greeting with a wordless grunt. We checked with Selwyn, who was organising the searches, with the aid of a large-scale map. We set off. Not a lot of conversation, mostly banalities about how the Powells must be feeling, possible scenarios of where Melanie might be, what could have happened. All in a context of bewilderment, of being lost ourselves, looking for a way back to ordinary life. An atmosphere of sadness, of depression. Two or three hours of meticulous searching produced no trace of her. We reported back to the Vicarage, with a flickering hope that meanwhile she might have been found. All reports were negative. I went home.

I thought of Melanie, of how she was seen by different people. Ellen knew about her, had mentioned 'that loony woman', had criticised the Powells for letting her wander about unsupervised, and had prophesised that she would come to grief one way or another. 'End up in a ditch, that one will,' she had observed one day, Cassandra-like. Now I had to admit the possibility of the outcome that Ellen had prophesied.

Most people had become used to her, some had seen her as an amusing, harmless eccentric, others as an object of pity. People were sorry for the Powells, not realising that in so many ways she brought them joy. 'A gift from God,' Bill Powell had often been heard to say.

I wondered if the police had decided to take official action. By now it had been explained to them that Melanie was not an ordinary young woman, could not react as you might expect. Had the Powells ever tried to make her careful of people she met? Warned her of possible if unlikely dangers? Would she have known what they were talking about, or cared?

Another silent evening. I felt lonely. If only I could write something. It was not possible. I poured myself a glass of wine, wished Selwyn were here to share one with me, and pondered on our odd relationship. Thoughts of him filled much of my day. I wanted and enjoyed his company. Love? I supposed so.

Can you love someone you hardly know? He never spoke of what he wanted from life, how he coped with his personal difficulties, I knew there had been many. Did he still feel the loss of his wife, did he regret his illegal, damaging, activities, born out of hate? What did he think of me? An incomer, female, unattached, successful, no shortage of money. Lacking a traditional Welsh reserve, curious, unconventional, argumentative, not pretty, but not bad. What more could I do to arouse his interest, without loss of self-respect? Nothing, I concluded, and went to bed.

I woke up early, as had become usual. Thoughts rapidly converging on the only thing that immediately mattered.

Melanie. The third day of her disappearance. Two nights spent away from home. What should I do with this day? Join another search party? The area was becoming well covered. There couldn't be a barn, a ruin, a wood, a ditch that hadn't been meticulously investigated and marked on the map. I was despondent. I didn't feel like another visit to the Vicarage. I was unhappy at the sight of the same blank despondent faces, the routine fruitless searches, the sadness, the Powells' agony. I was afraid of bad news.

If that's what the news was, it would find me soon enough. I must get out of the house, though, I didn't feel like another walk through the fields and woods, impelled to search repeatedly, as one does, for something you have been looking for a hundred times, in the same places, knowing perfectly well it isn't there.

I'll go to Shrewsbury, to the library, I decided. Maybe I'll look at some bird books, find a picture of the Mandarin ducks Melanie had spoken about. I couldn't see how this could help to find her, but it would make me feel in touch – you never know how Fate links things together. I was being fanciful, illogical and becoming mentally weary.

I found the pictures, and they brought me a little closer to Melanie. I projected a vision of these magical ducks on to the river as I walked back to the car through the town's beautiful Quarry Park. The riverside walk took me as far as Porthill Bridge.

A bridge makes a frame for all that lies beneath it, silhouetted against the brightness of all that lies beyond. It also makes a shelter for house martins – I remembered Melanie telling me about them. I spotted one or two flying low, swooping beneath and out the other side.

The silhouette I saw was a sitting figure, arms round her knees, gazing at the supporting structure above her head. I drew nearer, and I saw the familiar features, turned upward to watch the birds that lived there, that nested there?

Astonishment, hope, joy, all in my head and heart as I stopped myself from shouting her name. Slowly, keeping her in sight, I drew close, sat down beside her. Melanie spoke.

'House martins. They're often under bridges as well as house eaves. It's more sheltered.'

I tried to subdue the tremble in my voice as I responded.

'There's lots to see here, Melanie, but I need to get home. Would you like a lift back?'

She nodded, and rose to her feet. She looked fine, as far as I could see, and undisturbed. I would not ask her anything, tell her anything, her parents would know the best way to deal with her homecoming. Walking back along the riverside, under and over the bridges, my heart was thumping with joy and relief. I must get a message to the Powells straight away. We reached the car park. There was a phone box nearby, I could keep her in sight.

'I Just want to make a phone call, Melanie, I'll be very quick, wait for me in the car.'

I dialled Bill Powell's number. He answered immediately.

'Powell, the Vicarage.'

'Bill, it's Kay Francis here. What is the best news you could possibly have?'

He stumbled over the words.

'What is it that you want to tell me?'

'I'm telling you that Melanie is safe and well. We are in Shrewsbury. She is with me in the car.'

I kept her in sight as I spoke.

Silence. Then just two broken words in reply.

'Thank God.'

Another silence, then small sounds, voices in the background, commotion, shouts. He must have signalled his news; I imagined the theatre of joy.

'We'll be home in under an hour. I haven't questioned her at all. You'll know best how to deal with things. I'm so happy for you, – and for me too, and for everyone. 'Bye now, see you soon.'

I drove back with care, no point in tempting those Fates again. There was no conversation between us. I glanced at Melanie, her eyes were closed. I pulled into the Vicarage garden, parked carefully beside Bill's car. I sat for a moment. Melanie was getting out. No goodbyes, I didn't expect one.

Mrs. Powell came through the front door, took Melanie's hand. They walked into the house together. Bill Powell came to the car.

'Where has she been?'

'No idea. I found her in Shrewsbury. She seems fine. I've not asked her any questions.'

'You did right. Everyone has gone home. We thought it better. Our prayers have been answered, thanks to you, Kay. I don't know how to tell you, you can surely imagine, our feelings since your phone call. To have her back with us – it means our lives can begin again. We'll see what she tells us this evening, and I'll call round tomorrow morning, if I may, to hear exactly where you found her.'

I understood why he wanted no celebrations. Melanie's life was one in which she was comfortable, it would have upset her to have her parents showing strange and unfamiliar emotions. If things needed to be explained to her, it would have to be done quietly, in ways she was used to. I shed a few tears, gave him a hug, said that in the morning I'd tell him all I knew, and left. The air was sparkling, the clouds had lifted. Home again, I gave Jack his dinner, watched uncomprehendingly a programme on television, and went to bed. I hoped that Bill had been able to contact as many people as possible with the good news, to save them from another night of anxiety and fear.

He would be saying his prayers, in relief and gratitude.

TWENTY-ONE

Newfield, July 1980

'How is she?' I asked Bill.

'She seems the same as she's always been, perhaps a little excited. She seems to have had a wonderful time, in terms of what makes her happy.'

Bill Powell, looking infinitely weary, but peaceful, stirred his coffee. Telling him all I knew took only a minute or two. I knew remarkably little.

'Let's try and put it all together. I found her sitting under a bridge in Shrewsbury.'

'*Shrewsbury* was it! We'd been wasting our time, then, all those days, searching locally. How on earth did she get there?'

'No idea. But that wasn't my concern at that moment. It was purely fortuitous; I had a fancy to pop into the library and decided to take a walk by the river afterwards. I found Melanie sitting happily under Porthill Bridge, looking at the flocks of house martins that live there. I can tell you, Bill, that I had a difficult few moments when I first saw her. I wanted to run and grab hold of her, to persuade myself that she wasn't a vision born of longing, an angel, perhaps, or Melanie who had disappeared and might well do so again, if I took my eyes off her for one second. But I kept her in view, and tried to keep calm, I didn't want to do or say anything that would worry her, make her uneasy.'

'You did right, Kay.'

'We chatted for a few minutes, she told me about the birds above our heads, and I offered her a lift home. That's all I can tell you. We walked back to the car, and I phoned you about ten minutes after I'd first seen her. Has she talked at all to you about what she'd been doing?'

Bill smiled, 'only about the things that matter to her, the birds she saw. We've been picking up clues, though. She was not alone. She talks of what 'we' did. There must have been someone else with her. From the way she speaks I have the feeling that there were several. I'm not sure why I think this – she must have dropped a hint. But I can't stop her in mid-conversation and ask her why she makes that particular remark, or ask her for reasons for what she says. As far as she's concerned it's all perfectly obvious.

She showed us something, a memento of her absent days. It was a feather.'

I laughed. 'That's not surprising.'

'This one is. She says it's from a golden plover. She found it, she says "while we were sitting on a rock among the heather, waiting for one to arrive." I looked it up later, it's a very rare bird. Found in the Cambrian Mountains.

'The only people who might sit waiting for a particular bird to arrive would be a gathering of bird watchers.'

'That's what Jane and I thought. That somehow or other she'd got herself attached to a group excursion.'

'We could find out more. Look up trips organised by

various bird societies. We could tell them what we think might have happened, I'm sure they would help if they can.'

There wasn't much more we could say to each other. Not that it mattered a great deal. Melanie was home. We could all take up our old lives again, with, perhaps, a new knowledge of ourselves.

'Bill, you look so tired. Can you get a bit of rest?'

'A colleague has kindly offered to take Sunday service. And church members are wonderful, we have been inundated with cooked dinners.'

Who would there have been, I wondered, to do the same for a miserable unbeliever like me? The kindness, the sympathy would have been there, but unorganised and impotent.

'Well, Bill, if you like, I'll try and find out exactly what happened. Talk to bird groups. See what they've been up to recently.'

'Thanks, Kay. I'm not sure it really matters, but it might be a help if …' He lost his words for a moment, putting his hand over his eyes. '…if ever she went missing again.'

Heaven forbid, I thought, but heaven wasn't listening. It goes its own sweet way, impervious to the misery of one of its own.

The task was not too difficult. A three-day outing to the Cambrian mountains had been organised by a Shrewsbury bird group. Two nights had been spent in a Youth Hostel, food and expenses pre-paid. Unfortunately, the organiser had gone sick the day before and couldn't come along with the others, so there was nobody in the group who knew all the names and faces – including one or two unfamiliar ones from other birdwatching societies. Melanie had come across the group, who had stopped off at Newfield for coffee and to look at the river birds. She had happily joined in with their observations, and hearing that they were off to find more birds, simply got on the bus with them. It had never occurred to anyone that she shouldn't have been there. It would have been assumed that she was just another member, though perhaps rather an odd one.

Melanie had been in a hostel before, Bill told me, probably the same one, near Dolgellau, where she and her mother had stayed for a weekend's break a year or two ago. It wouldn't have been an unfamiliar experience for her.

There were other conversations between us, until all the facts were established. I asked Bill the question that no doubt all of us had been thinking about.

'Are you going to change the way she lives? I'm sure you're worried that something similar might happen again.'

'We have always been apprehensive that something might happen to her. An accident in a remote spot, the offer of a lift from a stranger. Don't imagine we haven't thought about such things. The alternative is not to allow her out alone. How we could achieve that I'm not sure, short of locking doors, and trying to explain things she couldn't understand. Her life is as happy, I think, as it could be, the way things are. I think that Jane and I will keep things as they've always been; she wouldn't understand the reasons for any change. However, there is a pleasant development on the horizon which will make things easier, and it's getting nearer every day. I shall be reaching retirement age soon. This'll mean that I'll be able to spend more time with Melanie.'

He smiled at the prospect. 'I'll find it hard to keep up with her. Tree climbing is not my forte, but my ornithological education will be enormously widened.'

There was another problem, though, that he hadn't mentioned. Selwyn had told me, as we were discussing the whole affair over the garden gate one day, that the Powells were worried about Melanie's future.

'They're thinking about what will happen when they're no longer around to look after her,' he said.

'A very natural concern.'

'And one that has no answer. Or rather, no answer that we can see, beyond institutional care.'

He paused. 'I did say to them that as long as I was in the area I would keep an eye on her, help as far as I could, whenever necessary. But I couldn't undertake any kind of permanent responsibility. They understood that. It's a pity they don't have any close relatives who might take her in.'

'Let's not spoil the day with such speculations. Come in and have some lunch. Scrambled eggs on toast. We can enjoy small treats now the clouds have lifted.'

He considered for a moment.

'Thanks, but I'd better not. I've got behind with so many routine jobs while Melanie was missing. I must catch up. Thanks anyway, another time.'

Another time, and another excuse. I was getting used to it, and the annoyance and frustration it produced.

'Been found, then, has she?' Ellen commented on her next visit. 'Some people have all the luck. Daughters are a worry, men always land on their feet. Wish I'd had a son instead. Second thoughts, p'raps I don't. Wouldn't have Laura, then, would I?'

The telephone rang, Bill Powell again.

'Hello Kay, Bill here. I've just discovered tracks of another S. Meredith. You still interested?'

I was and I wasn't. Finding her would make no difference to me or anyone else. But my curious mind would not let me pass by an opportunity to find out why my mother owed her money. I told him I would still like to find her. If it was a 'her'. At the back of my mind there was a feeling that my mother had caused difficulties for S. Meredith, and that I could afford to redress that wrong. If indeed any distress had ensued from a failure to pay a debt. I still had the two pencilled messages.

'There's one more thing I must tell you, Kay, odd and rather nice.'

'Good news is always welcome, Bill. What is it?'

'The secretary of the bird-watching group from Shrewsbury has been in touch. She had a suggestion, supported by the whole group. She said they were surprised and rather shocked at the whole episode of Melanie's disappearance. Could they make up for it, to a small extent, by offering her an official invitation to suitable group outings? If she came alone they would take great care of her, they said, but if we preferred, one of us could come with her.'

'Goodness me. Well, that was a nice gesture!'

'It was. We'll have to consider it – I can't see that there can be any objection.'

'It's a bonus. We have Melanie back, and she has the chance of a wider world to live in and enjoy.'

Thinking about Bill's reference to the elusive S. Meredith, I spoke to his contact, a young man who lived near Bridgnorth.

'My mother died years ago,' I told him, 'This Miss or Mrs Meredith was a friend of hers. I met her once, when I was about five. I'd quite like to get in touch.'

'My dad came from Newfield', he said, Worked as a sort of handyman for lots of different people. I remember him talking about a woman called Meredith – lived in an old cottage near the river, he said, pretty ruined it was, and needed the roof seeing to. He spent a couple of days on the job, re-tiling and filling in holes where the squirrels got in.'

'Do you know what happened to her? Where she is now?'

'No idea. I can ask him if you want.'

'That would be extremely kind of you.'

The answer, when it came, was barely a disappointment, I had become used to living with this puzzle, and had little real hope of ever solving it.

'She went off to London.'

I was not surprised. On the day of that memorable trip so many years ago, my mother had told me that we were going to see a former neighbour. I wondered if she had now gone back to her home area, to that part of the East End that had housed the two of them. There was nothing more I could do to find her. At this point I wasn't even sure that I wanted to.

A card arrived from the Patels, announcing the arrival of Rory Vikram, nine pounds and doing well. Laila was with her parents in Yorkshire, being instructed in the care of a first baby. She would stay with them for a few weeks before returning to London. I thought about our old home, which was now theirs, and wondered where they would keep the pram. Pram? How behind the times I was!

I wondered how the Patels were dealing with the modern problems that went with being both working people and parents. I looked forward to seeing them again.

TWENTY-TWO

London, August 1980

I had presents for Rory Patel. A warm infant's outfit for his first winter, and my first two books of stories for children. They had their origin in tales that had been told over the years to children in different parts of the world, one or two from the Indian continent, the home of his own ancestors. The books had sold well, and I hoped that one day he would like them too. The hope of reading them to a child of my own was becoming less and less likely, as was the man who would be its father. However, I was coming to accept that this picture was a pleasant fantasy, certainly not a desperate need. Simply a path that had not appeared. There was no anguished searching. Life was full of paths.

I deposited Jack with Huw, and set off for a week's break in London. I was looking forward to making the acquaintance of Rory Vikram Patel, a day or two in the National Library and a farewell dinner with Cherry, who was going back to Melbourne a few days later. I phoned the Patels.

'Can't have you staying in a hotel', they had announced, 'the top floor is all set for visitors, lovely view from there. Hope you'll stay with us for your first night at least. Lots to talk about!'

A beautiful child, I thought, on being introduced to Rory. But babies mostly are at this early age. Too young to have developed the irregularities of feature that spoil the symmetry of their little faces and contribute to their individual personalities. That will come later, perhaps, with Adam's elegant eyebrows and Laila's upturned smile. Just a picture post-card baby so far. I held him for a moment, till his lower lip trembled.

At five months old, he seemed a solid, confident infant, reaching the usual landmarks at the proper age and in the right order, hardly justifying his father's constant reference to his library of textbooks on child development, recently added to by his own published research. Laila was keen to return to her work as a general practitioner, handing over some of Rory's daily care to her niece, Rose, who was living with them while waiting for the start of her own medical career.

In a bedroom on the top floor of the house where I was born, I slept badly that night, kept awake by the raucous laughter of late-night partygoers making their way back home, and an unexpected sound that belonged in Newfield, not here in London – a barking fox. Hunted by humans in the countryside, they were discovering that they were being unintentionally fed by the residents of big cities and were wisely deciding to relocate there.

Laila had already left home for a stint in her medical practice when I joined Rose and Rory for morning coffee, together with the Patel's daily domestic help. Rory was entertained by the appearance of a window cleaner, not waving, but cleaning, I suggested, and encouraged the little one to wave back. By lunchtime the help had left, Rory was asleep in his cot, Rose was reading in the nursery, and I was finishing my sandwich alone in the kitchen. The basement door opened; Laila had returned from work.

'All well?' she asked.

'All well,' I answered. 'We had an entertaining morning. Rory was in good form. We had a visit from a window cleaner, which amused him greatly.'

'Your lady help left a note for you. It's by the phone.'

Laila picked it up.

'No problem,' she said, 'I'd forgotten to leave the money to pay for the windows.'

She tossed the note on to the table. I glanced at it. Looked harder. Looked very hard indeed. Caught my breath, seeing a flashback from many years ago. Dad and me, sitting at our kitchen table in our new home. Looking through a bunch of letters.

I read the one that Laila had casually tossed on to the table.

'*I payed the window cleaners you forgot to leve the money bedroom windows a bit*

smeery
S. Meredith'

There was not the smallest doubt in my mind. I knew that signature as well as I knew my own. I quickly stopped myself from uttering a sharp exclamation, and silently registered this extraordinary discovery. Laila was putting on the kettle for a cup of tea. I said nothing for a minute or two.

I ventured a question.

'Have you had your cleaner long? Is she a local person?'

'I think so. Susan has been working here since I left to stay with my family in Yorkshire. Seems O.K. When I took her on she mentioned that she'd been in this house before. Not surprising, she used to live round the corner. Knew one of the previous occupants, she said. She seems quite happy, thinking of getting married to her partner this year, they're house-hunting in their spare time.'

Immersed in my discovery of the elusive S. Meredith, I put my thoughts in order. For some reason or other, my mother had owed her money, made regular payments while we were still living in London, here in this basement where I was sitting now. But for some reason Susan Meredith had moved to Newfield, and my mother, with me in tow, had paid her a visit there. I had my post-card to prove it. All payments were made to the place with the Shrewsbury post-mark, to the tiny cottage by the river. WHY?

Simple. Identify myself and ask her.

Laila spoke to me.

'Hope you slept well last night, Kay, you look a bit pale. London's nights aren't as peaceful as in the countryside.'

'I'm fine, thanks Laila. Look, let's not cook tonight, let's break all the rules and buy a takeaway meal for all of us. I'll pop out now and buy something for tonight. Let's talk, not cook.'

Laila agreed, with some relief, I thought, and I set off for the supermarket, thoughts swirling round my brain. Did I really want to tell Susan Meredith who I was? Was it really necessary for me to know why Mum had owed her money? Both of us, she and I, were leading comfortable lives, Susan Meredith apparently 'managing' quite happily without the money Mum had owed her. I had imagined repaying her, but…pandering to my moral ego… was that for *my* satisfaction rather than for her benefit?

At last, I had found the writer of the letters written to my mother so many years ago, a perfectly ordinary woman, who had played a significant and puzzling part in my life and that of my father. Her final desperate pleas for the money owing to her had arrived too late, our family had already departed, the defaulter never to return.

My mind returned, as it often did, to Dad. I know what he would have said.

'Let it lie, Kay, let it lie.'

He would have been right. I should not disturb the balance of the lives we led, Susan Meredith and I. Whatever had happened in the past had already made its contribution to the present, the 'what if?' game was never worth playing. Why focus on one particular alternative, when an infinity of others are of equal power to change the world? and who knows what more distress might be caused if I made myself known to her? I shall most likely never know why my mother sent her regular payments of money while we lived in London. If she had ever found it difficult to manage without her monthly cash, she must have overcome the problems; she seemed perfectly well adjusted to her present life.

Sleep well, Susan Meredith, for better, for worse, your day has had no surprises for you, nor will your tomorrow.

The Patels and I enjoyed our takeaway risotto, and an accompanying bottle of Rioja. An early night for all of us, I slept well. I left in the morning, with goodbyes and thanks and promises to see each other again as soon as we could.

A visit to the National Library was as rewarding as I had hoped, enriching my understanding of those points in the early mediaeval history of Britain which might easily have been different, leading to a different today, to a different Wales.

I looked forward to seeing Cherry for our farewell meal.

She was going back to Australia; we wanted dinner together and hoped to make some plans for a proposed holiday. The destination had changed with every meeting. But Cherry knew instinctively what was concerning me most at present.

'How's the book going, Kay?'

'Not too badly. Originally I had been thinking that it would examine the effects of an individual in a new community. Then I thought it might be more interesting to locate the individual in a new ideology, a new mindset. Now I'm looking at the lives of individuals in a new *history*.

I feel like I'm moving in the right direction, though I'm not quite there yet. I'm getting down to some serious research into the history of the Dark Ages. I'm thinking of writing a story about someone who lived in a very different Wales, a big powerful country. It had won some crucial battles against the invaders from Europe – the Saxons, Jutes and so on – and now governed all of Britain. With the exception of a small rump occupying the eastern counties, which would be England. Great fun to imagine the language problems.

'Goodness, what a reversal of fortunes!'

'Sure. Makes me feel quite dizzy! But I'm happy with the idea. I'm looking forward to seeing what happens.'

'And I'm looking forward to finding out what happens to your life, Kay. You mentioned another man that you seem quite close to.'

Cherry, typically more interested in life than literature, keeps my feet on the ground. She must be thinking of Huw, I had mentioned him as the friend who was looking after Jack for me.

'Yes, someone who battles with classical philosophy while trying to train dogs for police work. His wife left a perfectly good marriage to become a peace activist. Makes me think I've been a bit too accommodating to the world's problems. Done bugger all about them!'

'Don't say that, Kay. Your job is to think and write about these things and bring them to a wider audience. It's just as valuable.'

'That's what Selwyn told me once. It's a kind thought. But tell me about *your* plans. You'll be back in Melbourne soon.

Will life be any different for you after this stay in England?'

'I hope so. I'm keen to get the divorce finalised and get Chris out of my hair. He bugs me, Kay, with his unreliability, his promises, his "you're the only one I've ever truly loved," and his so-called heartbreak at the prospect of the end of our marriage. It's got to the state where he gets on my nerves. Can't wait to see him go. He wants to stay good friends, he says, for old times' sake. It's for old times' sake, I told him, that I want to see the back of him.'

I thought of the handsome, muscled, shallow charmer who had dazzled both my mother and me. I hoped that he would be as uncomfortable and regretful in his new single life as he deserved to be. We both agreed that he would not be single for long. He would find a new base from which he could make new conquests. We tried to be sorry for him.

We parted, full of hope and plans for the holiday we have been promising ourselves.

TWENTY-THREE

Newfield, August 1980

Shopping for replacement items in London's street markets left me tired and disinclined to make the return journey back home on the same day, but home was where I needed to be. No supper, hunger would keep me awake, as did a strong black coffee at a motorway service station. The traffic was heavy through Birmingham, Spaghetti Junction a nightmare. There had been talk of a Birmingham by-pass, apparently the M6 was carrying far more vehicles than it was designed for. It certainly was that night. Even so, I would not be going straight home. It wouldn't be home without Jack, so I would stop at Huw's place and pick him up.

I rang the Huw's doorbell and was surprised to find it opened by a young woman.

You must be Kay,' she said pleasantly, 'Do come in, there's someone here who'll be very pleased to see you.' Jack emerged from the interior, out of control with delight. I was calming him down as Huw introduced his wife.

'Kay, this is Ffion. She's on holiday from the Peace Camp at Greenham Common.'

His designation of her visit as a "holiday" said much, the irony did not pass unnoticed.

Ffion regarded me with a smile. A small dark-haired woman, with huge soft grey eyes encircled by heavy, black-rimmed spectacles.

'I'm glad to meet you,' she said, 'can we get you a drink or something to eat?'

I was taken aback by her instant friendliness. It was obvious that she did not regard me as an interloper in her marriage. How she regarded me was a puzzle, as was my take on her – a quick revision of assumptions and prejudice was needed on my part.

'It's nice to meet you, Ffion,' I replied. But it's way past my bedtime now, I'd be very glad if you could call for a chat some time, if you're not going back straight away. There's a lot I'd like to ask you about the peace movement, if you're happy to talk about it.'

'I'm going back tomorrow,' she said, 'but I could call in on the way.'

I was pleased, as I wanted to know more about the cause that she now followed, and for which she had left Huw.

He looked on during our brief exchange, seeming a little lost. I said goodnight, thanking him for his care of Jack while I was away.

Home again, midnight. The river bright in the moonlight. I promised myself that on one clear night I would walk to its banks, to see for myself if there was an image of the full moon on its surface, but I would have to be in exactly the right place. I thought of the moon's waterless Sea of Tranquillity, its reflection in the river rippling in imitation of Earth's real oceans.

Ffion called next morning. She started talking while I made coffee.

'You probably weren't aware,' she said, 'that it all started here in Wales. We were so alarmed about the government's decision to site American nuclear missiles on British soil, that we formed a protest group. It was called "Women for Life on Earth" and we took it to Greenham Common, where the site was being established, to make our voices heard. The name has gone, but we are now part of a larger movement for peace. It is becoming more widely known and more successful as time goes on. It's *so* important.' She looked at me, hoping, I suspected, that she might find another recruit.

'I'm with you on its importance.'

'But not with us in your presence.'

'No. I know myself well enough to realise I would be a hindrance. Even with the best of intentions.'

'I can understand that! A life of protest doesn't suit everyone. Living is not easy there, we have no facilities, no water, no electricity, no shelter other than what we build ourselves.'

My mental picture of Huw's wife had changed. A nice woman, I thought; we could have been friends if she had simply been a neighbour, her social conscience buried under the layers of convention that our times had imposed on us all. However, there was one thing I needed to say.

'I think Huw misses you.'

She frowned. 'What I do is bigger than the relationship between two people,' she said. 'And it has other implications. It is a feminist movement. It's something we do for the women of the world, as well as for our children. I'm sorry if Huw feels abandoned, but he should make an attempt to understand our motivation.'

'I think he does,' I replied. 'But it's not just that he feels abandoned. He *is* abandoned. What is he supposed to do? Join you all at Greenham?'

Ffion laughed. 'Wouldn't be allowed,' she said. 'We don't have men there. Not even sympathetic ones!'

'Don't you miss him?' I asked her.

My life has changed,' she said, 'he is part of my old life. I can't afford to waste my energy on futile regrets, I have too much to do.'

She talked more, I listened. Some good sense, I thought. And the question came into my head, can good sense be the enemy of love?

'Huw has told me that you have been very kind to him. Encouraging his interest in philosophy, suggesting how he might take it further. I think that your suggestion of a degree course with the O.U. is an excellent one.'

'It will help to focus his mind,' I said. 'At the moment his reading is too random and diverse, he needs guidance in this area. But he has energy and persistence, as well as curiosity about the nature of the problems that we all think about. He'll do well.'

She gave me a quizzical smile, offering no further comment on Huw.

'I must get on my way,' she said, 'there's so much to be done.'

I wondered what it was, since most of what the campaigners did was locate themselves in places which would cause greatest inconvenience to the authorities. But I supposed that such a choice of action might require planning and discussion.

'Do you have much difference in opinion?' I asked her. 'About the choices you have all made, the best way of achieving your goals, about the minutiae of daily life in those primitive conditions? Do you *argue* about what you are doing, what to do next? You all run some risk to yourselves in your actions. Take it all too far, and you may find yourselves arrested, stopped from the very activities that are so important to you.'

Ffion laughed. 'We're human beings,' she said, 'we disagree all the time! But we're sisters too, and mothers.'

But not wives, I thought. Ffion said goodbye to me, a small woman dwarfed by her huge rucksack, refusing a lift, walking to the nearest bus stop.

I spent the rest of the morning thinking about Ffion, about the Peace Camps, about Huw, about what he really wanted from his life. Did he see me as a replacement for Ffion? Did I see him as a replacement for Selwyn?

Jack and I took the car westward in the afternoon, to that distant line of hills that Selwyn and Huw knew so well. Past a remote village or two, the road petered out into a wide but steep-sided valley. We walked along a track that started gently, with a stile or two which provided a problem for Jack, till he found gaps he could scramble through. The track went forever upwards, sheep scattering to our right and left. We left the scrub and the bracken, moved on to peat and rock – this was obviously a mountain, but I could see no top to it. I wasn't going back now, I was enjoying myself. The track wound between rocky outcrops, sometimes over them. Jack was less enamoured, his paws finding little purchase on the smooth boulders. I managed the more vertical rocks with their useful little cracks and protruding handholds, hands and feet working nicely together. Poor Jack whined anxiously when he couldn't follow; once or twice I had to retrace my steps to find a route that was easier for him.

Quite suddenly, the summit appeared, no longer hidden by the convex shape of the mountain. There was a ridge in front of me that led almost immediately to the peak, crowned with a cairn. Surprised and pleased to have arrived at the top, I placed another rock on the pile, in the tradition of summiteers. I looked at the view, on one side a vista of ridge on ridge, bleak hilltops as far as I could see, on the other the thin blue line of an estuary, widening in the far distance, approaching its final exit to the sea. I had walked without map or compass, with no idea where we were. But it was surely Heaven. I took a deep lungful of the crisp, holy air, it permeated my body till my fingers tingled.

We left the summit. At least I'd had enough sense to note a few landmarks on the way up, had turned round one or twice so that I could recognise our route on the journey back. One brief moment of uncertainty, but I followed Jack's preferred way, and he was right, of course. The sky was darkening, I hastened my steps, I was wearing jeans and tee-shirt, fine for a stiff climb on a fine autumn day. I felt a few spots of rain. I could see the car a minute or so away. We ran the last few hundred yards, wet and without mishap, but I spoke to Jack seriously.

'Your mistress is an idiot, Jack,' I told him, 'Don't ever let her do that again.'

The unaccustomed exercise put me to sleep during a writing session later in the evening. I went to bed in a pleasant cloud of stiff legs and a sense of accomplishment. After breakfast next morning I wandered into my paddock to pick some early blackberries for bramble jelly. Selwyn was there, kicking at some molehills that had emerged recently, I would have liked to tell him to stop – I could use that lovely soil for potting. But I did tell him about my expedition the day before, unplanned, I added, an impulse that turned into an unexpected achievement. I had climbed one of his beloved Berwyns.

I told him. he seemed angry.

'I'd have thought you had more sense! To go out walking in the mountains, without telling anyone where you were going. To go without waterproofs, without proper boots, without a map, a compass, without food, without ordinary common sense! What on earth did you think you were playing at?'

'I didn't have to tell you. I knew you'd scold me.'

'What you do matters to me.'

What was I hearing? A fleeting moment of joy, surely at last an admission that I wasn't just a neighbour, a friend, someone he felt it his duty to keep an eye on. I held my breath. We were in my paddock, the place that we both owned, in a sense, as although it belonged to me, I had let him use it as he wanted, a shared amenity, shared home ground. He swiped angrily at a thistle.

'These need cutting.'

Close to tears, I turned my back on him.

'Cut them then.'

I walked away from him, back to the house.

Why did these moments of anger, of stupidity, keep on happening? Not even a lovers' tiff, for we were not lovers. Fuck him, I thought, let him go his own way, lead his own life, we are not suited. If we cannot get on at arm's length, how could we hope to do so under the same roof?

At least the book was going well. My conversation with Bethan had been a catalyst for the first serious work I had been hoping to do since the move to Britain.

We had talked of the changing fortunes of the British and the various invaders from the east, from western Europe, from Saxony, from Norway, from Jutland. We had considered how far these forces had penetrated Britain, how the areas occupied had fluctuated, how the native British had fought for the land they had regained since the departure of the Romans. Maybe, they thought -if they had known anything beyond their own areas – maybe these strange tall people will get fed up and go away.

I could write about what might have happened if the invaders had in fact been driven back from our western kingdoms of Llewelyn and Hywel Dda. and finished up much further east. Still with a foothold in our island, but without the power of rule.

The story would explore the lives of the Welsh and the English if their roles had been reversed, that the English were the minority people in the British nation. Not just at the time of the battles of the Dark Ages, but today, in 1980.

The ideas were coming, I remembered and recognised the feeling, like a plunge into icy water, sharp, almost painful, exhilarating, a birth. The characters were storming the gates, each determined to fight their way on to the pages that were emerging in front of me. One at a time, I told them, you'll all get your chance. I counted my blessings; Selwyn was not one of them.

Laura was, though, I relished her rapid development.

'She's more than ready for school,' I commented to Ellen.

'She's starting next term.'

'It's a fair distance to Newfield. Will you walk with her?'

'As far as the main road. A man I work for has got a child who's starting the same time as Laura. He'll pick her up in the car.'

I was both relieved and worried. I knew teachers were trained to look out for problems at home. I wondered how many of Laura's would be visible in the context of school. No exciting trips to report, no summer holidays by the sea, no television programmes to talk about with her classmates. All she would bring of value would be the ability to read beyond her years. She would come to see the difference between her background and that of others. As I had to, growing up without a mother's love.

I had sensed in her an energy, flexibility, a determination that would serve her well in those difficult school years. Ellen didn't like dogs, disliked Jack in particular, feared for the safety of her grandchild. Wisely, she didn't voice these fears to Laura, but discouraged her from getting close, on the grounds of contamination from his unruly coat that shed hairs, I had to admit, all over the place. Laura soon discovered the brush I used every day, and her first act on arrival was to vigorously groom him. She was unafraid, and her arm was often round his gentle head. The relationship between them flourished. Sometimes, when they were playing together, she looked at her grandmother and smiled. A small triumph for her. She would survive the hazards of school, I was sure.

I had an encounter with Gareth, who I discovered in my yard one day, clutching a piece of paper.

'This is from Dad. I didn't want to put it through your letter box, in case you just put on a pile somewhere. It's a bill. You didn't pay for your last batch of logs.'

'Yes. Your father told me he would send a bill. I was expecting it.'

Why did he have to refer to the situation in terms that suggested I was at fault?

'I'll fetch my cheque book.'

I glanced at the invoice; something caught my eye. I made out the cheque and handed it to him.

'The name on the bill is right, but the address is wrong. The name of my house is "The Cottage."'

My visitor looked sullen.

'If you keep changing the names of places, you can't expect people who have lived here all their lives to remember what you want to change them to.'

'I haven't changed anything. 'The Cottage' was the name of the house when I bought it.'

'Well, the people you bought it from changed it. They were English too.'

'For heaven's sake, Gareth, you can't blame me for that!'

He shrugged. 'It's what the English do.'

He turned and walked away. His discourtesy was insufferable. And yet…I went after him.

'Gareth!' He turned. 'I understand what you're saying. I know you would have liked to buy this house. But I didn't know any of this before I came. And even if I had, it would have made no difference. The original owner was no doubt Welsh, but at some point the house was sold to an English person. The seller was Welsh, but he was also a human being.

Would you expect him to refuse the highest offer that was made because it was made by an English person? Shouldn't you be blaming the seller for taking the best price he could get? You are being unreasonable as well as unfriendly.'

He turned away once more. I felt cross. But I couldn't deny that, as far as the name changes were concerned, he had a point. Wherever in the world they happen to be, incomers should respect the society they move into. You can buy a house; you can make changes to it. You cannot buy and change its history.

I looked at the bill for the last delivery of logs, which had caused all the trouble. The name of my house was rendered by two words which I could not say, even in my head.

"Tyddyn Amlwg"

I resolved to find out its meaning, learn to say it correctly, and then consider whether I should give the name back to the old house.

My next chance meeting with Selwyn was many weeks later. I was sitting in the paddock, on the grass. He had cut the thistles.

'Hello' he said. I thought how our frequent misunderstandings never carried over to the next meeting. We resumed conventional greetings easily, on the surface at least.

'Hello. I've got a job for you. Would you translate a name for me? I've written it down, I don't know how to say it. It's the old name of my house.'

I handed him the scrap of paper. He smiled. 'It's quite a common name. Given to a cottage or a smallholding in a fairly prominent position.'

'Well, The Cottage is not a *small* cottage.'

'It's not the first dwelling that's been built on this site. Your Victorian house would have been a replacement for an older building, probably stone, maybe timber framed. And it's situated on a bit of high ground, you can see it from quite far away.'

I'm thinking of giving its old name back.'

'That would be a nice gesture.'

No mention of our last meeting. We chatted for a few minutes, it started to rain again, nature determined to limit our chance encounters. He departed.

I turned back to the house. 'Tyddyn Amlwg'. The name looked formidable, but fortunately all the sounds were those found in English speech, so there should be no difficulty in learning to say them. I liked the idea. I could think of others who would, too. The name would frighten a few English speakers. Many of them were used to Welsh names, and could speak them quite happily. Some would be as cross as Gareth was, and refuse to let go of 'The Cottage'. There would certainly be some confusion. I disliked cutting links with the history of a place, it seemed to me like losing a part of its structure and its personality. Selwyn would be pleased, of course, but once I had mastered the pronunciation, and everyone had got used to it, the new name would make little difference to the world.

TWENTY-FOUR

Newfield, September, 1980

The wind was rising, hurling the rain like gravel against the windows, keeping me awake. It was almost midnight when Jack woke up. The alarms were sounding. I tumbled out of bed, grabbed a robe, and went downstairs to the now familiar symphony of Jack's repertoire of reactive fury. He was at the door, vocalising enthusiastically, but not in house guard mode. His tail was wagging. I turned off the alarms, drew back the bolts, and opened the door. The rain and wind erupted into the hall, ferocious as an animal. Selwyn stepped inside, his waterproof jacket streaming with water, making a significant puddle on the slate floor. With difficulty he closed the door.

Yet another close, unconventional meeting – me at my worst, straight out of bed, dishevelled but not unduly embarrassed, I hoped.

I tied my belt closer, trying to look calm and dignified.

With a sodden sleeve, Selwyn wiped the rain from his face.

'Sorry to wake you, Kay, but I think we have a crisis on our hands.'

'What's happened? Are you alright?'

'My place is O.K., but the river's broken its banks. I could see it coming all day. I didn't want to go to bed – I'm worried about the caravans. I met someone from the site who had decided to move out today, he was expecting a flood. I thought maybe we ought to offer to help Ellen and her family move somewhere safer – I don't mind putting them up for the night, but I thought – as she knows you – she'd be more willing to come here. It would be familiar and more comfortable for them.'

'O.K. Give me a minute to dress. I'll be right back.' He called after me 'You'll need waterproofs and wellingtons!'

Pulling on my warmest clothes, I heard the storm raging round the house, looking for a way in. Shall I be able to stand up in that? Downstairs again, I put on a confident face and braced myself for a battle with the animal outside.

Ready for another blast, Selwyn opened the front door, holding my arm to steady me, and together we managed to cross the few yards to the car. We set off, temporarily sheltered from the outside fury, and turned into the small lane that led towards the caravan site. Twigs torn from their branches battered the windscreen, wipers barely able to cope. The storm had scattered debris over the road, rivulets were running down each side, ditches overflowing. We parked the car by the site entrance.

Lights were on at the office, but few coming from the vans themselves. Two people were leaving the site, struggling in the storm with bags of belongings. As they passed our car Selwyn half opened the door, and asked them, shouting above the wind, if they had any information about river levels, was the site in any danger? Had anyone phoned the police, was any help coming for people who needed it? They didn't know, were keen to get away.

We parked the car and left it, tried the reception area; a phone was ringing in the empty room. Selwyn turned to me.

'Looks like we're not going to get any information. we'd better go and find the van ourselves. You up for it Kay? I've no idea whereabouts their van is.'

'Of course', I said defensively, 'I've got my storm legs now. I'll be fine.' Back out into the wind and rain, we moved between the caravans, not speaking, the roaring of the wind making impossible any attempt at conversation. I thought of my last visit to the place, remembering how close to the river it was. Surely they must be preparing to leave.

The rising water was silent. I imagined how, freed from its banks, the river would find little in the way of obstruction, nothing to prevent the furtive spreading of its waters across fields and tracks, through hedges, over pastures, round trees, under fences, an explorer investigating unknown territory, a new world.

Selwyn spoke to me, I couldn't hear him. Just ahead of me, he'd stepped into water. Sloshing around our ankles at first, it crept up our wellington boots to levels that threatened inundation. I couldn't see the van we were looking for, must be still further on, downhill, in deeper water. Then came the sensation I knew I'd feel, sooner or later, the first icy overspill into my boots. Selwyn's wellingtons, I guessed, would give him another couple of inches of protection.

The water deepened, and I began to feel a touch of its power, a swirl that caused me a momentary loss of balance. I stumbled and righted myself. He has the advantage of another ten inches of height, I thought, he will keep going further than I can.

Passing dark, deserted vans, Selwyn bent his head as he tried to make me hear his words above the noise of the storm.

'Are you sure we're in the right area? Can't see any more vans ahead. Are you O.K. to go on a bit further?'

'Yes. I'll tell you if I can't.' We were halted by a sudden increase in the depth of water.

'The ground's not level here, would you like a hand?'

Yes I would, I thought to myself, but I can manage without. Ask me when the sun's shining. When you want to, not when you have to.

'I'm O.K. '

The caravan we were looking for was, I remembered, set apart from the others. When I had visited it, I'd wondered if it had been set aside for renovation, or simply because it was not up to the standard of the rest. No doubt cheaper to rent than the other ones, and an opportunity for a desperate home-seeker.

My wellington boots were now hindering my progress, both had filled with water. I felt unsteady, afraid I wouldn't be able to keep up. Shall I tell him when I can't go on? I'm not entirely useless, though, without me he wouldn't know where Ellen's van was located. A couple of steps in front of me, he looked back, I waved him on. I wished I were bigger, stronger, more confident.

I kept my torch focussed on his tall figure as he moved further ahead of me, and I began to feel the movement of the current. How cold it felt as it carried away my body's warmth. We had passed the main body of vans, and all we could see from the illumination of Selwyn's torch were small trees and bushes, all bending eastward in response to the driving wind.

'Is that it?' I felt, rather than heard his question.

I saw the caravan's walls beyond the bushes and brushed the rain from my eyes as the image seemed to waver. Selwyn turned towards me, cupping his hands to help the words travel.

'Stay there' he shouted, 'Don't go any further. I can see the van straight ahead. I think there's a light in it.'

I shone my own torch on his retreating figure silhouetted against the vehicle's side, realising that against Selwyn's steady upright shape, the van itself seemed to be rocking. He was searching for the steps. Rickety, as I remembered them, unsafe at the best of times. I heard his voice, but the words were carried away in the angry spitting wind. He was shouting, banging on the door. I knew I had reached the bounds of my usefulness, that he was stronger than me, and his extra height vital in the rising flood. If I moved towards him I would become a liability.

A feeble light was coming from the van, I thought I heard Ellen's voice. Why didn't she open the door? With Selwyn there, she should realise that help was at hand, no time should be wasted. As far as I could see in the light of Selwyn's torch, the door was still closed. Was Ellen refusing to leave? More banging, shouted words, then nothing, no sound but the intermittent fury of the wind gusting past and the steady accompaniment of moving water. For the moment I lost sight of Selwyn. I was alone in a nightmare of a cold wet element that threatened to unnerve me. *I will not panic.* The best thing I can do to help Selwyn is nothing. An easy solution. I'll be here where he left me, as long as I'm physically capable of standing.

I waited, aware that water levels were still rising. I moved my feet apart, to steady myself, wishing I'd brought a stick. Was that a faint light showing at a window? With heart-stopping relief, Selwyn was in sight again, moving towards it. I focussed my torch on his unsteady, erratic movements. The fanlight window was opening. and something, a large package, being pushed through it. Did they want to save some possessions? It was taken by Selwyn, who stepped out of my sight again. A few seconds, and there he was again, making his way slowly and carefully back to me. The bundle was Laura.

'Take her!' he shouted. 'The door's locked and Ellen can't find the key, can't get the mother out of bed. I've got to get them away somehow.' He turned back.

I took the child, clasping her over my shoulder with one hand, the other gripping the torch. I spoke a few words of comfort to her. Her head was close to mine, she could, I hoped, hear my words.

'It's Kay, Laura. I'm going to carry you up to the car. The water's too deep for you to walk. Don't worry, we'll be fine.'

'Gran'ma comin'?'

'As soon as she can.'

Adjusting my balance to the new weight, I turned my back on Selwyn's retreating figure, the rain mingling with my tears. I tried to see through the darkness for any light, any point I could focus on, to keep myself on a straight path up to higher ground.

I had lost all sense of direction. My first steps were taken with only the hope that in walking away from Selwyn I was retracing the route we had followed to reach the van. Burdened by the weight of the child, every step was hard work, harder than any step I had ever taken. Uphill, I thought, that's the only help I've got. Must make every step an uphill one. Concentrating my undisciplined mind, which, left to itself, was away with unrelated matters, anywhere to escape the nightmare of the moment, I sought to establish a pattern of words and movements. Each step needed a pause of seconds for me to regain my balance, and a conscious decision before venturing on to the next. Step, pause, rebalance, steady, step, pause, rebalance…a mantra to go with the movements that were keeping me on my feet, covering, inch by inch, the rising ground I knew lay between us and safety.

Step, pause, rebalance… the completion of each element a small success. Step, pause, rebalance… how long has this been going on? How will Selwyn manage when he gets the others out? Step, pause, balance... The child is so heavy. I shall not drop her, but I could trip or lose confidence and fall. Another step, pause, balance ... step, what if I can't do this? Christ, she seems so heavy. Step, pause, rebalance, wait, the water isn't so deep here. Another step, uphill, it's harder going but the water's a bit shallower, wish I could empty my boots. That last step seemed easier, try again, step, pause, yes, I managed that one better. Was that a light ahead? Step, yes, easier, less resistance from the water, step, another step, no need to rebalance this time, two continuous movements without a pause between them. More steps and now surely that *is* a light!

I tried to clear the rain from my eyes with the hand holding the torch and dropped it. I looked at it through the water below me; for a few seconds the light shone beneath the surface, illuminating a green theatre of plant life dancing in rhythm with the new medium, its surface pitted with the still falling rain. I couldn't bend down to pick it up. The brief drama vanished, I raised my eyes and found what I had been desperately looking for – a distant light that I could focus on, step by step, leading me to the site entrance, to people, to safety.

I spoke a few words to Laura, who was crying now, and struggling, I suppose, to look for a comfortable position, standing on her own feet.

Freed from the torch, I could now use both hands to hold her. If I can get to the lights, there'll be people there, surely they will have come to help, they know how near the river the place is…the child's weight was beginning to strain the muscles of my arm, sending a sharp shooting pain through to my neck.

I shifted her to the other shoulder, still keeping to the pattern of movement that had got me to within sight of help. Moving on, moving on. I wanted to turn round, to see if any light from Selwyn's torch was still visible, but dared not. With the child on my shoulder, I mustn't lose my precious balance. Voices now, and blessed lights. Another step – I was out of the water.

'I'm going to put you down, Laura, just for a moment. Just while I get my breath – what a heavy girl you are. We're going to the car first, while Selwyn helps your Mum and Grandma. Then we'll all go to my house for the night. There, now I'll carry you again, till we get to the car.'

I picked up the child again, wearied beyond imagination, but the worst was over, the tiredness, the pain would pass. I started walking again, slow, but with the lights growing clearer, brighter with every step. I lurched forward, but righted myself, still on my feet as I neared the brightness. I made for the group I saw gathering by the site entrance, lit by the headlights of two police cars, and, with its engine running, a tractor. That's what we should have had, I thought, high and safe above the water.

People were moving between vans, shouting, and banging on the sides. A policewoman approached us. Still holding the child, I called to her -

'Please send help down towards the river – there are people in the bottom van, please go quickly, the water's still rising…'

Pointing back towards the blackness, I said again, afraid that my voice would fail, 'Please will someone go and help them! The water's so deep there…please, they need help…'

'Let me take the child' a voice spoke to me and an arm steadied my erratic movements.

'No, I mustn't let her go, she knows me, she'll be frightened…' I clung to the little girl, hardly realising that we were safe, knowing only that I would not let anyone take her from me. 'It's the others …' The policewoman shouted to the group, then turned back to me.

'People are going now, look – they've got a tractor starting up and it'll soon be on the way, with good lights, they'll soon have everyone back here and safe.' She gently took my arm and guided me towards a police car. 'Are you from one of the vans?'

'No, I live in Newfield. We came to help a friend. We've got a car here somewhere, but I must leave it for Selwyn...' Is there somewhere we can sit down and wait?' I wondered if I was making sense.

'I'll run you home, you can't hang about in those wet clothes with that little girl. Don't worry, we'll soon have you and your daughter warm and dry...'

She's not...' but my voice faltered, and what did explanations matter? Letting us be ushered carefully into one of the cars, pulling the child close and putting an arm around her, I comforted the wet and frightened child.

'Soon be home, sweetheart, Jack will be glad to see us.'

I talked the driver through the wind, the rain and the darkness till we came to my house. I eased myself out of the car. I would make a bed for Laura on the sofa in the kitchen. The policewoman was helping me step out of the car. I turned and gathered up Laura for our last few steps towards the house. The mantra echoed in my mind, step, pause...but we were home now.

'Please go back' I said to the policewoman, 'I'm sure they need as many people as possible. I'm really perfectly all right. I'll switch on fires and make a hot drink... '

The policewoman looked doubtful.

'If you're certain you don't need a hand. Please get out of those wet clothes before you do anything else.' She glanced at Jack who had barely recognised a stranger. 'I'm sure I've seen that dog somewhere before.'

'Thank you for bringing me home.'

A brief touch, and she was gone. I started organising what needed to be done without dwelling on the night's events and its yet unknown consequences. The thinking would come later, breaking into my rest for many a day and night.

Getting us both dry and warm, comforting Laura as best I could, putting together a makeshift bed on the kitchen sofa, kept me occupied until I could sit with the now sleeping child, waiting for Selwyn. I looked at her, she's like me, I thought, missing a mother's love. But I had my father, and she has her grandmother, the love of both rock stable. She's small for her age, as I had been. Lucky for her, less so for me. It had been hard, but I had carried her, as the pain in my shoulder still testified. Did Selwyn realise how nearly impossible it had been? I closed my eyes, but saw again the dark moving water, felt the sharp shards of rain against my cheek, faced the threat I had refused to think about. I knew it now and trembled. I closed my eyes to feel the comfort of my kitchen, the sound and smell of the sleeping dog, and the touch of the child to whom I felt so close. I tucked her hand beneath the blanket that covered her. I thought about Selwyn, and how he could cope with the situation I had left. He would be focussed on getting access to the locked van, could he find a means to break into it? Smash the main window perhaps? Brave and resourceful, he would surely think of something. But I knew too, that speed was vital, the van had started to rock in the rising waters, sooner or later it would become buoyant, it could start to move downstream.

I glanced at my watch. Half-past-four. Would Selwyn bring them back here or take them to his own house, which was nearer? Ellen would not rest without knowing that Laura was safe, they will surely come here. Sluggish and comatose, Laura's mother would be a hindrance that would endanger all three of them. He couldn't manage the rescue of both women without help. I knew that there had been trouble with the key before. Laura's mother had often locked the caravan, to prevent her child from wandering away while she slept off the effects of whatever she had taken. For one reason or another the door had been locked with Ellen inside, and in the confusion the key had obviously been lost. How aware Ellen would have been of the danger I couldn't know. Fear, anger, darkness, muddle within the van, raging storm without – all playing a part in a delay that could cost them their lives.

I looked at the sleeping child, red hair damply curling across her face. Without Ellen, Laura would be in care. I didn't even try to sleep. I listened for the sound of a car, went to the door, thinking I heard it, but there was nothing but wind and rain. Indoors a sleeping child, a sleeping dog, and three missing persons. I looked at my watch, half past five. Should be getting light soon, in normal weather, but the clouds were still thick and heavy, though the rain had stopped. I knew that it often took days for flood waters to recede, the volume of water from the mountain streams would take time to work its way downriver, things were likely to get worse in the short term.

Laura was stirring. She sat up, looking around her.

'Where's Gran'ma?'

'Not sure, love. Remember last night? All the wind and rain? Selwyn was helping her get out of the van. We came straight here because we couldn't help him. The water was very deep.'

'Where's Jack?'

'He's gone to the door. Look, his tail is wagging, I think he knows who's here.'

I opened the door, Selwyn stood there, a sodden figure, his face dark, weary, hopeless. I knew what he was going to tell me. He stepped inside.

'Laura?'

'She's O.K. The others?'

We were both silent for a moment.

'I don't know. Couldn't get them out.'

'D'you want to tell me about it?'

'Yes. You need to know what happened.'

He leaned tiredly against the wall.

'Come in the kitchen and sit down. I'll make you a hot drink.'

He ignored the invitation.

'I'd felt the van shifting when I took the child and brought her to you. When I got back it had moved. The only way out for them was through a main window, it was worth a try. Easy enough to get Laura out through the fanlight, impossible for an adult to follow her. After you'd taken her I tried to get them to come to one of the main windows...Maybe we'd have managed somehow...but it was hard to get Ellen to tell me what the problems were...I don't know if Laura's mother was awake or conscious. Ellen kept asking me if Laura was safe. I told her, yes, yes, she's with Kay, she'll be all right, but she seemed to give up at that point. The van was shifting all the time and I was holding on to a tree branch to keep my balance. I could have wept with fury and frustration. I shone my torch on the window – Ellen was struggling with it – probably stuck, never opened before, I might have been able to break it, if I could've found anything to use... she could have broken it from inside, I didn't know whether to stay as long as I could or go back for help.'

Selwyn covered his face for a moment. I took his arm, wanting him to come into the kitchen, but he stood, still talking, still living through the night's events.

'I watched the van shifting in the water. If we could have opened the door and let some water in, it could have stabilised for a bit, but as it was, it was too buoyant, starting to drift out of my reach. I knew you'd send help as soon as you reached the lights. I waited till the police came but by then the van was out of sight and they'd have needed a boat to look for it. Their lights scanned the water as far as they could see, but there was no sign of it. They said there was nothing more they could do until daylight. They phoned the police and fire brigades down river on both sides, to look out for a drifting van. If it had reached mid-river it could have been carried away quite fast. They told me there's a good chance that it's caught up somewhere. ...I don't know.'

I looked at my wet, exhausted visitor.

'Come in Selwyn. I can find you some of Dad's clothes, at least get dry and warm, have a hot drink. Come into the kitchen.'

He shook his head. 'I'd best be going home.'

'Come in, you fucking idiot!'

He shook his head. 'I'd rather go home. I'll give you a call later. I'll keep in touch. Let you know when I hear anything. 'Bye Kay.'

I held back threatening tears, I wouldn't weep, it could have kept him there.

TWENTY-FIVE

Newfield, September 1980

The caravan was found next day on its side, half-a-mile downriver. The door was off its hinges, the body of one woman still in the van, the other in the river. The news was brought to me by the policewoman, who had called shortly after Selwyn left.

'I was worried about leaving you after such a traumatic experience. You were so wet and cold, and there was no-one at home to help you with the little girl. But I could see that your main anxiety at that point was that the people in the caravan needed help more than you did. You were right, of course, but … it was too late.'

'Can you tell me what happened when you got back to the site?'

'People had already gone to help, but it was difficult as we didn't know exactly where this caravan was located, and it had already drifted downstream. We found your friend who said he had tried, but couldn't get the people out. Now it was out of reach and out of sight. Poor man, he was up to his waist in water, said the van was locked on the inside and that the occupants couldn't find the key. We were glad to get him out of the water and on board with us. At one point we thought we wouldn't be able to find him, let alone the van.'

'He called on his way home and told me what had happened.'

'We're trying to locate the owner of the site, but just now there are so many other things to be done. One other person is missing. We don't know yet the full extent of the flood, people say it's happened once before.'

'Well, thank you for calling. We're both all right this morning, but the little girl doesn't realise she's lost her mother.'

The policewoman looked startled. 'She's not yours, then? You're not her mother?'

'No, but she knows me very well. I'll keep her here for the time being, until decisions are made about where she can go.'

'Well, I suppose the situation will have to be reported to the social services. Thank you for looking after her for the time being, it's the best thing for her.'

The policewoman left. I now had to come to terms with the knowledge, half expected, that Ellen was dead. I felt sadness, a kind of generalised sorrow for the disasters that befall human beings across the world, but not grief. I hadn't liked her; she had never made me feel anything but irritated and often uneasy. In spite of her strange moods, I was always aware of her devoted love for Laura, and forgave her much on that account. I accepted that her death would bring a whole new aspect to our situation, mine and Laura's, but I couldn't think about that now, everything was too recent, too close.

Laura was still asleep on the kitchen sofa.

The phone rang.

'Kay, Bill Powell here. I have heard your news from Selwyn.

He rang to tell me about the extent of the flood, so that I could keep an eye on Melanie.'

'Yes, we both had a difficult night. As did many other people. The village is O.K. I suppose, it's well above the river. Have you heard if there are any other casualties?'

'One person missing, I believe. Others found safe but with nowhere to go. We've decided to open the church as a temporary refuge. We can provide mattresses, food and some warmth. Not as much of that as we should like, though. Heating a church is expensive, and people have to wrap up when they come to services. Church members are organising everything, as competently as they always do. Will you tell anyone you think might need food and shelter, or knows someone who might? And what about you, Kay? We always think of you, Jane and I, as someone so efficient and sensible, that you never need help from others.'

'Well, I don't know about that, Bill, but I'm grateful to you both for at least thinking about me.'

'We do, Kay, and we pray for you.'

Days passed in a haze of phone calls, police interrogation, and caring for a bereaved child, though she did not yet know that her mother and grandmother were lost. I decided that the knowledge must be introduced gradually, at some point that felt right. She was just staying with me and Jack for a while, I told her.

She has enough to cope with, I told the visiting agencies, she knows me, has been here often, she will feel better here than anywhere else. Give her time to adjust, I'll keep in touch, just leave her here for the time being.

They didn't argue. At an appropriate time, I would tell Laura the truth, as gently as I could, that her mother and grandmother have both died, that it was sad, but accidents happen.

There would be an inquest, of course. Questions would be asked, particularly about the caravan site, its proximity to the river, flood risk. People remembered another flood, many years ago, but were vague about how far it had reached. In this part of the world the lucrative development of sites for mobile homes and holiday vans had taken place comparatively recently. Ellen couldn't have afforded to be too fussy about the precise location of the van she rented. A day or two passed in which the child seemed to want little other than to play with Jack.

She appeared at my study door. 'Gran'ma comin' soon?'

'No, love. You're going to stay here with me for a while. Shall we go for a walk with Jack?'

She took my reply with equanimity. I wasn't noticeably upset, so she would see no reason why she should be.

Her obvious delight at the suggestion of a walk cheered me. She will be able to take the change in her daily life without turmoil, I hoped, for the time being at least. Ellen was the only bright spot in her childhood, there would have been nothing else and no-one else for her to miss. She was not worried about the absence of her grandmother just now. I will see how she reacts as the days pass, wait for her questions, but try to keep her interested and occupied.

We took our walk, well away from the river. The flood waters had largely receded, the Severn high but contained within its banks. Some low-lying areas were still under water; come the spring we would see the consequences of the sediments deposited on the fields, becoming the fine grasslands that feed the rich farmers' cattle.

A couple of uneventful days went by before I saw Selwyn again. He telephoned me, we arranged that he should call at the Cottage after lunch. I hoped Laura would amuse herself quietly.

He looked tired. Farming activities didn't cease in times of tragedies, crises, unlooked-for responsibilities.

'I am glad to see you, Selwyn. Our last meeting was not one I shall easily forget.'

'Yes.'

He wandered uneasily around the hall. Sat down on the bottom stair. The chair by the small table that housed the telephone gave me a good view through to the kitchen where Laura was playing at the kitchen table. I waited for him to talk.

'There is a great deal of the past couple of years that I shall not forget. But Kay, I should have said this last time. You … did well. No, magnificently. It was a great deal harder for you than for me. To carry a child through all that water Not many women could have done it.'

'There was no alternative. I just focussed on staying on my feet.'

'Which is something you always do.' You are a remarkable woman, Kay.'

I don't want to be admired, but I would like to be loved. We have such an odd relationship. He crops up in my life, at moments of crisis, seeming to look out for me, seeming to want a role, but keeping a fixed distance between us. An occasional friendly hug would be nice, a pass would be even more welcome. What the hell does he want?

'I have been thinking about how all this will be resolved. Are you managing the care of Laura? Your life must be disrupted.'

'It is. But I can cope for now. I hardly dare think about the future, I tell myself that I must make each day as trouble-free as I can, for Laura's sake. She is not a difficult child; she is a self-sufficient being. Sometimes reminds me of myself at that age. Things could be worse. What about you?'

'No consequences from the flood, I had already moved the sheep. We shall be back to normal soon. But the world has shifted a bit. You've had a tough time, Kay. If you feel the need to talk, any time, I'm not far away.'

He rose from his seat at the bottom of the stairs and wandered round the hall.

Why did Selwyn always manage to arouse my resentment and bad temper in our conversations? Never lasting, never lessening my fondness for him. But regularly provoking me to respond.

'But you *are*, Selwyn, you are far away *all* the time. What are you afraid of? That we should become too close for comfort? For *your* comfort?'

He was silent for a moment, not looking at me.

'I know. There are reasons, Kay, some you know about, or can guess, others you don't. One thing you don't know is the time I have spent thinking about you. About the possibilities of things between us being different. Of the possibilities of a future together.'

At last, he looked directly at me. 'It wouldn't work.'

'And you're not prepared to try?'

'Our priorities are different and become more so as each day passes.'

'Is your life to be ruled by your obsession with the wrongs that your country has suffered?'

'It consumes me, Kay. As the future of your child consumes you.'

'*My* child?'

'Laura. My guess is that you will keep her. One good thing to come out of Ellen's anger, her fear and the disaster that has put an end to her sad existence. We shall never know what went on in her mind, but the one thing that held firm was her love for Laura. That never wavered, as yours never will.'

One thing he was right about. Unkind of the Fates, I thought, to throw me and all my problems into a life that was clearly marked by an obsessional love of country, with an equally obsessional determination to do something about its future.

'I am sorry for you, Selwyn. You have become involved in my life, my problems, through chance, certainly, but you haven't washed your hands of my troubles. I am grateful. *More* than just grateful. But I don't know what I can do to repay you.'

'Nothing. But I shall always think of the woman I knew, honest, direct, loving, brave.'

He was already putting our relationship, such as it was, into the past.

'For me, I have decided to deal with my beliefs and hopes for my country in a quieter and more sensible way than the one I used to take. I can't abandon the cause I have fought for all my life; I can't abandon the friends I have always supported, even when I have disagreed with some of things they did. Things some of us went to prison for. Things *I* went to prison for. You know enough about recent local history to realise what went on. You once told me of a cottage you were searching for. It had disappeared, there was talk of a fire. The fact that I didn't light the match didn't make me any less guilty than the others.

I shall leave the farm here and move back to Welsh-speaking Wales, to the family farm I left so many years ago, when I started joining protests against the sale of Welsh properties to English incomers. I was very young. I did more stupid things than I would care to tell you about.'

'I think I could beat you in that department.' I said, with feeling.

'Political opportunities are opening up for me, I can't tell you what they are at present, but you will get to know in due course. These shall be my priority, yours will be your next books and Laura. There is a chance of happiness for you, content for me, if we are sensible.'

He looked at me directly.

'Don't think, for one moment, that between our meetings I forget about you. All I can say is that a decision to live together would not be sensible, could even be wrong for both of us. We are too different, too far apart, moving in different directions.'

Too far apart. Angry and sad, I could still recognise the ring of truth in his words. Attraction was one thing, compatibility was another. I knew that the future I had been hoping for depended on too many factors, some I recognised, some I guessed, but all involving changes in us both that were not sensible or even right.

He is slipping away from me. I want to hold on to him, to tell him that we should give our relationship, such as it is, a chance. But I can't, and if I could, he would not like me any better for it. There is so much truth in what he says.

'Thank you for coming, Selwyn. This conversation had to happen sooner or later.'

He rose to leave, just as Laura's footsteps announced her presence. How could I think about all that Selwyn has been telling me with a child wanting her tea?

He said goodbye quietly and left.

I would not, *could* not think about what he had said, Laura was waiting for me. I smiled at her. 'Shall we make some pancakes for our tea?'

The day continued its new pattern, I managed to complete one or two of the tasks that came with my new life, Laura played with Jack and reported their conversations to me. Bedtime, story, a kiss, and goodnight. A few hours to myself, time now to deal with our future. *Our* future, mine and Laura's, for they were inextricably bound together.

I thought about having Laura living with me. I had even contemplated this before as a temporary solution to Ellen's fears – having Laura to stay for short periods, while she cleaned up the caravan, organised counselling or some kind of treatment for her daughter, made the necessary arrangements for the child's school. She may well have thought of such an offer as patronising interference in her life, the kind of thing done by people with more money than they know what to do with.

I doubted that she would ever have agreed to such plans. Her fear of losing Laura made her suspicious of any actions by an outsider. I had spoken to one of her other employers, sympathetic to her plight. We had talked of possibilities of help that Ellen would not fiercely reject. I think she was fearful of losing control of their lives. Some of that control might have been lost if they had been living under someone else's roof.

Selwyn was moving away from Newfield. I wondered if he would come and say goodbye. As it happened, our last meeting was unplanned.

Laura had been invited to visit the school she was going to attend. A neighbour with a child of similar age had offered to take her, and bring her back to their house for tea. I had a few hours to myself.

My walk took me, as it often did, back to the few stones that remained of the cottage where my mother and I stayed that night so long ago. I had no wish to encounter Mrs Hayleigh again, so my approach to the place took a different route. I walked as far as the stones and sat down to watch Jack pottering among the rubble. I heard Selwyn's voice.

'A bit of history we share!'

I hadn't noticed him arrive.

'*You* spent one night here,' he said. 'And years later *I* did nothing to stop the fire that was being lit.'

'Not by you.'

'It makes no difference. We were doing something for Wales, warning off the foreigners who were taking over our country. I think I felt a sense of regret that others were braver, had more initiative, and fewer doubts than I had, but a feeling of relief too. Something was going to be done, but it was not me that had the responsibility for doing it. The courts found us all guilty, and rightly so.'

'Do you have regrets?'

'My life is full of them, Kay. But there is one thing I can do, which is relevant to the situation then and now. I'd like to tell you about it – I think you'll be pleased. Look at this field.'

I looked at it. Neglected, with the remnants of a small cottage, perhaps a smallholding at one time.

'I can buy this field. It has been a long and tortuous journey to the point where I can say that with confidence. When the idea first occurred to me, nobody seemed to know who the land belonged to. It has taken me years of research, consultations with local government authorities, expensive conversations with lawyers, frustration and sheer weariness to arrive at last at this point. But I have success at last. Very shortly the field will be mine.'

'But Selwyn, what on earth do you want it for? You told me you were going to move back to your home area. What are you going to do with – a field, so far from where you are going to live?'

'Keep a few sheep on it! I know someone who'll look after them for me.'

'Who?'

'Gareth. I don't need planning permission to rebuild the cottage, and it will be a lot bigger and better than the old one you remember, the one my group set fire to. Gareth can live in it rent free, for the time being, depending on how he gets on with his forestry work. I know he's looking to expand his timber business.'

I decided to ask him a question that had puzzled me since I learned of Gareth's misfortunes.

'There's something I don't understand. What was stopping

Gareth from getting married and living in his farm with his wife? Presumably he'll inherit it one day.'

'This compromise simply doesn't work. It's a potential disaster, and the farming community recognises this. The new woman has to conform with her mother-in-law's domestic routines, her likes and dislikes. She's expected to help, but can't please herself. How could it be otherwise? The woman who was there first shouldn't be made to feel pushed out by her son's new wife. The son would continue to work for his father, continuing to do what *he* was told. Gareth is already feeling fed up with having no say in how the business is run. He's got lots of ideas he wants to put into practice. He's after independence, and I can't say I blame him. He knows I'm sympathetic to his predicament, and he's keen to come in with me in getting a new house built. It's a small way of righting a wrong, and will satisfy me.'

I could understand how Selwyn felt. You can't always undo wrongs that you have done or been involved in, but you can do something else that will help to restore the moral balance.

I smiled at him.

'I'll watch the progress of the new building with interest, Selwyn. Maybe Gareth will forgive me for buying the house he wanted, and invite Laura and me to tea. You should tell him of the unpleasant woman who lives in one of the bungalows – she knows of your involvement in the fire, and won't miss any opportunity of referring to it.'

'I shan't be here for much longer; my family are expecting me back before the end of the month. I must say goodbye to my friends and neighbours, but I would rather not call on you for the sake of the formal words that convention demands from both sides.'

He put his hands on my shoulders and kissed me. The first and last kiss. It would have to do.

'Goodbye, Kay.'

I walked home along the river back, ready to welcome home the child in my life, my writing and my future. I shall not be alone.

TWENTY-SIX

Newfield October, 1980

I watched Laura perched on the window ledge, gazing into the bright autumnal morning. We should be outside.

'Shall we take Jack for a walk?' I suggested. Children needed exercise, I supposed, at least we can combine the two daily excursions, fitting them into an increasingly crowded day. She was starting to collect things – a shiny stone, a piece of patterned china, a fossil one lucky day – snail-like in shape, but tough, unpatterned, yellowish, – a devil's toenail. I decided that learning the name and the reason for it could be left till later.

'Where we goin' to keep our things Kay?' she asked me on the way home.

We. Our. These were the words she used. The direction we were moving in was clear.

I shivered; it was cold for late summer. There was no rule that said I couldn't light my fire before October. But firelighters had been left off my shopping list for months. I'd have to find some paper to get the kindling started. I'd told Ellen to put the accumulating copies of the local paper in the cellar, so I opened the rarely used door in the hall, switched on the light and made my way carefully down the stone steps, followed closely by Laura. I glanced round, it was a quite a large area, one wall showing the remains of built-in wine racks. There was an unnecessary plastic Christmas tree, left behind by a previous owner, one or two cardboard boxes, a crate of still unpacked books. If you can live without stuff for a dozen or so years, forgetting that you have it, do you really still need it?

Laura was intrigued, looking at the perfect spider's web that spanned one corner, poking her finger down a mousehole, examining a heap of old rope and tut-tutting over various damaged items.

People do interesting things with cellars these days – a games room, a sauna, a gym perhaps, all activities for families with a need for more space to accommodate their diverse tastes and requirements. Perhaps Laura, as she grew older, would like a room for table tennis. The only ball game I'd ever had any success with back in Melbourne.

There was my old typewriter! I had forgotten about it. A large cardboard box in one corner, what on earth was in that? I opened it. We both looked inside. I was surprised at its contents – a collection of items, most of which I recognised. A gold bracelet, a twenty-first birthday present from Dad, I thought it had been lost in the move from Australia.

'Ooh Kay, that's pretty!' Laura had found something that caught her fancy.

A rather nice silk scarf, green and black, art deco inspired. I had regretted its disappearance, but as is the way with scarves and umbrellas, I supposed it had been left behind somewhere. Laura picked up a ring and was sliding it up and down her finger. My mother's wedding ring, Dad had kept it, not giving it to me, he knew I would not want to wear it. A rather striking pair of silver high-heeled sandals, with a thin strap that had impinged very painfully on my little toe. Thinking the same thing would happen to any wearer, I'd told Ellen to throw them away. A framed picture of somewhere or other, a print that had been given to me by students at the completion of a course I'd been teaching. A silver spoon, goodness knows where that had come from. A ten-pound note.

Laura was trying on the scarf.

'I like this, Kay. Don't you want it?'

She rummaged further in the box, found an expensive watch Dad had given me, and I thought I'd lost.

I sat on an old stool, Laura still amusing herself with the contents of the box. I considered the implications of my discovery, this collection of objects and money. Made by Ellen, of course, no other person had access to the cellar. Dad and I had dumped odd items there that we couldn't find a current use for, but with the hoarder's instinct that perhaps they might come in handy one day. Had there been another hoarder with the same idea?

Why had Ellen made this collection of stuff that was not hers? I remember hearing that shoplifters often take things from shelves and put them together in one place in the store. You can't be accused of stealing if you haven't taken anything out of the store. But you can return to the spot and remove the whole lot in one single action rather than several separate ones, a single risk rather than multiple ones.

Was this a similar strategy? Was she removing items from the household and putting them in one place, ready for a quick and easy removal when the opportunity came? Relying on the fact that I would become used to their absence, forgetting about them or believing them to be lost? Small things, of little value to me, but maybe with some cash-raising possibilities for someone who needed the money and knew where to go for it.

I felt deeply sad. I would have given her the lot.

I looked at the pile of newspapers in front of me. The reason I had come to the cellar in the first place – newspaper for lighting the fire. Ellen had known that old newspapers were kept here.

Lightning struck. Of course. *Of course.* Understanding came in the presence of this place and its contents. it was all so obvious, *now*.

In that instant, a mystery was solved. Not just the one involving the strange collection of objects, but another, more profound, more disturbing, more dangerous. I knew, directly and simply, what had happened seven months ago. I looked beneath the top few issues, and found the one I was looking for. I knew its date; I would never forget it. I knew also that it would not be complete. There it was, the front page headlining some matter of local importance, the next one re-telling it in greater detail. The next few pages were absent, as I knew they would be.

The rest was intact. The issue before me was missing only the pages that had found their way into the external chimney of my log-burning fire. The paper that my engineer had found, handed to me, puzzled and worried and refusing payment for the job I had asked him to do. No stupid prank by a drunken idiot, but a deliberate action from someone who knew exactly what they were doing. Someone who knew exactly what *she* was doing. Ellen was the only person with unlimited access to the Cottage and knew where the old newspapers were kept. The person I had visualised on that day, stepping down the rungs of the ladder, who had never turned round for me to see his face was not a man. She was a woman. She was Ellen.

Can envy, dislike, fear, a wretched life, so twist a mind that it devises a scheme to kill? Was this a temporary aberration, a fleeting loss of sense, of reality, a revenge on the life she had endured and that had found its focus on a person who, in her eyes, had everything? Could such a mind hold at the same time a profound and fierce love? Laura was her only hope, the only light in the darkness of her miserable existence, and a light that flickered dangerously with every perceived threat that her granddaughter might be taken from her. And yet... how would she have benefitted from my death? Only through the satisfaction that revenge can bring. Revenge on the Fates that gave everything to one person and nothing to the other. Madness takes many forms, disguises itself cleverly, has its own logic, its own morality, it lives in its own world. It throws a stone through the window of a stranger, steals stuff it doesn't want, bites the hand that feeds it...She had failed, a new strategy had to be devised.

'Should we put the stuff back in the box, Kay?' Laura's voice brought me back to the present.

'Yes, love, for the time being. But you can keep the scarf. We can take it in turns to wear it!'

We left the cellar to its lonely custody of secrets, and went back up to the hall, closing the door behind us. I brushed the dust of the cellar and the past from my eyes.

Small face round the door, Laura came into my study.

'You lightin' the fire, Kay?'

'I was cold after lunch and I was thinking about warming up the place a bit, but I've changed my mind. If we light a fire too early there'll be nothing to look forward to in October. It's nice to have a lot of little things to look forward to as well as the big things like birthdays and Christmas!'

I screwed up the pages I'd been holding and threw them on to the empty fire. 'That's where they belong!' I said to Laura, 'What would you like to do before tea-time?'

Laura took my hand eagerly. 'We can read about Alice!' she said, the book that Gran'ma got for me.'

I caught my breath. Was she going to ask about Ellen again? The moment passed. It would be like this, I thought. She might ask once or twice more if her grandmother was coming for her, but other things would claim her attention, and I would wait for her acceptance that this was her life now, and tell her, as I must one day, of what happened on the night of the flood. Other things I would never tell her, but I would make sure she knew that her grandmother loved her. And that I did, too.

Selwyn, as the father of the child I would never bear, was fading from my picture of the future. The figure of Laura was becoming the reality. A sadness and a joy. I didn't see this outcome as a compensation for loss but a gift in its own right. There would be problems, of course there would, but I would cope. The future was beginning to have a shape, and now there was one permanent figure in it. Not the one I had originally hoped for, a different figure, a small one, but one that warmed my heart with every day that passed.

Huw called in the evening. I had been wondering earlier whether I should tell him of my discovery in the cellar. My two discoveries, though only one was a police matter, and that beyond investigation. He hadn't needed to bring me his failed police dog, after all, there had been no intruder. I decided against telling him for the time being. However, it was obvious that he had something to tell me.

'Glass of wine, Huw?'

He accepted happily, and I settled down to hear what he had to say.

'I've had a letter from Ffion. In it she says that she's been thinking about our marriage, – such as it is – and decided that she can't continue in it unless I make some changes.'

'Oh dear, Huw. But since she's never there, I can't think that any change you make can affect her.'

'It's my job that's the problem. She says that being married to a policeman is against all she stands for. It's demeaning, she says. She says a whole lot of other things too. To be paid for upholding the law is anti-freedom, anti-change, anti the love we should have for all humanity, no matter what they do. It's a weapon of the rich in their exploitation of the poor and underprivileged. She wants me to give it up. It's not me, she says, but the institution I stand for.'

I was nonplussed. Ffion was going rather too far, I thought. The stigma of being married to a policeman was surely her problem, not Huw's.

'Has she set you an ultimatum? '

'I'm not sure. And I'm equally unsure what difference it would make if I changed my job. If I could find one that fitted her moral requirements. There's no way she would come back in the foreseeable future. Not while the cold war continues, and we continue to arm ourselves with nuclear weapons.'

'I'm sorry about this, Huw. Sorry for both of you. She seemed a nice woman, I liked her.'

'So did I, once.'

'D'you want her back?'

Huw took a deep breath. emptied his wine glass, made his confession.

'What I want is an undemanding job that I enjoy, time to read and mull over some philosophical stuff, a bit of female company, and I wouldn't say no to a bit of sex thrown in as a bonus.'

'Not an impossible goal, Huw. You're halfway there already.'

He smiled appreciatively. 'I think you're going to say that I should look for another woman.'

'That would be a good idea.'

'You know perfectly well I've found one, Kay. But she's got her eye on another man, and goodness knows what he's got his eye on. Bit of an idiot, if you ask me.'

255

He twirled his empty glass.

It was getting near bedtime. It amused me to think that both he and Laura used the same delaying tactics, indicating that they needed another drink. 'You've had enough,' I said to him, as I usually said to her. He grimaced, and left, reluctantly, as he always did.

I went to bed, thinking as I dropped off to sleep, that there was no need to worry about that long past shadow, the attempt on my life. I could sleep with all the tranquillity I had ever wanted. Ellen, poor mad soul, is dead. She can do me no harm now. In fact, the realisation that it was she who had tried to kill me came as a profound relief. No longer did I need to suppress lingering, subconscious fears, tell myself it was a mistake, a warning, a joke – nothing to worry about. There was no threat from an unknown source, there was no living man or woman wanted me dead, waiting in the wings for another attempt. One question answered, one mystery solved. I shall get on with the things I have to do, the first being to set in progress the formal adoption of Laura.

TWENTY-SEVEN

Shrewsbury October, 1980

I was on the phone to my solicitor.

'Alex, I want to adopt a child'.

'Goodness! That's…a big decision. Not what I was expecting this morning. Last time I saw you, you were expecting to talk about matters of copyright concerning a new book.'

'That's still on the cards, but meanwhile I want you to deal with adoption formalities.'

He paused for a moment, no doubt to bring before him the relevant legal procedures.

'Have you chosen a particular child?'

'Yes, I have. She's already living with me. Her name is Laura Parry'

'Parents?'

'None. Her mother has recently died, together with her grandmother. She has no living relatives that I know of.'

'Do you have her mother's name?'

I realised that I didn't know the name of Ellen's daughter, who had only been bitterly referred to by her mother as 'her'.

'I think she had been married, but I don't know her name. She was the daughter of Ellen Parry, who worked for me as a cleaner. I hope you'll be able to find out all these details. All three of them lived in a caravan not far from my house. The site that was flooded – you must have heard about it. Laura's mother and grandmother both died. It was all in the papers.'

'Yes indeed. A terrible tragedy. Ellen Parry, you said. Leave it with me, I'll need to check one or two things before we can proceed. Must be hard work for you, caring for a child under these circumstances, especially when you're not used to it.'

Unreasonably I felt cross.

'Tiring even when you are. Ask any mother!'

He burst out laughing. 'Don't lose any opportunity, do you, of a feminist dig! I'll think very carefully before I attempt any sympathy again.'

'No, you are right. I am tired and unreasonable and prickly. It is a fault, and I am dealing with it. I promise you I shall be a nicer person one day!'

He laughed and forgave me, as he always did.

'But Kay, we must have a proper meeting. You must come into the office. We can't do everything by phone.'

'It'll be difficult…'

'Absolutely necessary, I'm afraid.

'Anyway, it looks as if you're happy with your decision – there shouldn't be a problem with the formalities, but it might take a bit of time. I wish you the very best of luck with your new life – and your daughter's.'

A week later, a phone call from Alex summoned me to his office.

'I need to talk to you. It's about the adoption process.'

'I'll have to find someone to look after Laura. It's not easy, can't we talk on the phone?'

'Sorry, Kay, there are documents I want to show you.'

'Couldn't I bring her with me?'

'I really don't think that would be a good idea. I don't know how much she understands. We would be talking about her mother and grandmother, she might be upset. And I shall need all your attention. Can't you find someone to look after her for the afternoon?'

With misgivings, I called on Bethan to come to Tyddyn Amlwg and stay with Laura. I had not wanted to leave her so soon after the flood, but at least she would be in familiar surroundings, with Jack, and Bethan had met Laura several times. Learning the reason for my absence from home, she came willingly.

Once again I set out for Alex's pleasant office in Shrewsbury, hoping that what he wanted to discuss would not take long. Over Welsh Bridge, up to the town centre, down an impossibly narrow street that leads to an ancient cluster of black-and-white houses, now mostly an expensive location for sources of advice on everything that might involve litigation or money. Car park located, I walked the few yards to the building that housed Alex's office.

Past reception, up the polished staircase to a door on the right, half-open. Alex called me in.

I can see the interior of his office even now, as clearly as if it were in front of me. His desk, telephone within reach, a wrought-iron lamp behind his chair. Two files, one open, before him. The back of a framed photograph, – wife? child? Filing cabinet to the right, bookshelves to the left. Dark red Turkey carpet, worn thin by the door. Potted geranium on the windowsill, scarlet flowers blocking a view of yet another fabulous half-timbered building across the road. Another door, slightly ajar, a glimpse of a small kitchen beyond. Kettle still steaming, is he going to make tea for us?

Everybody knows exactly where they were when they heard that Kennedy had been assassinated. The moment of shocking news is fixed to a picture of the place where you were when you heard it. Your immediate surroundings are part of what you are reading, hearing, being told, time and place becoming one.

Alex's pleasant, unremarkable office, that day, became such a picture. I would leave it a different woman, with a different past.

He grasped my hand warmly in greeting, indicating a chair, and sat down again behind his desk.

'Good of you to come, Kay. Some odd things have cropped up. I know the name Ellen Parry, she was one of the two women who lost their lives in the flood, wasn't she? As you say, it was all in the papers. I believe you had something to do with the tragedy?'

'Yes. I was with a friend. We managed to get the child out of the caravan they lived in, but the water was rising so fast – with hindsight perhaps we could have managed better, but it was dark and we didn't know what we would find. A rope would have helped… a hammer would have helped…almost anything…but we were carrying nothing with us…we…'

Alex interrupted, apologising.

'You're going over and over it in your mind, Kay. You're bound to. Disasters are unforgiving, they make us think of what might have been, what more we could have done. To do one's best at the time – that's all anyone can do. You've saved a child, and you've made a new future. That's a wonderful thing.'

'Yes'. I stepped out of the flood waters, rebalanced in Alex's comfortable office.

I knew that he was trying to re-assure me, assuming that the events of the night of the flood would not be soon forgotten, that they were still vivid in my memory. He was right of course, and I was grateful for his words. But they had brought back those hours in the flooded river, and I needed time to right myself. He waited a few moments, glanced at me, and resumed, elbows on his desk, hands clasped under his chin.

'But I want to talk about Ellen Parry, as in fact, – and you didn't know this, – she was a client of mine.'

I was surprised, to say the least. I couldn't imagine Ellen needing or affording a lawyer.

'She wanted to consult me some time ago on some complicated matter of inheritance – all hypothetical, and, as things have turned out, unnecessary. She left with me a batch of papers for safe keeping. As she is no longer alive, I suppose these should go to Laura, as her only living relative. No doubt you will keep them for her – or they can stay with me if you prefer. They include birth certificates for Laura, for her mother and for Ellen herself.'

A wise move on Ellen's part, I thought, as things had turned out. These documents wouldn't have survived the flood. I told Alex all I knew about her past, which was very little. She had been vague and dismissive of anything I'd asked her about her past life, dwelling only on how difficult and unfair it had been.

'She once told me that her mother had left her as a child. 'Buggered off' she said. I wonder who brought her up? Her father?'

Ellen had told Alex more than she had told me. He knew the answer to that.

'She didn't know who her father was. Nor did her mother, she said with some bitterness. She was fostered by some woman in this area. Had a pretty rough time, I imagine. Apparently, the money for her keep dried up, and the carer couldn't contact Ellen's mother.

'She said that her foster mother berated her for her birth mother's disappearance, made it perfectly clear that she was not wanted there. Or anywhere, I suppose. So the poor child was made a skivvy, and blamed for it. I guess she had never known love. Not surprising that she went off with the first man who showed an interest. She must have hoped that the man she married would give her some affection and support, but she seems to have been unlucky again. I have tried to trace her foster-mother – the woman who was paid to look after her – no luck there. Mrs. Parry was your cleaner, you say?'

'Yes. I found her a difficult woman. But when life treats you like that, you're bound to be distrustful of the world. But she had this one over-riding passion, which was the care of her little granddaughter. Her own daughter was a hopeless case of drugs and drink. Ellen had to manage to keep the three of them going somehow or other, earning such money as she could, and trying to keep an eye on Laura and Laura's mother at the same time. A thankless task, but she had her little granddaughter, a focus for all she did, a compensation for a loveless life. Her worst fear was that the Social Services would consider their home in a caravan as unsuitable, possibly dangerous, particularly as Laura was frequently left alone, locked in the van.'

Alex looked shocked. 'Well, I can see why she was afraid of the child being removed.'

'The van was usually unlocked if the mother was at home, usually asleep or comatose. It was on one such occasion that I'd first come across Laura, walking by the river. I'd taken her back to the van as I was worried that this little girl I'd found might be lost, and not know the way home. The situation as I saw it on that day looked pretty dire. Ellen turned up while I was there, and behaved most oddly. I was sorry for them, and when Ellen appeared on my doorstep looking for more work, I didn't feel like turning her away, particularly as I felt a cleaner was a good idea. A decision I frequently regretted, but never got round to doing anything about, as her work was always satisfactory; there would have been no grounds for dismissing her.'

I thought back to our odd relationship. I knew how difficult life had been for Ellen, but sympathy doesn't preclude dislike. A resentment for her many discourtesies, her unfriendliness, her envious sarcasm. There'd been more, though, there had been times when I'd felt a subconscious threat, a gut reaction of nausea in her presence. But logic had told me that none of this was a reasonable excuse for dismissing her. And of course, there had always been Laura to think of. I'd been reluctant to lose touch with the child. Strangely so.

Alex frowned. 'I realised things were not entirely satisfactory, but the facts as she related them to me, seemed accurate. You say there were no living relatives. I wonder why she wanted to consult me on inheritance matters. She did say that she had recently acquired new information about her birth mother. But I really shouldn't be talking to you about a client, though in this case I can't think it matters. Especially as you'll want as much information as possible about the child.'

I felt uneasy. The room was beginning to feel stuffy. I'd like to have opened the leaded-light window to let in some fresh air. Alex continued.

'Mrs Parry left a few documents with me for safe keeping. Marriage certificate. Birth certificates. Looking through them, I noticed that she was born in London.'

He paused. Nothing to cause alarm, why should it? Why did I feel a tremor, the smallest movement of the world around me? A hint of vertigo? I'd felt it once before, in the caravan. I leaned back in my chair, closed my eyes for a moment. Must make sure I keep well, get enough rest, today is being a bit of a strain. I heard Alex's words again. *Ellen was born in London.*

'She didn't tell me that. Go on'.

'Kay, you told me once that you were a Londoner – an East Ender – born just off the Mile End Road. Ellen Parry was born in the same civil parish as yourself.'

The words hit me like a physical blow. Again, the world around me shuddered.

Do you find that an odd co-incidence?'

Now I was fighting for my composure. Fighting to stay the person I was when I arrived at my solicitor's office. Flashbacks were blocking coherent thought, flood waters swirling around my feet. One step at a time, pause, rebalance…keep hold of Laura – she must be kept safe.

The desk between me and the figure behind it were becoming unstable images. I felt the presence of something imminent and unknown, outside the door. it was waiting, as it had been waiting for forty years. It would be appallingly familiar when it appeared, as I now knew it must.

'An odd co-incidence? No it was no co-incidence, it was how things were, I knew.

I felt in danger, I half rose, but could not trust my legs, my balance. I sank back into the chair. Alex was moving from his place behind his desk.

'All right, Kay?'

I could not answer him, I could not speak. I saw the figure of Ellen in my mind. She had rarely looked directly at me, but once or twice there had been something there that came from some far distant time and place. Why had she reminded me of my mother? I asked myself, *who was she*?

Things were changing, dissolving, re-forming while Alex spoke. I could not see him, images in my mind were blocking those I saw in front of me. I put my hand over my eyes.

'I can see you're upset, Kay. I have no idea whether Ellen Parry's life story has anything in it which affects you. I'll go on, shall I? Her marriage certificate states that her maiden name was Ellen Quentin, born to a woman called Kathleen Quentin. There is no name for the father.'

Ellen was born Ellen *Quentin*. A child of my mother.

Time must have passed. I have no idea how much. At some point I heard Alex's voice, concerned.

'No hurry, Kay. Take your time'.

Time seemed irrelevant; it was passing in another place. I was a child again, but not alone. Another child was with me, coming and going from time to time. Nellie had played with me, bossed me, laughed at me, disappeared, returned, was part of my life until I grew out of her. Then a final disappearance. After my trip to Newfield at the age of five, I never saw her again. Never as a *child*. Never as a playmate. All that was in a different world.

Later, as I fought to come back to the present time and place, I realised that Alex was putting a cup of tea on a small table beside me.

He drew up a chair, his kindly face anxious.

'Are you up to going on, Kay?'

What with? My life, I supposed, but it was not the one I was living when I entered his office. I spoke with difficulty. The words coming like a stranger's.

'I suppose so. It has to be done.'

He asked the question I'd been asking myself.

'You knew Ellen, in those days?'

I heard the words, pulling me back to the present, but carrying with them a changed past, and I knew that although the question had been asked of the woman who had arrived at his office half- an-hour ago, it would be answered by a different one, with a different history.

'Oh yes. I knew her. She lived with me and my mother.'

Uncomprehending, Alex frowned, silent. Outside, a clock struck three.

'I remember her as clearly as I remember the house we lived in, the bedroom we shared, the games we played. She was my imaginary playmate, she was Nellie.'

Alex started to speak, but I could not, had no wish to listen to anything further. I knew I was not, at that moment, fit to make any contribution to the meeting.

'Alex, I can't talk any more. I want to go home.'

I rose to my feet, unsteadily, holding on to the back of my chair. 'I'm sorry. I'll be in touch. I must get back to Laura…'

Alex took my arm. 'I can see you've had a bad shock. I can call a taxi for you, I don't think you ought to drive…'

He spoke worriedly.

'I"m expecting. another client at four, otherwise I'd drive you myself.'

'I'll be alright. I just want to see Laura, I shouldn't have left her.'

As I spoke I knew that that she was well and safe, it was I who needed her.

I was through the door and out of the office, leaving Alex uncertain what to do about his unceremoniously disappearing client. Seated in my car, I determined to keep the afternoon's revelations out of my overwrought mind, and concentrate on getting myself home safely.

I drove home with the text-book care of a learner, trying to keep my thoughts on the mechanics of driving, I must not lose concentration. No, I won't overtake here, keep safe, keep safe. I must not think of the last hour. I have a dependent now. Laura is my focus, just let me get back to her. Too close to the car in front, mustn't hurry. Complicated intersection, concentrate. Wish I hadn't left her – but what else could I do? Must find a good nursery. Clutch, change gear, brake. Keep safe. When I get home we shall say goodbye to Bethan, make a hot drink, she will play with Jack for a bit, go to bed, and I shall read a story to her.

We are related by blood, we belong together. She is my great-niece. She is my family; she is all I have that matters in the world.

In learner mode, I drove on carefully, attention on the road ahead, determined to keep the rest of the day as pleasant and uneventful for Laura as possible, that none of the emotional turmoil I was suffering would affect her and our usual relationship, and, mercifully, in acting calm, I became so. She was glad to see me, telling me about what she had been doing with Bethan. Bedtime as usual, as I had been promising myself, the hot chocolate for both of us, finally a story, a good-night hug, and the bed-room door left slightly ajar.

Making my way slowly downstairs, I wished I had someone with me. I had a sister once, but she has died, and I hadn't known who she was.

We could have worked through this terrible story somehow or other, she and I.

I would have looked out for her, made sure her life was comfortable; surely she would have forgiven me. But she had chosen another path. Alex had mentioned that she wanted to talk to him about some matter of inheritance.

She had probably intended to consult him on the possibility that if I died, she would have a case, as my only relative, for inheriting my assets. A crazy path to take. And crazily embarked on, poor soul! Oh Ellen, why didn't you talk to me! But that would have made a different life, and I must live the one I have. I paused at the foot of the stairs, my hand on the banister. I turned and went back up to Laura's room.

I sat down in a chair next to her bed and wept bitter tears for Ellen. Fate had taken from her the only thing she had to love, and given it to me. I fell asleep in the chair, exhausted.

Waking early, I was relieved to feel myself calmer, went downstairs to let Jack out, make myself a coffee. Still time, before Laura wakes, for another confrontation with my early life. A quieter assessment, I hoped, getting to know the new version of myself. A woman with a sister who had recently died, a woman with a great-niece.

The jig-saw pieces were re-arranged, making some sense at last. Mum already had a child when she met and married Dad. Attitudes were so different in those days, today you could barely begin to understand the implications of what she had done. Women didn't work after marriage, a married man had to support a wife and family. But not many men would want to bring up another man's child. Some would, of course, but they were perhaps exceptional. Maybe Dad was one, but I would never know. In him, Mum had found a man who wanted to marry her, but she was not prepared to take the risk of telling him that she already had a child, an illegitimate one. The inconvenient little girl was hidden, to be brought back once Dad had gone to war. How long could she have hoped to keep up the deception? How long could she afford to pay for those times when her first daughter had to be placed with a child minder? Those times when Ellen's presence became a risk? And when my father came home, a potential disaster?

She must have been worried stiff that some accidental slip would bring down the whole edifice of lies. And what an unexpected release was offered by the family's move to Australia! She could disappear from the lives of her older daughter and the woman she paid to care for her. S. Meredith, whose monthly payments had dried up so unexpectedly, whose messages had lain unread on the floor of the deserted basement flat, to be salvaged by the Patels. Of course, had she decided to make the journey from Newfield to collect her money, she wouldn't have come alone, Ellen would have been with her – living proof of the reason for the payments, should my mother been foolish enough to deny everything. I would have recognised my imaginary playmate.

But the scheme had collapsed with the disappearance of the three of us, Mum, Dad and me, well on our way to a new life in Australia. No more scraping of payments from the housekeeping money, fear of discovery gone for good. My memorable trip to Newfield had been to make final arrangements for Ellen to be deposited with S. Meredith, with the agreement that money for her maintenance should be paid monthly. Ellen never saw her mother again.

There was, however, one weak link in her chain of deception. Me. The set-up she had devised involved the relegation of her second child's memories, *my* true memories, of a sister, to the role of imaginary playmate. No wonder this particular playmate never returned after my father came home.

However, there could have been no expunging of the truth from my mother's own besieged brain. As a young girl she had made a mistake that would scarcely raise an eyebrow today, one that had been painfully but successfully erased from her daily life, but never from her own mind. How could she have stopped herself wondering, from time to time, about another life developing in another place, in parallel to the one developing in her care? This one with a loving father, and all the opportunities that anyone could wish for – the other, a blank. Small wonder that emotional distress sometimes surfaced, that her relationship with me was fraught with difficulties.

I sat in my study, scarcely registering the passing of time. Re-living my childhood, mysteries which I had thought to be self-generated revealed to be genuine and now, with this new knowledge, solved at last. From time to time my lips moved, always with the words 'Of course, of course', as all the puzzling episodes fell into place.

I heard a sound from above, Laura was waking. Not calling out but talking to herself. That's good, that's a good start to the day.

I'll go up to her, we'll have a little chat, and she'll start to learn how to dress herself, when to wash, that bed-time is at the same time every day, and that routines make a pattern to our lives. Surprises are nice but not every day.

She will come to understand that all puzzles and misunderstandings will be resolved with honesty and kindness, that we will love and trust each other, and that as far as possible, our lives will be fun. There's so much I want her to learn. So many reasons for hope and joy. I bounded up the stairs.

TWENTY-EIGHT

Newfield October, 1980

I had been trying to make a pattern to the days, Laura's and mine, so that she would learn that for an hour or two after lunch, I had things to do, and she would have to amuse herself. After tea I would share activities with her, reading or playing games, or cooking. Gardening in the summer. Writing would have to be relegated to evenings, after her bedtime. We'd work out a routine that would suit us both.

Today, after yesterday's profoundly disturbing revelations, I was sitting with Jack in my study, thinking about all that had happened, when he woke, ears pricked, body geared for his usual response to the arrival of a car. I quietened him and went to the door. I saw a vehicle I didn't recognise but emerging from it a figure that I did.

'Alex!'

'Hello Kay. I had to come. I tried to phone but there was no reply. I was so worried about you.' He looked at me closely. You look ...'

'Yes?'

'Surprisingly well. You had such a bad reaction to the information I gave you yesterday – I really hardly understood what you were saying – I expected to find you … well, still shattered, to say the least. I was so worried about letting you drive home.'

'Come in Alex. It is good of you to come. We need to sort things out.'

'If you feel like it and have time. I'm free from appointments for the rest of the day. Thought I'd drop in and see you. He looked at the little girl that had appeared beside me.

'And this must be Laura.'

'Yes, this is – my new daughter. Make the necessary arrangements come through as quickly as possible, please.'

'I'll do my best.'

'Laura, this is my friend, Alex. We're going to have a chat in my study. Will you play in the kitchen and keep Jack company? Come and find me if you need anything.'

She assented happily and Alex and I settled into the easy chairs by the window.

That's some view, Kay.'

'It has a history. One day I'll tell you about it. But we have things to talk about.'

Alex reached for his briefcase.

'Our discussion came to an abrupt end yesterday. I've brought with me the documents I was going to show you. Do you want to look at them?'

'Let's leave it till another day, Alex. I'll make proper arrangements to see you in your office, but I don't feel like formalities today.'

'Thanks. I'm so relieved that you're recovered from your experience in the office yesterday afternoon.'

'Since I saw you I've been trying to come to terms with a new life – my own. For it is not the one I have always *thought* I remembered. You asked me a question, you said, did I know Ellen in those days?'

'And you said, yes, you did. She was your playmate, you said.'

'She was my imaginary playmate.'

'Imaginary?'

That is what I was told. That is what I'd been brought up by my mother to believe. That all those small things I remember about her, the things she did and said, the clothes she wore, the games we played, all these were figments of my imagination, in the same category as all the made-up little stories I used to tell. They were worse than stories for my mother because they were true. She was afraid of them. She called them lies, and used to punish me for telling them. She had to stop me from repeating any reference to Nellie, as we called her then, in case there were elements that might be recognised by someone as fact. I can see how afraid she must have been when my father came home from the war. He used to ask me things about my life. So, Nellie became my imaginary playmate, and I believed her, and of course my father did, too.'

The silence in the background bothered me. I got up to check on Laura, but I needn't have bothered, she was engrossed in Cinderella's night at the ball, the devil's toenail representing the fateful slipper.

'I'm still thinking about it all, Alex. I will never know the full story, but the pieces are beginning to fit together. I've had to re-think all I knew about my early life. I'm not a hundred per cent certain about everything, but what I have just been saying is what I've put together after the things you told me yesterday. You have a birth certificate for a child, a girl, born to Kathleen Quentin, of the parish that included Mile End, where

I was born. Kathleen Quentin was my mother. On Ellen's birth certificate, you say, there is no name for the father.'

'I have the certificate with me, if you'd like to...'

I interrupted. 'Not just now, Alex. I'd rather do all the necessary official stuff in your office. So, it's apparent that when I was born, my mother already had a child. Our generation can hardly comprehend the effect this would have had on the lives of this unfortunate girl and her family. I guess that at the time, my mother's life was one of constant reproach from *her* mother, continual reminders of the shame she had brought on her family. I was aware that my mother didn't get on with my grandmother, because I knew that we had moved out of her parents' home, which puzzled me a lot. Surely, she would have had an easier time at home with parents as built-in child minders, but I guess relationships with my grandparents were making all their lives impossible. Moving out, to our miserable basement flat, was a lucky decision, as their house received a direct hit from one of the bombs that were falling all over London in the early part of the war. My grandparents were both killed.'

'A sad story, Kay.'

'One of so many. I don't know what financial resources my mother had. Maybe she found someone to leave the child with, so that she could get a job. She certainly managed to get about during those dangerous days and nights. She told me how she'd met my father at one of the local dance-halls and that they had fallen in love. I don't know whether she was on the lookout for someone to marry, or whether it was a case of love at first sight. But she had obviously decided that she dare not risk his discovery that she already had a child. One way or another she kept the knowledge of Ellen's existence from my father, who was whisked away to the war almost immediately after they were married. Once he had gone, of course, she could have the child back again.

This would have saved her the payments required to whoever was looking after her child whenever her presence at home became inconvenient. My birth must have been an expensive time for her. How she foresaw the future I have no idea, – I guess she just lived from day to day in the hope that nothing would happen to give the game away. Such a foolish thing to do. But the age and the culture were a world away from present day attitudes, and I suppose she herself was not a strong enough character to face the problems that would inevitably arise, if the truth got out. Another woman might have made very different decisions.'

I was talking to myself as well as to Alex.

'And having determined from their first meeting that her new husband, my father, should not know about this inconvenient child, there was no way she could tell him in the future. That would have compounded the shame of having had the child with the massive wrong she was doing to him and to Ellen. The main risk to the success of her plan was me.

I paused for a moment, the memories were leaping out from my childhood in such a wealth of new understanding that I was overwhelmed with the realisation of their truth.

'At some point before Dad's return from the war, she must have had the opportunity of getting Ellen well out of the way of accidental discovery. I suppose it was her usual child minder who moved to Wales, and was willing to take on the care of Ellen there. I remember very clearly a trip to Wales, which must have been in connection with making a permanent arrangement. Thinking back, so much that happened makes sense now. We were always short of money. With only Dad's army pay, she must have struggled to keep up the regular payments to Ellen's foster-mother. There were arguments about her housekeeping money, Dad couldn't understand why all the cash seemed to disappear, leaving her short. She always had some excuse, but it caused a few cross words and some tears.'

Over the years Dad's voice floated back to me.

'But Kath, love, where has all the money gone?'

'Now I can see why my mother was over the moon at the prospect of a move to Australia. The risk of disclosure completely removed. She would have become untraceable, certainly by anyone without resources. Her constant worry, of course, was that I would mention this other child, the other little girl who so often lived with us while my father was away. She just denied her existence, over and over again, till I wonder if she almost began to believe her own lies.'

'And you, Kay, were told that all the things that happened while she was living with you, did not happen – you had imagined them all. The child who lived with you and your mother, was *redacted* from the story of your lives. That was cruel.'

'Once she had started on this route, there was no way back. Other than a full confession. She lived with this huge risk, until the heaven-sent opportunity of our complete disappearance to the other side of the world.'

Laura appeared in the doorway. Alex looked at her with interest. However I wanted a little longer with him, there was something else I wanted to say. A request he could hardly refuse.

'Laura, would you let Jack out into the garden for a few minutes? Take his ball and play with him for a bit. Alex and I have nearly finished.'

She brightened and disappeared with Jack – a mutual occupation that neither of them could have enough of. Alex watched her go with some amusement.

'Do you realise, Kay, how extraordinarily alike you both are? Easy to say with the knowledge that you're related. I am puzzled, though, that you had no inkling that Ellen was your half-sister.'

'Why on earth should I? I was an only child, according to my parents. You don't look for likenesses in a stranger to a sister you never had.

'There were other things, though, hints of a constantly repressed emotion, things Ellen couldn't help saying, mostly unpleasant. I think she was looking for ways to get money from me, at least some of which she must have believed was rightfully hers. She couldn't know how I would react to any revelation that she was my half-sister. Most likely she thought I'd be angry, ashamed, shocked, and want nothing more to do with her, and that she'd certainly lose her job straight away. Better to bide her time and hope that something more favourable might turn up. She made one attempt at bringing this about, something that you are not aware of.'

Alex looked at me enquiringly.

'You don't need to know it. I didn't know at the time, and it makes no difference now.'

I spoke the words only in my head. 'She tried to kill me.'

'You must wonder how my father and I ended up here, in the place where Ellen lived. Sentiment, I suppose. My mother needed to come to the place where Ellen's child-minder was living, having moved from our London neighbourhood to Wales, I have no idea why. She had told me that the journey was to visit a former neighbour who now lived here. The trip was exciting for me, my first journey out of London. My first sight of fields, woods, cattle, villages. I loved every moment of it. I wanted so much to come back, I promised myself I would, one day. So, back in Britain 25 years later, where else would I want to visit? Dad and I found the place, liked it, found a house, and here I am.'

Alex looked at me wonderingly. 'I cannot imagine, Kay, how it feels to have your past life changed. Not just a trivial mistake put right, not just one false memory, but the knowledge that the world you remember was not the real world. I think it is one of the most extraordinary stories I have ever heard, and I can assure you I've heard some weird ones in my office. And I've had worse reactions from some clients. Hysterics are routine. And abuse. Now I've had this chat with you, I understand what you must have felt yesterday. I think that adopting Laura is a wonderful idea, and a natural, obvious outcome. What you need now is peace and quiet, and time to think, so I shall leave you and your little daughter to get on with the rest of the day. Give me a ring when you're ready and we'll deal with the legal side of things.'

'There's one more thing I want to mention, Alex. You said that Ellen was a client of yours. I was surprised at the time, and later on I thought, how could she possibly afford to go to a solicitor for advice?'

He looked embarrassed, starting to say something. I stopped him.

'I know this much about you, Alex. You have more compassion than is wise for a lawyer. My guess is that your advice cost her nothing, or a ridiculous amount that was enough to save her pride, together with some comments about legal aid if necessary. She would have no knowledge of legal practice and would have believed whatever you told her. Tell me the truth. You didn't charge her for talking to her and looking after her documents.'

It's all history now Kay. It's cost me nothing, but I got from her the information that helped me to sort out your difficulties. A good thing in the long run…'

I interrupted him.

'Alex. I can't tell you how sad I am that I couldn't do anything to help Ellen. She's gone now, but there's one thing I can do for her. For my own satisfaction, of course. I can pay for whatever amount you would have charged an ordinary client. I know you will try to refuse, but do this for me, Alex. Let me pay her debt. It would help me start to make some kind of symbolic restitution for a little of all she suffered. Don't refuse, please.'

He smiled. ''If it means that much to you, Kay…'

'It does.'

Laura was coming indoors, flushed and happy after her games with Jack.

Tactfully, Alex realised that I had things to do. We said goodbye, and I spent the afternoon cooking with Laura. Bedtime for her at seven, and a chance for me to bring some order into my house and my life. Laura's care would occupy most of it, but I felt immensely glad and happy that she was here. To have someone at last, who was truly my family, with a future that I could follow with abiding interest and love, – that was something I had never dared to hope for. The other dream, that Selwyn and I might became lovers, could live our lives successfully together, had been looking increasingly unlikely even before this monumental revelation. It seemed impossible now. I *almost* didn't care. I could write again. I had Laura. I had a family. A child who would sit at my kitchen table, painting, rolling pastry, doing her homework. A child in my life.

TWENTY-NINE

Newfield October 1980

I looked at the little girl who was having breakfast with me. My great-niece. So nearly lost in more ways than one, and found so casually on a walk. Had I not come across her that day by the river, it's unlikely that I would ever have met Ellen. Although she was aware that the Cottage had been bought by two people with a name she knew very well, would she have forced an acquaintance somehow? Just in case this Kay Francis might turn out to be her half-sister? I suppose I'd inadvertently confirmed all the details she needed. Knowing that there might possibly be some physical resemblance to her granddaughter, she would have found it in Laura's colouring, her red hair, and mine. Faded now, but recognisable enough to provide the genetic bond that had missed both her generation and her daughter's.

Ellen had surely made up her mind to escape as soon as she could from the miserable circumstances in which she found herself as a girl. This would have led to her very early marriage, mirrored by the child she had with the man who married her. A rush for freedom which led to three generations telescoped into a shorter period of time than would be usual in a family. Only a few years older than me, she already had a grandchild, while I was still fertile enough, I believed, to become pregnant if my life had taken the course I had once hoped for.

I wondered what Ellen would have made of the outcome – that Laura would now have everything that she herself had missed – but through me, the person who had everything that she considered hers by right.

A small voice broke into my musings.

'You goin' to be busy today, Kay?'

A week ago, she was the child I had grown fond of, who I didn't want to part with, and who I was going to adopt because our lives had become entwined. Today the voice I heard was that of my own great-niece, my sister's grandchild. My only blood relation. A new incredible discovery, but I loved her as much and no more because of it.

'We want a few things from the shop in the village. Would you like a walk?' I asked her, 'the rain's stopped and there might be a rainbow.'

'Kay...'

'Yes?'

'Where does a rainbow go when the sun stops shining?'

I gave her the answer my father gave me when I was a child.

'The same place your reflection goes to when you move away from the mirror.'

'It's a like a sort of reflection then?'

'Very like.'

A slow process, a walk with Laura. Not through lack of energy, but a determination to examine everything of interest that she came across. I remembered the same curiosity when I was a child of her age, and my mother's refusal to 'loiter', as she called it. Picking up things from the ground had been frowned upon. They might be dirty.

Laura took a bag I had found for her, specially designated for the collection of interesting things. It held a jam jar for housing the odd caterpillar or beetle, and I explained that whatever plant a creature was found upon should accompany it into the jar, and that once we had examined it, any animal must be returned to the wild. We made an exception for caterpillars, if we judged them to be happy with the diet provided. Pupation and the eventual emergence of a butterfly or moth was always magical; Laura would watch the creature emerge, shake itself, spread its wings and fly off.

'I wish I could go to sleep and wake up with wings!'

Time to introduce her to Peter Pan and Wendy.

Our walk took us past a group of half-grown oaks. Laura looked up into the canopy of leaves.

'There's someone up in that tree.' She stopped. 'Look, Kay.'

It was true. A face was looking down through the branches.

'Melanie!' I exclaimed, alarmed. 'Are you O.K. up there?'

'One of the boxes is broken.'

From where we were standing her position looked precarious.

'D'you want any help, Melanie?' I asked nervously, unable to see what I could do.

Help from me, or anyone was obviously not required. Melanie was as at home as a squirrel among the branches. With grace and agility, she moved quickly down the oak trunks, grabbed a horizontal branch and dropped the last couple of feet to the ground. Whether or not she remembered me I have no idea. Dressed in tough dungarees and tee shirt, face glowing with the exercise, she looked the child she was.

'Box is broken. Need a new one.'

'Where do you go to get new ones?'

'I get them from Gareth. He makes them from trees.'

'That's nice.'

Bits and pieces from his tree felling enterprise, I supposed. Poor Gareth who couldn't find a house to live in, making little houses for Melanie's birds.

A car drew up beside us, Bill Powell emerged.

'Hello Melanie and Kay, and…' He looked enquiringly at Laura, I introduced them. He looked puzzled.

'I've a lot to tell you, Bill. All good, I'll call by some time. We've just met Melanie. She dropped out of a tree in front of us.'

The vicar smiled.

'Yes. People don't realise she's as much at home in the world above our heads as on the ground, where most people's feet are. This so much alarmed one passer-by that she sent for the fire brigade. Melanie was down before it arrived, much to the embarrassment of the Samaritan in question. Was there a problem with the box, Melanie?'

'It's broken. Something broke it. We can go to Gareth and get a new one.'

'Good idea. Jump in, Mel.'

We declined his offer of a lift and went our separate ways. We did our shopping and filled Laura's treasure bag with enough items to keep her happy for the afternoon. I put in a couple of hours' work with one or two interruptions for the purpose of identification of her finds, but on the whole a productive session. It finished with the appearance, once more, of Laura.

'What you doin' Kay?'

'I'm writing a story.'

'Will you read it to me?'

'I'm afraid it's a grown-up story. You can read it one day, when you're older.'

Her face crumpled in an unfamiliar mixture of anger, frustration, and disappointment. I had not seen her react in this way before. My failings were evident to her, she wasn't going to give up without a battle. She shouted at me through her tears.

'Gran'ma would read it to me! I wish Gran'ma would come!'

So, this was the time to face the moment I knew would arrive sooner or later. We had to talk about why she was here with me. I took her on my knee, using the soft fabric of her dress to wipe the tears from her cheeks.

'Laura, there are things we need to talk about. Things sometimes happen that make us very sad. I am very sorry that your Grandma won't come back. She died, that night when there was so much rain that the river couldn't take it all away and it came over its banks and as far as your caravan. Do you remember that night? The time when I carried you through the water, and you came back with me to my house?

She sobbed, I hoped she was listening and remembering.

'I came with my friend Selwyn, and we couldn't open the van door to help your Mummy and Grandma get out. I think the key to open the door from the inside had been lost. Your Grandma managed to get you through one of the windows, but she couldn't get out herself, and Selwyn and me couldn't get in.'

Another burst of sobbing convulsed the small body, but her anger had turned to misery; I stroked her hair, wondering what was going through her mind.

'Do you remember, Laura? Do you remember being carried out of the caravan and through the water till we got a lift in a car back to our house?

Your Grandma and your Mummy couldn't climb through the window so they couldn't get out, and the van got taken away by the river. They both drowned, Grandma and your Mummy. I'm so sorry, Laura. There was nothing anyone could do. We'll always remember your Grandma and talk about her whenever you want. You and me, we're on our own, now. We'll help each other, won't we?'

I put my arms round the crying child, until she stopped, exhausted, hiccupping. She was quiet that evening, went to bed without the usual delaying tactics. I started to read her a story, but she was asleep, exhausted, before it finished.

Grandma was not mentioned again for some time. I was anxious that she should grow up knowing that her grandmother had loved her very much. What part her mother would play in the story I wasn't sure, but I think the relationship was barely relevant to Laura's life as she had known it.

The episode was not a set-back, life went on as it had before, she was quieter for a day or two, but was soon back to the lively, curious child I knew. I was glad that her memories of that dreadful night had finally surfaced and had been confronted. There would almost certainly have to be more discussion of the drama at some future time, there would be images in her mind that would never be erased, but I hoped they would find their place and be absorbed gently into our shared history.

What a strange story I had to tell. Laura must know everything. I shall always tell her the truth, – with one exception. The one thing that no-one else in the world knew. That Ellen had tried to kill me. I could keep that secret, I thought. Why burden Laura with information which would certainly distress her, and that she didn't need, that she could never find out by accident? She must know one day that I am her great-aunt, that her grandmother and I were half-sisters. But not yet, she had enough to cope with and to understand at such a young age. How and when it will be done must depend on how her life evolves, and when the time seems right.

I needed to think carefully about to whom the truth about our blood relationship could be told, to whom it *should* be told. What would the world think? Was I just that nice lady who had helped to save a child on the night of that dreadful flood, and who had subsequently adopted her? Alex knew the facts already. Selwyn, Huw, Bethan and Cherry knew of my fondness for Laura. So far, Bill knew only that she was the child that Selwyn and I had managed to rescue from the caravan. There was no point in keeping the truth from them, they would all exclaim at the extraordinariness of the story, rejoice with me at the outcome. But how much of it should be in the possession of the world we lived in? How much of it might get out in the course of time? It really depended on Laura herself. I decided that it was her right to tell or withhold the information that we were related. It didn't matter that much; at worst the disclosure might be embarrassing.

Eyebrows would be raised. There would be amazement, speculation, stories, most of them completely wrong. Much gossip would follow, but I thought we would be tough enough to deal with that. I hoped the world would see that we were happy and making a good life for ourselves.

THIRTY

January, 1994 Melbourne

Dear Kay,

What a birthday present!

I woke up this morning forgetting that I'm half a world away from home. I've got so much to tell you and wanted to phone, but couldn't work out what time it would be in Britain, my head is still a bit fuzzy from jetlag. So, I thought I'd send you a letter to tell you about some of the things that have been happening here. Anyway, I like writing letters – you can think about what you're going to say before you say it.

The first thing will amaze you. You will never guess who was at the airport with Cherry to meet me. Someone you know very well…wait for it…Jonathan! And even more exciting, Kay, they're an item! They met, apparently when Cherry was trying to contact you when she came to England all those years ago. They had one or two dates then, I think. Not sure how long Cherry spent in Birmingham, but she went back to Australia at some point, and when Jon decided to open an office here, who did he contact for a bit of help? They seem awfully happy together, and are getting married *very* soon. They would like you to be here as a witness, but they know you're at a crucial point in that new book, and can't just drop it all and come. But don't forget to ring and congratulate them, but check the timelag first!

The next exciting thing is that I'm to be their bridesmaid! Representing you, they say. I'm to have a special dress as nothing I've brought with me is suitable. We're going shopping this afternoon. Cherry doesn't want a honeymoon as she's got a part in a new play that's just started at the theatre in the middle of town. Can't remember its name. I shall go and see it of course.

Melbourne is lovely and the weather is beautiful just now. Tomorrow we're going on a sight-seeing trip to Torquay, which Cherry says is a good surfing area. She's an expert of course, and Jon is learning, and they have promised to help me have a go.

The weather's not too hot, but I have bought a nice hat because of my fair skin. Cherry says that people are more careful these days, and the hat is very fetching. I wore it to the beach yesterday. In a way, having to wear a hat when everyone else is dashing around getting a gorgeous tan is a bit of a pain, but you always used to say that wearing a hat makes you more mysterious and ladylike and fragile, like a Jane Austen heroine, so that's the image I'm aiming for. No-one's taken in by it, Cherry says.

I brought with me the final draft of your new book, have you got a title for it yet? I love it Kay, but it's so different from the others. It's hard to remember that the story is all taking place in an alternative universe. Everything seems so natural, it *is* natural, of course, for that universe. As it is for the one *we* live in. I love the idea that England and Wales have exchanged histories.

I have been thinking about my sixth form choices. I definitely want to keep on with Welsh, together with history and perhaps politics – as I have a reputation at school for being argumentative! What do you think?

Hope Jack is well, give him a hug from me, tell him I'll be home again soon.

Lots of love and a million thanks for the best of all possible birthday presents. So much to talk about when I get home!

Laura, XXX

Dearest Laura,

Fantastic news! I had no idea. I knew Jon and Cherry had been out for a meal once or twice, she told me he had been sorry for her all alone in Birmingham, and had been very kind. Both divorced, so no complications. I rang as soon as I got your letter, and Cherry told me all about it. I am so pleased. We'll try to organise a get-together as soon as we're all free.

Huw Penry Jones dropped in yesterday for one of his regular visits to check that all is well with Jack. I pointed out that Jack had been with me for ten years now, and was settling in very satisfactorily. He was dropping hints about another dog to take over as Jack's getting old. Apparently he's got another failure in the pipeline, that he thinks would be ideal! He says that a puppy often gives an old dog a new lease of life. He's still training dogs with the police, but has discovered an aptitude for academic work. He got his degree with the O.U. and is considering a master's at Aberystwyth. He hasn't seen his wife for years and has no idea whether she ever found herself, supposes she's still looking. Doesn't seem to bother him much!

Had a day out yesterday with my old friend, – Selwyn Hughes. He had a day off from campaigning for the next election, still a year or two away – but you can't start too soon, he says. He suggested a trip we had spoken about many years ago. We'd always been keen to see the Severn Bore, so we took the car down to a well-known spot near Hereford and joined several other on-lookers to watch it. Such a strange phenomenon, an incoming tide with not enough room to contain it. The water piles upwards as there's less and less room for it to spread sideways. At least I think that's what happens. Tennyson has a more beautiful account of it. If you're learning surfing at Torquay , you'll be able to ride the Severn Bore with the best of them! Selwyn has been visiting Gareth and his new family in the house they have built. I'm planning a welcome home party for your return with all our friends, Sel will be coming too.

I'm glad you've been thinking about A-levels. Dear me, the last ten years have gone by so fast! You grow up while I'm not looking. Hope I recognise you at Heathrow next month.

Much love,

Kay

EPILOGUE

'Kay!'

'Yes love?'

'Cherry mentioned that when she was trying to contact you, Jonathan said that you had just come out of hospital after some kind of accident. I didn't know you'd ever been in hospital. What had happened to you?'

'Lost consciousness through breathing air that was mostly carbon monoxide. There was a blockage in the external flue pipe, so the fire couldn't burn properly. Fortunately, I was found and carted off to hospital. No permanent damage done. I was home again within a few days.'

'What caused the blockage?'

'Oh, the usual thing. A bird's nest.'

This book is printed on paper from sustainable sources managed under the Forest Stewardship Council (FSC) scheme.

It has been printed in the UK to reduce transportation miles and their impact upon the environment.

For every new title that Troubador publishes, we plant a tree to offset CO_2, partnering with the More Trees scheme.

MORE TREES
LET'S PLANT A BILLION TREES

For more about how Troubador offsets its environmental impact, see www.troubador.co.uk/sustainability-and-community